Persona

a novel

Aoife Josie Clements

LittlePuss Press, Brooklyn NY

Published by LittlePuss Press, Brooklyn, NY
littlepuss.net

Cover image by Cat Graffam
Sink, 20 x 20 in., Oil on Canvas

Proofread by John Sweet
Designed and Typeset by Cat Fitzpatrick
Edited by Emily Zhou

Printed and bound in Canada

This product is GPSR-compliant for sale in the European Union.
Authorised Representative: Easy Access System Europe
Mustamäe tee 50, 10621 Tallinn, Estonia,
gpsr.requests@easproject.com

ISBN 978-1-9643220-6-3 (print)
ISBN 978-1-9643220-7-0 (e-book)

3 5 7 9 10 8 6 4

Praise for *Persona*

• CIBA Booksellers' List Winter Pick •
• A *Lit Hub* Most Anticipated Book of 2026 •

"This is the best book I've read in years. Clements walks onto the scene with the skill and confidence of an old master; *Persona* disgusts its reader past endurance, then breaks their heart before they realize what's happening. It brings together everything from the films of Ingmar Bergman to *Neon Genesis Evangelion*. It's a churning black spiral of misery, nausea, and anxiety, and woven through it all an infinitely fragile thread of human connection. Clements has written the year's great work of literary horror. This is not something to miss."

—Gretchen Felker-Martin, author of *Manhunt* and *Cuckoo*

"The most stomach-churning, upsetting, thoroughly cursèd queer book of the year."

—Alison Rumfitt, author of *Tell Me I'm Worthless* and *Brainwyrms*

"Harrowing and gorgeously written ... fearless and sharp."

—*Publishers Weekly* (starred review)

"I can't imagine I will read a better novel this year, it is just that brilliant."

—David Demchuk, author of *RED X* and co-author of *The Butcher's Daughter*

"Nightmarishly realistic and immersively terrifying."

—*Booklist*

"A captivating, terrifying experience ... *Tell Me I'm Worthless* meets *Coup de Grace* ... what a debut, what a ride!"

—Red Newsom, Blackwell's (Manchester, UK)

"It feels almost impossible that this is Clements's debut novel, as it is so disorienting and disturbing it seems to have been written by a master."

—Manda Barker, Raven Book Store (Lawrence, KS)

"Is identity a thing that belongs to you? Or is it something you've forcefully inherited? Is there really life beyond the internet? And why is it so hard to pay rent?! Part poetic acid trip in a hall of mirrors, part sci-fi horror creation myth, part Gen Z character study, *Persona* makes you wonder what you'd do if you came face to face with the parts of yourself you'd worked to exorcise—and then wonder if those parts ever belonged to you at all."

—Breton Lalama, Type Books Junction (Toronto, ON)

"An old pain made unreal and vivid in the sputtering, intermittent, blue-lit blight of now."

—Andrew F. Sullivan, author of *The Marigold*

"Like picking scabs off old wounds, *Persona* is horrifying, addictive and wonderfully satisfying."

—Avalon Fast, Director of *Honeycomb*

"Pulls at the scabbing scar-tissue of transsexual flesh in these existentially terrifying times."

—Willow Catelyn Maclay, co-author of *Corpses, Fools, and Monsters*

"The best novel I read all year."

—*The Needle*

"An ungovernable spiral-down-the-drain story that stuns until its bitter end."

—Charlie Jones, A Room of One's Own Bookstore (Madison, WI)

"Eldritch, beautifully personal and (somehow) very funny, *Persona* presents horrors both earthly and cosmic in a uniquely nerve-shredding way. Aoife Josie Clements' brain is an intoxicatingly terrifying place, and we're all the better for it."

—John Toews, McNally Robinson Booksellers (Winnipeg, MB)

"THIS BOOK IS ABOUT YOU! We are all doomed."

—Sybil Lamb, author of *I've Got A Time Bomb*

CONTENTS

PERSONA

I. SLEEPWALKER

It isn't necessary that you leave home. Sit at your desk and listen. Don't even listen, just wait. Don't wait, be still and alone. The whole world will offer itself to you to be unmasked, it can do no other, it will writhe before you in ecstasy.

—*Kafka,* Zürau Aphorisms

1.

It used to feel like I was a part of something in this place, and now I can feel it drifting away from me. I admire the topography of the landscape, everything right where God intended it to be: two-month-old dishes on my computer desk growing blue mould forests; the walls of accumulated garbage bags forming sprawling hills and fields of reflective black down the hallway and through the living room; the popcorn ceilings smiling down like an image of these mountains, earth and sky mirroring one another. God did not put these things here, but I did. Maybe I am God. Maybe I have been lied to about anything at all happening outside these walls.

There's a chill in the air and I can smell small death in the world around me. The insect and rodent populations are going through their annual culling, and as they make their last stands, I welcome them in. Come in, I say, little guests I formed from the dirt, brought into the world against your will, come and feed from your plentiful mother as you need. I hate myself for creating this world but accept the responsibility of managing it now I have done so. I just got off the phone with my boyfriend. He called to tell me that he's started seeing someone else because I haven't voluntarily left my apartment in a year.

His deep monotone, stiff in inflection, echoed from the desktop speaker, its green light blinking. He explained to me that while he'd never thought he'd meet someone like me, the work of keeping me together had become too much; that I never expressed any interest; that it was always him wrestling me for any little bit of time. He looked at me with eyes drained of sympathy while I cried and apologized, thinking to myself but never saying out loud, *You never wanted anything but an hour on call to watch me jerk off. And you saw how bad I was getting out there, and I swear, in here it's comfortable and it's safe and I don't have to consider how much I'm constantly failing. I've just been so busy trying to keep myself afloat, and if I'd only understood you were feeling this way, I could have tried to do something.* I thought this, but I didn't say it. I just said *sorry* again and begged and supplicated myself to him, and he said I was a liar, that I was just keeping him at arm's length, and I made a pleading noise like a dying dog. It must have been too much for him to take. He dropped the call and left me here, hands shaking, face hot, staring at the boxy monitor. I tried to call him back over and over, for what feels like hours. But he won't answer me.

After my last attempt, before I can think of anything else, I think about eating all my sedatives. Then I give myself an internal slap for thinking about eating all my sedatives. I go back to whatever I was doing before he called, some chat room, but it's difficult to focus on conversations with strangers because I am still thinking about eating all my sedatives. I remind myself, as so many have reminded me to remind myself when I think about eating all my sedatives, that if I eat all my sedatives I am not very likely to release myself from any kind of suffering at all and am really much more likely to debilitate my body and mind so badly that I'm just left immobile, the poor girl who ate all her sedatives, to be shown on TV as the life-affirming story of why you shouldn't eat all your sedatives. I am still assuming that I will still exist to watch the aftermath, and the reality is that I can only understand the scope of the decision I've just made in the microseconds after, and I will not be happy with myself when I realize what I've done. I decide to give the urge an acknowledgement by taking a few extra as I drift off to bed. A reward for my impulse control.

Fuck it. I wake up in the middle of the night and I swallow the bottle. Three gulps of wine, seven pills in each, fast enough not to think about it. That should be enough.

2.

As the adults drank wine and prepared Thanksgiving dinner upstairs, me and my cousins were preparing a show for them downstairs. The basement was a seventies pit design, all orange shag carpet and brown wood panelling. Patches of concrete from unfinished renovations poked around the edges of the carpeting like they were trying to modernize it. It felt like a little cave. I was playing the prima donna, directing the littler kids, getting in arguments about which skits to draw out, which songs to cut, which dance moves were too controversial.

"We can't dance to 'Hit Me Baby One More Time,' my mom told me that's a dirty song."

"What do you mean?"

"You know, like sex. Grown-up stuff. Hitting is like a thing, with sex. It's a metaphor."

I had a severe headache that day, a persistent pounding in my skull, which no amount of water seemed to be able to cure, and I felt like vomiting, but I also felt completely unstoppable. I was finally about to prove that the things that made me hard to talk to could be put to good use. There was nothing stopping me from putting on the best show I could. I'd planned it out perfectly: My big moment was a song, some vocal jazz number my mom had shown me on the radio, an ambitious choice for my range. Once everyone's parts were set, I spent about two hours staring at myself in the mirror and thinking about how the lights would go down and there I would be, fully formed at the centre of the room, carrying all the gravity of the song and bringing the family to tears. I mouthed along to the words over and over again, ensuring I had every line absolutely perfect, thoroughly freaking out my little cousins. If anyone came in, I'd snap at them whenever they got near for breaking my focus.

Eventually, we went upstairs and ate. I ate and ate until my belly hurt. Then, realizing I was bloated and desperate to look good for my stage debut, I went out into the blue autumn dusk and pumped as hard as I could on my uncle's swing set, thinking I could take the weight off in the space of a few hours of continuous cardio. I gave myself a pretty bad cramp this way and had to tell everyone the show would be delayed by a couple hours. I sat on the floor and played *Mario Kart* with my cousins, livid that I'd become so lazy and disgusting. By the time I decided to let the adults know we were ready, there were a few more empty bottles of wine on the table. They cheered when I came in, and someone made a joke about where I'd been since dinner. I told them to be downstairs at 8 p.m., a little mad at how nonchalantly they were treating my commands.

Finally, the sky was dark and the basement glowed a deep auburn. We'd fixed the rail lights towards the centre of the room, illuminating the little elevation in the pit we were calling our stage. I welcomed everyone in, *no smoking in the theatre, please stay in your seats*, and so on, and as my littler cousins did their dances, everything was going to plan. The adults weren't paying quite as much attention as I'd have liked, but everyone seemed like they were enjoying themselves. It was hot and felt kind, and I had a lot of energy to work with. I walked into the light when it seemed like they were starting to leave, I told them that *now, ladies and gentlemen, there is one final performance*.

I hit Play on the boom box, and muscle memory locked in hearing the first chords. I primed my voice to ring out, but when it had escaped my throat, I heard it the way other people heard it. My tiny falsetto carried through a line or two before everything went white.

Without control I start moving forward, my tiny frame pushing directly through the crowd of five or six adults, out up the stairs and out to the street and out into the night *oh my god oh my god what have I done why did I ever think I could sing, why did I ever think I could be seen, be known*. I'm producing a noise I shouldn't be capable of producing. Lights in the windows of my uncle's neighbours turn on halfway down the cul-de-sac. People run out into the streets to stare at me, poke their heads out between blinds to look from windows. I'm a few blocks away by now and I can tell that I've been doing something to elude my mother and father and family. I only know that I can't return to that place, I can't be seen there, whatever I was trying to say was nothing, must be forgotten by everyone. I feel hotter and hotter, tension building up inside my chest as I keep moving, until finally I feel arms around my back. My dad picks me up in his arms sideways and tries to make comforting animal sounds to encourage me to rest, but I slip from his grasp and resume my howling march up the street, back bent, neck stuck up screaming to God, walking fast, and now the retirees of my uncle's neighbourhood who have stumbled sleepy-eyed into their yards start asking if they can help, if everyone is okay. They are assured by members of my family that yes, yes I am. I keep moving until I can't anymore, nearly reaching the main roads that lead out of the suburb, the adults grabbing me by the ends of the dress to pull me back in whenever I stumble off the pavement. Eventually I collapse. My dad picks me up again and carries me back up the street, and I am staring at the night sky frozen in his arms. Time stops watching the stars slowly slide along, every part of me shaking. Once he reaches the end of the street, my mom quickly unlocks the door of our old sedan and he drops me into the back seat. Once the door is closed and he thinks I can't hear, he apologizes and I am mortified.

After a while, I can see again. The breaths in my chest start to slow down. I try to make sense of what happened and I decide it just wasn't what I thought it would be like.

3.

Dark parallel shapes soften in the car window, seas of void and specks of light, white and red on black, my mother's car running languid and warm, soft and round, blankets covering me as I shake in the back seat.

I wake up on the floor next to the bed, staring at trash. I'm wrapped in dirty sheets — I must've rolled off in the night, lost between the pills' deep hold and the dream's sense of motion. My head is fucking splitting open. I can't believe I did that. Why did I think that would work? There's red all over my arms, and it's tough to tell what's blood and what's wine. It's all sticky, there are some places where fresh wounds have congealed into the sheet and the sheet has become a part of my skin. I peel it off, revealing the stinging wounds underneath, vicious, crimson, breathing. The cuts are deep: I can see muscle undulate like steak under my skin. Stupid, stupid, fucking stupid, junior high business. Still bleeding at a slow drip, I push myself up from the ground and limp my way out of the bedroom and into the hallway towards the bathroom, over the garbage bags stacked up by the door. I half trip over a bag in the hallway and stick my hand out for balance, feeling the greasy film on the walls. The cuts burn as the muscles tense to catch me. The wounds tingle and beg to be touched, aching with creeping infection from whatever organisms managed to crawl their way in in the night, and I can hear movement from underneath the bag I've disturbed.

My hair gets in the way as I try to pull the oversized pyjama shirt over my head, and I have to make a little animal jerking motion to get it over. It feels like my arm's going to fold over and split in half when I strain my wrists like that. I turn the shower on and let the room start filling with steam before I step in, leaning against the tile to stay up. Eventually, I let myself slide until I'm sitting down, folding myself into the tub's edge, knees bent and my head in my hands between them. The reality of what's happened here sinks in. I'm really still here. I'm crying. A stream of watery puke dribbles from my throat, the blackened red from the wine. It runs down my chin, catches in the blond hair trailing over my barely there tits, flows on over my stick limbs, shrivelled cock, nasty desiccated feet, drenching my body in my own waste. The steam is thick enough that I can hardly see, but my head is still ringing. I stand up, letting the searing water clear the commingling of blood and chunks of vomit away from the cuts, open skin shuddering under pressure until the surface below is red and clean.

When I started living on my own, I kept waking up in the strangest places, not always in the best shape. Finally coming out of the bathroom, I check the double padlock: I didn't get out last night, thank god. I guess the pills kept me sedated enough that all I could do was flop over the edge of the bed.

I sit at the desktop and take a deep breath. Today will be like every other day, but Sam won't call me to say good night. Thinking of this, another round of convulsions runs over me, but I have to work, so I try my best to block it out. I open up my delivery site, like I do every morning, and put in for two packs of cigarettes, a bottle of shit red wine and three packs of top ramen. It arrives at about 3 p.m., totals out to about fifty dollars a day, and just as long as I can make that at work for the next morning, I will get to eat and be happy.

I couldn't go in entirely unless I was financially secure. For the longest time, work kept me tethered to the world: a late night shift busing tables at a diner, a place where people would be upset with me if I didn't smile, if I didn't bathe. After a while it got to be too much, just like everything else. There was too much heat and too much screaming in the kitchen. I felt the patrons' eyes penetrating me as I'd drop a glass or deliver to a wrong table, and I saw looks of pity in my co-workers' eyes as they saw me overreacting to it. I was just shit at the job. Never focused, always upset, late all the time, gradually accruing condescension and disdain from both co-workers and regulars until they finally found some excuse to just get rid of me. The morning they fired me, my boss was gentle with me, but he made it clear that I wasn't welcome there anymore. It didn't take long to reach the end of any money I had left after that, and I got desperate enough to click on a pop-up ad: "WORK FROM HOME: UP TO $500/DAY COMPLETING MARKETING RESEARCH MATERIALS." I assumed it was going to bring me to a page asking for my credit card information, or unleash a torrent of malware, but the possibility of never needing to go outside again was too tempting.

What it led me to was a company called Chariot Marketing Solutions, which I could find zero information about online except for a dead website full of stock photos of people in offices pointing at computers, one logo and a series of dead links, but which now sends me a zip file of 10,000 fifty-question surveys per week through their employee portal. They've been paying me for my year inside at a rate of ten cents per survey completed.

I was a little surprised by the size of the surveys: At fifty questions per survey, there was no way anyone could afford to live on this while answering each question sincerely. So I started by just clicking each question's first answer. I quickly realized that you didn't need to answer the questions at all, the real challenge was how fast you could click. They had pretty strict controls in place for automation: The employee portal locked me out any time Itried to set up any sort of bot software to click on my behalf. I bought one of those medical mouse pads with a wrist support and studied videos of pro RTS players to maximize click speed, practising ripping through as many clicks as quickly as possible. With a few hours a day speed-clicking like this, I could make a few hundred dollars in a week, while also giving myself a cramp in my wrist that hasn't gone away since. I spent a little while trying to find another job, but I'm a trans woman with little to no work experience who barely finished high school. The more the rejection and silence piled up, the more the Chariot surveys seemed like the only way to keep from ever going outside again.

So I decided to try to do them for fun. I started to actually read the questions and, more importantly, to decipher what they were really asking.

Typically, the first question is:

1. Are you familiar with [brand]?

1 (not at all) 2 3 4 5 (very strongly)

These are usually 1s. The only people who hire Chariot are start-ups trying to get a foothold; bigger corporations would carry out these sorts of studies in-house rather than outsourcing them, let alone to a company with little to no record of its existence.

The next section could be characterized as "establishing familiarity with the field":

2. (If no to Q1), are you familiar with [company specialization]?

1 (not at all) 2 3 4 5 (strongly)

Then follow about a dozen technical questions, usually more 1s, though occasionally I can give a few 3s if the client is in the IT sector. Twenty questions out of fifty in, having established a total lack of familiarity with the field, I am then presented with some of the client's key ethical dilemmas. As with any great innovator, our intrepid entrepreneur has had to cut some corners in sourcing materials and has perhaps had to destroy more than a handful of human lives. They would like me to gauge for them just how much damage control needs to be done. These questions are generally in the form:

21. If [company] took part in [war crime/dubious labour practice] in [developing nation], how likely would you be to boycott [company]'s product?

1 (not at all) 2 3 4 5 (strongly)

I always answer 1 to these in hopes it might contribute to relaxing the client's scruples to the point where they might get themselves in trouble.

A frame of reference having been established (what the client works on, how evil their actions have been), we are ready for section four, which might be described as the word association section.

37. Does [company] remind you of luxury?

1 (not at all) 2 3 4 5 (strongly)

38. Does [company] remind you of family?

1 (not at all) 2 3 4 5 (strongly)

39. Does [company] remind you of citrus?

1 (not at all) 2 3 4 5 (strongly)

After these semiotics comes the demographic stuff (my gender, race, etc.), and then finally a section marked "How did we do?," always the same, always culminating in the same last question, number 50:

50. Did the process of answering this quiz trigger any traumatic memory, repressed, epigenetic or otherwise?

1 (not at all) 2 3 4 5 (strongly)

My default answer is 5, as doing anything for money reminds me of my reliance on others. Though, in the spirit of trying to stay engaged, question 50 can offer a vital moment of reflection: Have I been traumatized by microprocessors? Do corn chips return me to the secret horrors of birth? Can I access true reality by thinking very hard about laundry detergent?

When I was focused solely on click speed, I might complete five surveys in a couple minutes, but I would need to take a break afterwards and rest my wrists. But this way, I can sit through the whole night, ramen on hand, music on or even listening text-to-speech to chatroom posts, giving emotionally honest answers, and get better numbers over more hours without really noticing that I'm at work, the passive reading crossing some line between disinterest and interest, to a point where simply watching the number marked as completed feels satisfying.

Frankly, I'm lucky to have found something stable at all. You can adjust to anything if you have a good enough reason to, and it's not like I have anything better to do. To make my daily quota for food and needs, it takes about fourteen hours a day. Anything else on top of that, if I have the energy for it, goes to rent or for hormones, which get skipped more than I'd like to admit. Sometimes ramen or wine get skipped too. Cigarettes are the first priority.

I met a new kind of bug today in my apartment while I was working. He had a round black shell, horns on his head, and was swimming in the trash. Despite everything, it's turning out to be a good day. I didn't think I could meet any new kinds of bugs.

4.

Ninety-nine miners say goodbye to their families, unsure of how long they will be gone or whether they will be back. They light a candle for the god of the underworld, and march past dancers in great red-horned antlers. They line up at the foot of the cave, trailing into the distance, most moving steadily, some crying, some already getting drunk or into spats with one another. As they make their death march, their forms bend and reshape themselves into silverfish, forming a path up the side of my dresser and into my clothes.

Around hour nine or ten of working, I will relax a bit, take a few minutes to grab a glass of wine from the full bottle surrounded by the empty bottles on the kitchen counter. I will usually keep going for another couple hours like this, just dribbling the occasional sip from the bottle. Sometimes, when the wine starts to affect me, I will play a silly little game with my last few surveys of the day, a kind of weak protest, and try to answer them all with the exact opposite of my real feelings. Logging off, I light a cigarette. I don't notice the bittersweet smell of the tobacco in here anymore, but I think it does help block out the scent of the mould and mildew growing under the garbage, at least for a second. Then I open the anonymous chatroom where I spend most of my spare hours.

You might expect, as many people once expected, that fungible anonymity would allow for more fluid and sincere personal expression than the limitations of a singular identity. In reality, though, in the chat room, anonymity instead boils down the chaos of a conversation with multiple participants into a single voice, shouting at itself into eternity, in a beautiful, worthless mass expenditure of energy. It strips away our individual features so that we all emerge as, talk as, the Default Persona. The Default Persona within this empty space is a white male, approximately eighteen to thirty years old, who has been gifted with historically miraculous comforts but whose shameful masculine pride bristles against him. This is an easy thing to be, a safe thing to be. As long as you follow the code of anonymity, as long as you talk in this voice too, you can slide by, an unnoticed witness.

Or, you can try to depart from it. But there are only a few outlying foils to the Default Persona: the older man who warns of the dangers of following this path too far, the person of colour who statistically is certainly here but who seems to appear only to defend users who are accused of being racist, and the most mysterious and challenging, The Girl.

The Girl, according to the Default Persona, has the following traits:

She does not belong here. Having none of that wounded masculine arrogance to heal, the assumption is that The Girl, full of inherent or socially constructed meaning, could just as easily opt to exist Out There. If she has become a refugee In Here, if she has decided that, already possessing absolute dominion over Out There, she wants to take In Here as her own as well, this is a choice. Whereas the Default Persona, he would argue, does not have this choice. Therefore,

She is far worse than us for being here. As the Default Persona believes the deck to be stacked in her favour Out There, The Girl's having ended up In Here is a perversion at best and a sign of complete and utter failure as a human being Out There at worst. Of course, he'll say, we are all complete and utter failures here, but he saves his deepest contempt for The Girl. If challenged on this, the Default Persona would of course then say:

She just needs to learn the rules of the game. The Default Persona might admit, okay, yes, it could actually be nice to have some women who share the same interests as me. However, the Default Persona is too tired of being bullied to give an inch of compromise to anyone trying to fit into his new world. He demands that you sacrifice your identity wholesale and wear his mask for the sake of appearances, that you share his opinions, and that you never speak outside of his range of experiences. He only exists due to the maintenance of social codes, and so in order to protect his own invisibility he must punish any exception to his own rules as viciously as possible. This is because:

She represents creativity and the world, and the Default Persona demands eternal negation. It is unlikely that the Default Persona really holds any of the strong beliefs he claims to, young and still trying on ideas like his father's coats, all empty elbows and shoulders. The only true conviction his minuscule lived experience has gifted him with is of the centrality of himself in the universe, and therefore of the centrality of his pain to the universe. The return of "identities," recognizable markers of the outside world, would involve the intrusion of the real into the fantasy of non-existence. He cannot accept the reality of other people, because doing so would be too deep an acceptance that his own pain is mundane and non-total. And so he cannot accept The Girl.

I still occupy the Default Persona online most of the time. I've grown comfortable in his contradictions. While the Default Persona says he believes in things, the things he believes rarely tend to line up. Instead, any conversation with him, as him, is a game of invention and reinvention, the constant creation and destruction of identity for rhetorical advantage, scoring cheap points off the naive enjoyment of anything. To come into his world attempting unguarded connection is to invite total evisceration, consumption and excretion by the hall of mirrors, a thousand voices the same as your own declaring you less than worthless, better dead. You are of the shit, you are in the shit, you are shit.

I grew up in his world, and spent most of my teenage years in an empty house seeing how deep I could tunnel into myself. Then I spent my short adult life Out There trying and failing to re-create that feeling. Just walking or taking a bus with headphones on to a store where I had no money to spend, letting my mind wander, inventing plots for made-up TV shows or pretending I was describing the album I was listening to to a stranger in detail, overwhelmed with interest in my own ideas and with so little worry for how to execute them. I still visited the chat rooms then, but at that time they seemed like a spectacular underground cultural centre, exposing me to every kind of pirated media, the enlightening and the traumatizing. It felt good learning forbidden things: I was being taken seriously as an adult, even if I was constantly being torn down as a human being, let alone as a Girl.

Eventually, I found boards that announced they were intended for me, but even on them the Default Persona never seemed to change, even as the subject matter became more grounded in the things I was trying to avoid. To use these boards seemed to defeat the point of being anonymous, of disappearing into the mass. I just wanted to listen to people talk about video games, or anime, or whatever else they felt like passionately tearing each other apart over, without having to expose myself to the judgments of the real world, where I was a human being, with limitations and with an identity that could be pinpointed at a glance.

By the time I went In, or not long after, I realized I had crossed a line where I had had enough conversations with the Default Persona to predict his movements. Which meant that I was too far gone.

Me and him are one and the same now, Girl or no, and in my head I carry his voice, his opinions, an awareness of what he would say in any given situation, the desire to say it, and the knowledge that silence is always better.

5.

After the incident at Thanksgiving, I started waking up in different places. When I was little, it was fairly standard sleepwalking: a parent stumbling into the kitchen, seeing me standing there mumbling near the fridge, not knowing where I'd been, shaking me up and sending me off to bed with a hug and some warm milk; or they'd find me in the attic, two floors removed from my room in the basement. By the age of twelve, I'd figured out how to unlock the door, and for every one of those funny little stories, there'd be nights where I woke up on the front lawn and everyone was mortified. This happened a couple times a month without fail. My parents installed childproof locks on the front door, which worked for a little while, but I still figured it out eventually, and I started going farther and farther at night, sometimes a block or two out from the house. More than once I was woken up by a member of the neighbourhood watch, my parents on the verge of filing a missing persons report, but always curled up in some grassy place unharmed by the time they found me.

Eventually, my mom let everyone in our neighbourhood know that this was a common occurrence, and to look out for me if they ever saw me late at night. This reduced their panic around my disappearances by a lot. By the end of junior high, I was more often waking up on schoolmates' couches than on front lawns. I didn't have many friends, so it was always awkward getting breakfast from the mom of a stranger with a somewhat-familiar face, but it was still a nicer start to the day than search parties. Occasionally I would dig a hole while asleep and wake up lying in it, blood and dirt caked under my fingernails, or it would rain or snow while I was out on my night walks or I would catch a nasty cold for a day or two, but I was somehow always safe with strangers. This was a small miracle for a child wandering around alone at night, even in a small, tight-knit suburb. Still, I would imagine myself through the eyes of the strangers on the street, how they might feel seeing me out at night, the power they held over me in that moment.

After about a year of this, I noticed a change in my father: His skin started to become more and more translucent, his eyes dark and his frame gaunt. Whenever I'd sleepwalk, he'd stop me before I could get to the door, wake me up, and state flatly that I needed to go back to bed. Some nights, I could hear him pacing around the house for hours on end, muttering to himself, waiting to jump.

My mom's response to my sleepwalking was almost completely opposite to my dad's: After the first few scares, she was inured to my disappearances, and thought the only truly effective interventions would be medical and psychiatric. She shipped me off to therapist after therapist, trying to root out some core trauma at the heart of it, but they never found anything substantial.

My dad started to wear a somewhat heavier layer of cologne than normal in the mornings. Eventually, this failed to conceal the smell of liquor below. The look in his eyes became apologetic, like he desperately wanted to stop himself but no longer knew how. I remember wondering whether the drinking just helped him stay up to watch for me, or if there was something else going on. Neither he nor my mom would tell me anything.

One night, up late online chatting with some internet boyfriend, I noticed his silence and went to the door to check if he was in his usual spot. I stepped towards the door softly, hoping not to call him running my way, and pulled the handle very slowly, as I had many times before, to crack the door and peer down the hallway. There was a squeak, and then an unusual click, and the door would not give. I gave it a couple hard pulls, feeling tension in my wrists but achieving nothing. Then checked the door jamb: A new metal bar, locked from outside, ran above the knob. I knew if I screamed out, the fight between him and my mom would be explosive. I went back onto my desktop, and told my internet boyfriend how terribly unfair it all was, and how I couldn't wait to move away from home, how he shouldn't say those things about himself, and that the pictures were coming eventually. The next morning, I woke up in my bed, so either nothing had happened or the locks had done their job. I approached the day as normal, got dressed and started to slip out towards the kitchen for breakfast, but the door was still locked. My parents both drove into the city, so neither of them would be home.

My chest ached and I was ready to burst into tears or pass out or start screaming for help before I remembered I had my phone. Opening it, I passed by my mom's contact and jumped straight to my dad's.

please come home, i'm locked in my room.

I waited for a few minutes, terrified of being trapped, grimly realizing that I had to pee. I tried to make a plan. This is only about as bad as I feel at school, I told myself, and I'm sure it won't happen again, so the day in here won't be the worst, besides the pee issue, and I'll get to spend some more time with my online friends. I opened a game on my computer, hoping to forget my body and my situation, hoping that the time would pass on its own. After about twenty minutes, I heard my cell buzz.

dad: Oh no, k

dad: 20 minutes

dad: Thank you for letting me know

I felt some relief in my lungs. My bladder still hurt, but I went back to my game and tried to focus on that rather than on any bodily sensation. It was a first-person shooter. I kept getting sniped from across the map before I could get any sense of my bearings. *I suppose that's what I get for playing at 11 a.m.*, I thought, when the only people online are the ones for whom dissociation is a full-time commitment. I used to feel jealous of people like that: Even if it was only useful for humiliating teenagers on sick days, they had developed a mastery of something and claimed control over at least a single place in their lives.

I heard shrieking brakes in the driveway and felt the rest of the pressure melt away, warm, calm. *I'm going to be fine,* I thought, *Dad's going to save me and I'm not going to have to hold this anymore.* The keys in the door spasmed for about thirty seconds before the door crashed open, and the galumph of sprinting steps came down the stairs. I ran to the door of my bedroom on instinct, too close when he appeared in the doorway, still stinking drunk from the night before.

I'd never felt afraid of him before like that, but in the years that followed I could never fully shake the fear of having seen him that way. He told me he must have forgotten to unlock it, and to get used to this going forward because there were people out there who wanted to hurt me. He asked me why I had to make life so hard for him, and he told me to shower because I had pissed myself.

6.

Four high walls in three small rooms extending to a high ceiling and towards a picture window, sliding doors out to a balcony, all made smaller by the mess now reaching near shoulder height, a mess that seems to extend and contort at these late hours. I trip across the bedroom, drunk now, deep in the night, bumping into trash bags and things I attribute enough sentimental value for to keep. I had tried to sleep and couldn't get comfortable, sweating through the thin sheets, producing zones of unwelcome that eventually sprawled entirely over the bed until there was nowhere left, so it was time for an old ritual.

Sometimes I wonder if I dreamed pornography into existence, as it only seems to exist between waking and sleep as a guide back into the dark. I press a key on the desktop and watch it light up blue. I open the browser, entering private viewing, and click on the first thing I see, something half-kinky and relentlessly hetero, just as I have for as long as I can remember. The footage is lower-budget than the algorithm normally gives you when you ask it for something that will get this over with quickly. The camera is digital but about a half decade out of date in its faint pixelated muddiness, and the shot is positioned oddly, the camera angled up from the ground next to the bed around which the subjects are posed, facing into one man's ass, which is pressed awkwardly against a desk, though the other man's body is fully visible up to his beard, only his eyes cut off at the edge of the frame. Between the two men, a trans girl is on her hands and knees on the bed, face obscured behind the man's ass as she fellates him.

The tall man with no eyes fucks her in the ass from behind. Between the middling quality of the footage, the weird and obscure angle of the shot, and my own vision-blur, I am barely processing all this, but the media is only there to initiate some movement in my own mind, a recollection of fantasies, and it is doing its job, hand in my panties on my knees deep in the blue light, nearly tipping over.

The only relationship I've ever had started about eight months ago and ended yesterday. Sam and I met in the kitchen, where he was a line cook and I was busing tables. I thought he was obnoxious. He made soft fun of all the front of house as we bustled in and out grabbing plates, but he always somehow singled me out in a way that seemed pointed, even relentless. I kind of hated him for it, wondered if he was trying to draw attention to me. He claimed later that it was just the macho culture of the kitchen. He asked me out for the first time at the work Christmas party, where he'd gotten way too drunk. He had tears in his eyes, and he told me he had always felt bad for me, stood up for me when I wasn't around, when he said the other guys in the kitchen would get especially cruel. I didn't know what to say, I'd never seen him do that, but I was sort of flattered, even if he'd been the main one bullying me to my face. He asked me if I wanted to grab a drink after work some night, and I said yes, if only to escape the situation as he got more and more intense, slurring his words. I wasn't really attracted to him prior, but I was flattered by it, and his vulnerability made me see him in a different light. We went to a bar late after a shift, and he told me he'd moved around a lot as a kid with his father, a diplomat, and had become used to being alone too. He said he saw that in me immediately. I could tell he'd also spent a lot of time online and understood the chat rooms and the Default Persona viscerally; I'll still hear a post on the boards in his voice sometimes and wonder if it's him.

Both of us were unused to dating, and we made a show of ourselves; *baby*, *honey*, we'd call out to each other over the metal racks and the heat lamps, with the delivery of any plate. Sam took a lot of shit from the other line cooks, but he seemed so taken with me that he didn't care that they called him gay. I used to be afraid of even going back into the kitchen, drawing their attention, but I started to actively seek it out, dressing a little more outwardly femme, flirting with the other line cooks. They still mostly responded with jeers, but for the first time that didn't seem to matter. Sam was easy to get jealous, jumping to getting fuming mad easily if it seemed like I was looking at other guys. I know he got a lot of shit for dating me at all, but we were in our own little bubble and none of that seemed to matter anymore. On a warm night, we'd grab fast food on the way home and sit out in the parking lot surrounded by brown bags of garbage, smoking cigarettes until our throats were dry from the heat, drinking cold soda to break up the phlegm. Being around him made me feel like a grown-up for the first time: the first person who really took an interest after teenage years largely spent alone, years blurred slowly together in a painful, listless longing for something I could never quite find the words for. When he was there, there was someone to tell me I was good, that I was valuable, however much other people still seemed to be disgusted by me, and that was proof enough that I mattered.

Eventually, he quit the kitchen to start school, and though I was excited for him, I didn't have anything to distract myself from the pressure and the noise of the place anymore. I decided to leave too, not long after. I'd been living in this apartment back then too, but before I quit I was never here, and the garbage never really had a chance to accumulate until I started spending my days at home. The apartment was practically empty except for the computer desk, and I always tried to push things to Sam's place when we'd meet up, embarrassed by it. But on my own, watching the little bit of money I'd saved whittle away as I tried to search for jobs, I felt myself ceasing to care for myself. It didn't matter who I was when no one could see me. I felt the distance between us profoundly whenever he wasn't around, and I would message him non-stop trying to set up dates or making it seem like things were okay, but I became completely contemptuous of the person I was without him. I could feel him drawing away, like he could smell my desperation, his read receipts torturing me for days on end. When he'd finally respond, the dates were usually the same: I'd take the train across the city to see him at school, an hour each way in chilly autumn sleet, and we'd sit at a coffee shop for an hour or two and he'd tell me about his courses, fuck me in his twin-size dorm bed, chafing my thighs against the vinyl and sending me back out into the night. I could feel him less and less present in these meetings, but still I was rapt, fighting for dear life to hold on to what felt like my tether to the world, the one thing that ever made me more than that empty kid, floating aimlessly without an identity or a friend to speak of. I started going out less and less in my own spare time, learning to avoid the world except for absolute necessities. Over time, the gawking from the strangers on the train got to be too much to be worth whatever Sam had to offer in terms of spiritual healing. I could feel myself losing him, but it just made me push harder. I thought things had balanced out: I had found a way to live where I could minimize the panic attacks, the silent judgment I seemed to feel wherever I went. I had left him to his important work, and I could still hop on a call every now and then to help him get off. I was still useful. But I guess he probably met someone, or realized he was carrying me and was better off just letting me fall. Maybe we held on for too long after I went in. Either way, he's gone now.

I try to summon a memory of the sensation of him, but I can't. I feel completely numb, utterly estranged from anything that happened before the other night, before that deep sleep into the void. Everything that happened between us feels vague and abstract now, mixed into the childhood blue light ritual in ways that make it more comfortable to try to pretend it never happened at all. I'm trying to create a corner of my mind where I don't need him, where I can tuck him away when I don't need him, but he still appears somewhere in the ritual, inseparable from it. This or that angle of a man's body, some stupid thing he'd say about his *cock*, how it's *all yours, take it*, would put me back in a moment I remembered, and I'd feel that same faintly embarrassing warmth come over me that I used to feel on those summer walks home.

I force him away, out of my mind, a few times over, focus and vision blurring and twisting through the blue light. Eventually, my hands tense and the ritual is completed. I need a moment to recollect myself, and go to the washroom, white light streaming from fluorescent bulbs above the mirror. There are a couple cigarette butts lodged in the soap rack on the sink, one of them still has a little left, so I pick it up and light it. Looking at myself in the unflattering light through the smoke, I can see my skin is breaking out, my hair getting stringy and broken at its ends near my chest. By the third drag, the cigarette is burning my mouth and I put it back out where it was, marking the plaster. There's some brown grease on the wall behind me, or is it the mirror? I can still hear the quiet, distorted moans still coming from the computer, the video still playing on.

Somewhat more awake now, the noises coming from the screen have a sour note I can't place, and I trip back through the dark to make it go away. When I move the mouse to take the computer out of sleep, the man in the foreground has pulled the girl's blond hair back to spit in her face, and it takes a second for it to register, but eventually I can see it clearly.

I see my own face looking back at me, frozen in ecstasy on the screen. My eyes rolling, back bent down, but then clearer, raising my neck to stare up at the man as he spits. The fluid hits my face and dribbles off my chin, my eyes sinking down to the camera, my expression on the screen turning from pleasure to blank shock, a deer in headlights into the camera. I stay locked in eye contact with myself in breathless silence until the man pulls my head back down into his groin, obscuring me again. My face is gone, and I grip his thigh tight. I close the tab and shut off my computer in an instant. I feel a weight in my chest, and though I feel more awake than I have in weeks, I climb over the trash, sending mice scurrying from below, as I rush into bed to hide, shaking.

7.

I wake under a dome of concrete and moss, stirred by dripping water on my forehead: *pat, pat, pat*. A little blue light is cracking through shadow what seems like miles above. I am prepared to accept my new home, until suddenly I'm bathed in white light. My body tenses in anticipation of everything that's about to happen: the undercarriage of the train that will fold my feet upwards into cracking shins, my body that will be compressed and bent backwards, pressed up through the femoral and over the spine, my digestive system that will be pressurized at the point of bisection and extruded from the new entry, shredded under rust and steel and electrified against the third rail, my neck that will be bent forward into feet in an inverse-fetal *O*, my face that will be pressed against gravel erasing all identifying features, shards of skull slicing into exposed backs of my eyes and neck, my arms and hands that will be removed even as my brain begs them to enact agency. All of this will occur in the space of a little under two seconds.

I feel every muscle constrict and contract painfully. I am curling up, despite my efforts not to, into the precise position I'm imagining being forced into, as the train stops about a foot away from me.

The platform is full of morning commuters and they are staring at me. Everything is white-hot. I'm shaking. I extend an arm back to hold myself up on the ground. The conductor of the train steps down onto the tracks and, pointing his flashlight towards me, reaches his hand out, as if expecting me to sniff at it like an animal. He's maybe in his fifties and moustachioed, doing his best towards what I'm assuming he assumes is some fallen angel, some lost innocent. I think for a second of letting myself be sent to a psych ward, how comfortable it would be to live without expenses for a while, then remember I would definitely have lost my apartment by the time my brief vacation ended. I wait until his hand has nearly settled into its *there there, champ* shoulder pat and then I bite down hard, catching his palm between incisors and molars at about his thumb's knuckle, squeezing until some little bit of his palm bursts and I taste blood. I faintly realize that this is the closest I've been to another person in a year.

The man's face bends into a scowl as soon as teeth hit flesh. *What are you* is all I start to hear as I take off, half-bent, and scrabble onto the platform. I hear someone calling after me as I push and shove my way through the crowd, the commuters' faces indistinct. A hand tugs at my wrist and I jerk myself away. I can't look back, there are still certainly people chasing me. I can hear more shouts in waves and a clanging growing closer and closer behind me. Any tiny pause will allow them to reach me and pull me back into the din. I keep sprinting, forcing myself violently through the gap in the automated gate. There's a shrill pain in my chest. I can taste blood in my mouth, crawling up my throat, and I'm bleeding from my arms as well—*scrapes from the rails? walking off the edge of the platform earlier? ripped-open scabs from the other night? are the police coming?*—and I'm pulling people from their standing positions on the escalators now to push past, olive-and-black crosshatched tiling and black industrial rubber and stainless steel, like climbing an endless mountain somehow blurring into blue-green outdoors under the white-lit awning of the station, where there's pouring rain and looming glass office towers all around. I keep up my pace, no direction in mind. The dead skin on my bare feet itches like hell against the concrete and loses its grip against wet, dead leaves in the gutters, sending me face-first into concrete. I am in traffic. A car with foreign licence plates jerks to a stop inches in front of me, a mother and son. She covers his eyes while making an unintelligible hand gesture.

I no longer know where I am. I have to keep moving. I can feel the muscles in my thighs ache, pumping faster and faster. This is much farther out than my night jaunts have ever landed me before. I take in the misery and squalor of these blocks surrounding the train station, the hundreds huddled under tarps and in tents, selling broken and worn shit to try to survive, and it makes me quicken my pace guiltily. I know how little separates me from these people, how grateful I am supposed to be for that, but all it does is remind me I would like to get home. A man in dirty clothes shouts at me and asks if I'm looking for something, I keep my eyes focused on the ground, my head down. I am starting to slow into a jog. I jog on and on until I can feel the neighbourhood change.

Then suddenly the pain is gone and I can't feel anything anymore and I'm not moving anymore. An old couple tower over me with umbrellas, casting a pale light through the yellow canvas onto my face. They start asking me questions. I try to explain that I woke up in a subway station and bit the conductor, and now the police, or the commuters, or the demon in the screen, have all come to get me, to pull me back into the mess I've made and have me trampled by all the people I've inconvenienced so much, or to institutionalize me and take me away from my happy middle-class life. I don't think anyone understands what I'm saying. Someone starts dialing 911. I am able to make sounds that indicate not to do that with enough urgency for them to stop. The old woman reaches out her arm. I don't grab her hand, so she pulls me up by my shoulders.

Now I'm moving again but not so fast anymore. I circle the perimeter of the downtown area, disoriented, trying to find my way back to safety. My hair is flat and hard, matted with rain and blood. I'm being stared at by everyone I pass and I cannot make eye contact in return. I try to emit vicious energy, to prevent anyone from saying anything to me or acknowledging my existence. This isn't that different from walking home at 2 a.m. from the diner after my shifts. Day is worse than night in some ways. The rarity of seeing another person in those night hours offsets the lingering threat of violence in anyone who does appear.

So I imagine it is night. I imagine I am ready to call Sam and apologize for waking him up so late when he has class in the morning to talk to him on the phone until I get home because someone is walking behind me or because the same car just passed by twice. I imagine I am ready to drink myself asleep and wake up at one again the next day, an hour ahead of the next shift of being stared at by everyone and getting *sir*'d in a full face of makeup by people who didn't know any better. Everyone seemed able to tell that there was something very wrong, very fundamentally *off* in how I was coming across, leaving me out of the great secrets of my own essence, which they had determined on my behalf. I would think maybe I just smelled bad, or wore too much perfume, or not enough, and would shower and scrub until I bled and shave four times over to cleanse myself of any marks, never able to stop lingering on the possibility that maybe there was really just something truly, deeply off-putting about me at a base chromosomal level. The men always seemed to be plugging their noses to some indescribable unpleasantness, and the looks of other women felt imperious, like an ethereal being denigrating me as an earthly body. It seemed best to spare myself the embarrassment, and everyone else the annoyance, of letting the hollow shell of me wander around half-assing entry-level food service jobs before its inevitable exile.

Daylight has grown dim when I finally find the park next to my building, its rows of street lights running parallel to the brick wall along the back of the apartment. There's a dirt path along the side, a little patch of grass covering about a half block, and a bright plastic jungle gym. I slip around the edge, up the elevator and through the green metal hallway. The quiet must in the hallway reminds me of what leaving here on purpose felt like, before it's gradually obscured by the familiar stink of the apartment.

I'm in. I pour myself what's left of yesterday's wine and sit down in my bed. I sneeze. Did I catch something while I was out there? I've adjusted myself to a pretty specific microbiome in this apartment, after all. I listen to the rain *pat pat pat* on the window and stare out at the city at night. I sob hard for a while, then I collect myself.

8.

At 12:35 a.m., the power cuts out and I'm surrounded by pitch-darkness. I try to feel my way out of my bedroom over the crinkling garbage bags, each reflecting a little moonlight but not enough for me to situate myself by. I trip over one and land on my hands and knees, ripping the bag a little. Something with too much mould on it to recognize spills out onto the floor. I can deal with this later. I can hear my friends moving in the darkness. I reach out my hand to greet them, hoping not to be bit by anything unfamiliar. I find the door and crawl out into the hallway, full of dread, preparing to check whether they've cut my power. It's not that I can't make the money tonight if I have to, but I'd need power for that.

The wall's shroud reaches its end and I peer around the corner. There's the picture window, there's the balcony: no lights outside, either, seas of darkness, no islands, everybody in the same boat. I sigh with relief. I sit on the floor in the black and light a smoke to be able to see, fingers jittering. Some other windows in the dark now have candlelight in them. In the apartments across from mine the faces of people become visible. I try to observe the silhouettes in their faint detail, the rare few others up at this hour. A young woman taps away on a laptop; a man sits slack in a kitchen chair, a beer in one hand and his phone in the other, bleeding light in his face; a couple lie in each other's arms, craning their necks to try to read. I've stared into these windows so often, trying to make connections, seeing if I can see the same shape twice or draw out any kind of coherent pattern for any particular apartment, but none ever seems to arise.

I keep smoking although my smokes are low, and I can feel my muscles relax. The scent of the room disappears for me again, and for a second it feels like I'm in Sam's arms in that parking lot in the summertime. I can hear music faintly from somewhere when I crack the window, and a chill creeps into the room. Finally, the lights come back up. I don't know what time it is. I stand up, brushing ash off my hoodie, and wearily march back into my room and start to clear a space to work. I shove mouldy food from the desk, sending it clattering onto the garbage bags on the floor at the foot of the bed, then log back in to my computer, skipping past the obligatory "you did not properly log out" screens and opening the Chariot employee portal.

The portal gives me an unusual prompt:

NETWORK INSECURE

PLEASE SIGN IN FOR BODY SCAN

There's a link below it. I exit the screen, force-quit everything and restart the computer. There's no "you did not properly log out" message this time. I click on the portal, and again:

NETWORK INSECURE

PLEASE SIGN IN FOR BODY SCAN

And that same link.

All jobs are scams, and I'm comfortable with the idea that mine might be more of a scam than most, but the point of working from home was to not have my body seen by strangers. I consider emailing Chariot, but it's four in the morning, so I go to the instant help chat on their website instead.

CHARIOT: Hello! How can I help you?

annexe: employee services please

CHARIOT: Thank you for requesting EMPLOYEE SERVICES! Are you looking for payroll, technical support or another service?

annexe: technical support for employee portal

CHARIOT: Just a second! We're sourcing a technical support rep, they'll be right with you.

A couple seconds with the little "dot dot dot" typing symbol on the screen.

CHARIOT: Hello! This is Chariot Marketing Solutions' technical support team, how can I help you?

annexe: this is a little odd, but my employee portal is giving me an error message

annexe: NETWORK INSECURE, PLEASE SIGN IN FOR BODY SCAN

annexe: what is a body scan and why is the portal asking me for it, i don't feel super comfortable clicking this link

A little while with the dancing dots again.

CHARIOT: Thank you, Annie! Yes, this is a built-in security measure for the Chariot portal, and is required for all staff. Generally, a body scan request will pop up approximately once per year in order to ensure that a person and not an automated program is filling out the surveys. It is required in order to proceed, and staff are suspended without pay on refusal to participate.

annexe: so before i put whatever this is on my desktop, what should i know? what's it going to do?

Those dots again. I go to the kitchen for a cigarette and a glass of wine, standing in the kitchen lightly bouncing my head against a wall and tapping my fingers against the white-and-grey-patterned countertop for a minute or so.

The dots are still bouncing when I get back, but eventually it blings.

CHARIOT: The body scan process is entirely within the browser and will not download any additional software. It does not require that your webcam be turned on. It will determine whether there is a real person behind the screen, then it will auto-close the browser.

annexe: and there isn't any way to get around it? can i verify my identity with you, or call back into the office?

Instant, now:

CHARIOT: It is required in order to proceed and staff are suspended without pay on refusal to participate.

annexe: Okay, so if the webcam doesn't have to be turned on, will it still work if I put tape over the camera?

CHARIOT: It is acceptable to put tape over the webcam if you prefer. The body scan does not require a camera and will work either way.

annexe: thanks for your help

CHARIOT: Thank you, Annie! Have a good night and let us know any questions, we're happy to help. :)

I close the browser and take a sip of wine. I rub on my forehead a little with my wrists. It hurts at first when I really push into the soft tissue, but it starts to feel good after a minute. The webcam was taped over before, but I haven't put any back on since the last time I talked to Sam, so it's back around the corner to the kitchen to look for it.

Uncommon-use items like this are a nightmare for me. I rip open each kitchen drawer, digging through forks and knives and marbles and rubber bands and spare change, dead lighters and dice and other lost parts from board games, can openers, dust, sticky spots, pens, a photo of Mom and Dad, a notepad from work. Scrawled in the margins between bits of forgotten orders I see: *there was never any reason to worry. he sees me as i am :)* I remember a hot day and start to soften. Then I remember that he's gone, and that he's gone because I am not good enough. I wish I'd been pulled into a car while sleepwalking and chopped into pieces by some maniac before I could ever have let him get my hopes up. The tape is right in the back, almost wedged into the boards of the cupboard. I pull the end and there's a satisfying sound of stretching as the old glue gives. The camera is covered. Just for good measure, I restart the desktop one more time. It has a nice sound when it boots up: old struggling fans humming in unison with the old familiar chime from the operating system. I open the portal and click on the link under the error message. There's a sudden full-screen blast of large white text on black, no border on the browser, and no sound at all. It says:

CHARIOT BODY SCAN INITIALIZING

Then it goes dark. A digitized voice, monotone, androgynous, cuts through the hum of the fans:

Please stand in the centre of the room.

I stay sitting down.

Please stand in the centre of the room.

I stand up and move up and onto my bed. My head is nearly at the ceiling. I set my arms at my sides and stand stiff, waves shuddering throughout my body. The computer is now producing a low humming noise, barely perceptible under the fans' hum. There's a revolting fraction of a second of low, crackling distortion before the voice speaks.

Initializing.

I am standing on my bed in my little stance doing what the computer tells me to do. Colours start to flash on the screen, cycling fast enough that the moments of transition blend together, forming a writhing mass of incomprehensible grey, too intense to bear. There's a void in the centre of the screen — not dark but a ripple effect, creating a sense of depth that seems to tunnel on forever, crawling out of the screen and along the walls, a spectacular light show that seems to poison everything it touches. A high-pitched frequency emanates from the speaker now, an ear-rending shrillness that fills the room and seems to keep getting louder. Roaches are skittering across my feet to escape from the noise. My eyes are watering, salt tears dribbling down my neck, I'm starting to see a shape like a star emerging in black around the edges of the screen. Just as I'm about to vomit, I remember I can look away, and turn my head to the side, closing my eyes tight.

Immediately, the room goes silent and dark, and a low, distorted noise replaces the siren squall of the process's own sound.

Reposition please.

I hold my breath and try to compose myself. I sit there in the dark a second longer, hoping it will forget me and proceed without me. Distortion.

Body scan interrupted. Reposition please.

I tilt my head forward to face the screen, keeping my eyes closed. This has to be enough, right? Please, God, let it be enough.

Distortion. It can definitely see me through that tape.

Body scan interrupted. Reposition please.

I open my eyes and it starts right back over. I can't tell if the hum is getting louder or if the sensory overload has just moved to my ears now that my eyes are thoroughly fucked. The colours start to just look white, and I can feel my eyes running again. I choke back the tears and remind myself that I've dealt with worse, lights on a screen cannot kill me. *Maybe it's not so bad, maybe it's not so bad.* I remember that I do not want to die. I hate whoever is doing this to me. Why did I ever sign up for this, I will never give these people another part of myself again with all they've taken, I will run back out into the light of the world and into my beloved's arms and everything will be okay. *Everything will be okay.* I'm submerged in the light now and nothing they do anymore can kill me, and I recognize the litany of faces and eyes dispersed in the noise and call out to them, open-throated, hollering into the white. Strange, animal-like grins emerging from every corner of the light extending out past the edges of the screen, now up onto the edge of the bed and towards my feet, and in the centre of that blinding light I see with sudden and terrible clarity a pair of eyes, defeated, sunken, paranoid. My father's eyes as he's carrying me away. Sam's tired eyes as he sweats onto my face, my knees bent back. My own eyes on sedatives, blissful, no longer suffering. My own eyes paused forever in the porno unremembered in the light of day.

Focus returns to my body; a faint tingling sensation seems to move in waves in tandem with the frame, shivers almost knocking me off my unstable balance on the bed. The sheets and laundry are wrapped tightly around my feet. It feels like they are about to be pulled over the end of the bed from underneath, and could easily take me under with them. I stay completely still. I can feel the eyes on me. They're still in the room and I'm feeling we're approaching the exact point at which the blanket will tug, and now the walls are moving, at first in the shaking movements of the texture and of my body but soon spinning spinning too hard to see and stars are the room and the stars are the eyes and the eyes are as inescapable here as they ever were anywhere else and I was so impossibly naive to think I could sing I could hide I would be allowed to exist in society even from this kind of distance and

The room is black again. The bass frequency is back. I flinch hard at the distortion.

Thank you. The current time is 2:02 a.m. Please proceed with your work as normal.

I drop from standing onto my hands and knees in the bed. My elbows are shaking, and I feel the hot trails of tears on my jaw. An arm gives out, and I fall face-first into the sheets. I am okay, it's lights on a screen and there was tape over the camera and the camera was disabled. I let out one more deep sob into the sheets.

9.

It's 9:37 a.m. and I still haven't slept. My hands are still shaking, body still cold and numb from the body scan, but the survey packet arrived as soon as the process was complete and I've been working long enough to eat now. I place my daily order with the entry code attached, it should be at the door in forty minutes. I make myself the last of yesterday's ramen and sit back down at the desktop, back hurting, neck bent. I feel like I'm going to pass out, but I have to be awake to collect my order. And I need to try to find that video and get it pulled as soon as I can.

In my mind, I run through some of the scenarios that could have led to its existence. None are great options: It could be an AI-generated fake, but I don't have any social media, and I don't think I've allowed someone to take a picture of me since I was a little kid, so I don't know how someone would have a big enough collection of photos of me to do that. I could have been drugged, but I can't remember the last time I was in a position where that could have even happened. I could have been so deeply drunk and tired and miserable when I saw it that I hallucinated my own face. Or, like my father warned me, something could have happened when I was sleepwalking.

Nothing seemed coerced about it, and the me I saw there seemed at least conscious. She seemed like she could see me from in there, like she was as horrified to be looking out into the camera as I had been looking into the screen. No one who'd seen me sleepwalking ever said anything about me talking or opening my eyes. Something deeply evil needed to have happened for the girl in the video to be me, but it's impossible to imagine how it would have happened. I wonder about the permeability of the screen during the scan; what other ways could the boundary be broken?

If I can at least get it pulled, I might be able to get some control over this.

Trying to remember where my drunken predilections may have lain, I go to the first porn tube site that comes to mind. I try "mmf threesome" and filter by most recent, and am hit with a rapid, vicious flood of strangers' asses, way too dense to parse. I add a few more filters: "blonde," "teen," "amateur," finally giving in, "shemale." This has not gotten it much further down to something controllable.

I start scrolling down through pages and pages of trans girls' bodies, mousing over each to try to find my own face in the search. Scraping over preview after preview, I never see myself, and I try to refresh, but that just seems to replace all of them one thousand times over. Eventually, I start seeing chunks of thumbnails I've already seen, too many videos being generated too quickly to be properly archived.

I don't often look at this stuff sober. The total decontextualization of the bodies, interlaced with the rare and cathartic entry of the actors' faces, seems even more jarring than it does when I'm wasted and half-asleep. After I transitioned, it began to seem almost inevitable I would wind up doing sex work. One of those ideas you just sort of absorb through cultural osmosis. The fear, the mental image, of ending up street soliciting, or half-dead down some alley with a needle in my arm, was a recurring factor in the decision to go inside for good.

Sitting on page 78, seventy-two hours after posting, I see some familiar, fuzzy security cam–looking blue footage in a thumbnail under the title "june 23rd" and click. *There it is.* The men's asses crowding the screen at first, the girl bent between them, then the awkward stumbling reposition as the second man moves around from standing over her to fuck her from behind. They're both skinny, tall guys with beards and tattoos, not the beefy Adonises of a mainstream production. Then the moment finally comes, the face pulling up from the first man's cock to the camera, and there, undeniably, is my face, looking back with that listless look.

I pause it again. There's no way that's anyone else.

My guts twist up. I need to take a second away from the screen. I run down the hallway, into the bathroom, kneeling on the foul tile. I breathe hard and retch over the toilet, straining my chest and my neck, but nothing comes up.

Coming back to my desktop, my back cracks halfway down. I'm shaking, but determined. I have the video now, and I know I can stay awake another hour or two, and I know how to proceed. First, I report the video to the tube site for non-consensual content. Either they'll pull it or they won't, but I suspect I'm not going to get very far with an anonymous claim. I bite my tongue and start an account on the tube site. I also DM the user, but this is the only video they've posted, and the name is just a bunch of numbers, so it seems unlikely I'm going to hear back.

Now the next step. I'm sorry it has had to come to this, but the real answer to my problem is undeniable. It's time to consult the Default Persona. I pull up the message board, sadder than normal to be there, and after getting distracted for a minute by some kid's baffling ranking of the Radiohead discography, I start a new thread, simply the video embedded with "Source?" as the thread title. I know it will get me my answer eventually. I also know exactly what will come before that.

The first reply calls me a faggot and accuses me of participation in a Jewish psyop trying to turn the denizens of the chatroom into a bunch of chasers, or, worse, to get them to transition. Next I am told repeatedly that I would be better dead, and asked how it feels that no one will ever really want me. They point out that the men in the video are hiding their faces because they're ashamed. A subset of replies to the initial accusations reply that yes, we aren't women but in fact sick fetishists, but that's good, and it is our goal to force-feminize every person on the board, so here's the link to a guide on starting HRT online, start now — the medication under the link will be poisoned. Several complain that jacking off to trannies is really a lot better when the girl passes; others ask with conspicuous intent why post-op girls never seem to be in these things. There are hellfire sermons warning of the dangers of sodomy for both the body and the eternal soul, then about a dozen sub-arguments spilling off each of them, some joking that the great and holy proclaimers are doing their proclaiming only after having just watched everything they just watched, others responding that the fact that God hates them for jacking off to this makes jacking off to it even better, actually. There's a torrent of other clips. Some are simply responding to the thread with more porn, most of it substantially more niche. Several appear at first to be the sort of clips that overlapped with this on the tube site search results, but hard-cut after one or two seconds to an identical video of a man's face being peeled off with a machete and the skinless eyes underneath burnt with metal rods, as he shrieks alive in agony to the howling laughter of his captors in what looks like a child's playroom. Others cut between so many different clips so quickly that the brain can't really interpret what it's seeing anymore. There's a subset of respondents for whom these are the only clips they can jerk off to anymore. In the middle of this (I am clicking through everything to make sure I catch it when it comes), someone has replied to my original request:

ripped from destiny k's camsite, she's cute but she doesn't go on as often as she used to. i hope they take this down eventually.

The post includes a link. I click it desperately. A simple white-and-grey streaming client pops up, with a chatbox to its right, and I'm shocked to see it's currently active, although no one is onscreen. The footage is the same grainy blue as the clip, and there are a couple anons in the chatbox sending death threats, but the chat notification sounds are just ringing back from the screen, feeding back into an audio channel that's otherwise null. It's a small bedroom, with a bed and the camera positioned towards the upper corner of the frame from below, a computer chair sitting square in the centre of the room. There's a visible hallway leading out of the bedroom and towards a bathroom, and I can faintly see that around the corner from there there's an entry to a living room with a large picture window at the end of the hall. I realize it's the exact same layout as my unit, but completely clean, almost unoccupied.

I stare and stare at the screen, hoping to summon this demon, this not-me girl, to abjure her to come out and show her face, but she never comes. It's dead silent, except for some distant sounds of traffic. The longer I look, the more it starts to look familiar. There's a tiny slice of the view from Destiny's window in the upper left-hand corner of the frame. I can't stop staring at that corner. It's too small from the blurry webcam footage to really make anything out but the vague shapes of the blackened windows and balconies of a set of rows of apartments opposite. Still no girl. Silent, empty, fuzz. Focusing on the top corner, I walk slowly across the room and reach for the light switch, flicking it on. I run back to the computer chair and lean in deep, but it's all still enmeshed in shadow.

I hear a half second of what sounds like a man's voice projected from a tinny speaker from the other side of the wall, and then the screen goes fully grey:

This stream has ended.

10.

When I wake up, it's pitch-dark. I stay still for a moment, hoping I can just ignore it, whatever it is, and go back to sleep, but I can feel a tightness in my lungs, so, trepidatious, I reach my arm out to see if I can feel a way out of the dark. I seem to be cramped into a tight, small space, coffin-like, fitting my body close. It's dirt. There is dirt pressed tight on all sides of me. I can hear the calls of the foremen guiding me towards the surface from above, the mockery of my betters, chiding me about how slim my arms are and how soft I've become. *Can't he take a joke? Does something seem off? You're gonna get yelled at sometimes if you fuck up, so just stop fucking up. We all did it.*

I am light-headed. At first breathing seems easier than I would have expected, as easy as it would be anywhere, if not for the little particles blown off the wall each time I exhale, and sucked into my lungs each time I inhale. I wonder if this might be a good place, a place where I can keep sleeping and let the hands of the earth take me in. It's freezing at first, but quickly my body heat starts to warm the space around me, first to a nice warm hug and then to a swelter.

I hear Mom's voice, and I think of Mom and the pills, how much of her own life's worth is tied up in me, how impossible the story that undergirds her life would be to maintain in my absence, and I wonder if, if I stayed in the earth, it would stir up another round between her and Dad, maybe push them to divorce for real this time, instead of just sitting in their miserable quiet. I hear Sam's voice, and I think of Sam, and whether he would blame it on himself, and I doubt it, but maybe it would at least upset him, set him crying to whoever the next girl is about how badly I hurt his ability to trust another person. I hear Destiny K.'s moans, the odd reticence in them ringing hollow in the night's cool breeze outside this hole.

I can hear them all now, on the other side of this wall of dirt, compressed inches from my face, voices that I can never seem to get out to the other side of, even as they seem so close.

He really needs to pick up the pace. I don't know why he takes things so seriously. I mean, we have a three-strikes policy for talking that way with customers, he must have known he was on thin ice.

That temptation to fall back asleep is coming over me again, I want to close my eyes but never quite get there. The skin on my hands is peeling back, flaking and irritated from sweat. I peel this skin back and rip through until it bleeds. My fingernails are filthy, grime under them mixing with the blood and getting into my wounds, the new wounds on my hands and the open cuts on my arms. Bugs are crawling on me, each one tickling and waking me again. I just want to sleep, but I have to tend to them, flipping, reaching towards and shooing away and taking them away to safety, but there are too many getting into the hole now, there must be a nest somewhere here, too little space for me to be sure I won't crush them in my sleep. I wish that I could see the queens in the walls of dirt surrounding me, that I could congratulate them on their babies' beauty, that they could teach me to lie on my back and be served and release thousands of spawn in pods, to dig into little corners and warm, dark places and hatch when the time is right. Turning, I see a Davy light over my head in arm's reach, and I reach into my coveralls for a lighter. Flicking on the little candle inside, I can see the dirt in front of my face, soft, near black, with flecks of lime-green vegetation throughout, and I reach out to feel its soft give between my fingers. Very quickly, I start to feel my breathing become even more strained, and realize the flame has been eating up my oxygen. I spit on my hand and reach up to try to snuff it out, sour saliva dangling in strands across my fingers and down my wrists. I open it and reach in to snuff the flame. The darkness is sudden and total. I have nothing to focus on but my lungs, wheezing from all the cigarettes, forcing in air in choking gasps. I scrape blindly in front of me, pulling hunks of dirt to the ground, trying to get to where the voices are calling me, but it's of no use, my skin is peeling and my nails are cracking under the pressure, and I am hyperventilating, exhausting air faster than I should, blood from my cuticles dripping down my fingers, making my hands slippery in their dog-paddle claw shapes. It's hot and wet and sticky. I keep scraping and pulling endlessly until finally an opening emerges, but there are no foremen, only a hole the size of a fingertip, with nothing but black on the other end. I force two fingers through the hole, then three, and pull at it, making room for the other hand, shoving until both hands are knuckle-deep into the crevice.

The voices are coming from above now:

She's smart, but she's really taking a lot of dumb risks lately. I hope she just moves home. I think she's probably always gonna need somebody to take care of her. Some people are just like that, and that's okay. Poor kid.

I pull outward from inside, creating an opening a couple feet wide, but there is no cool autumn breeze, no Dad or Sam, just another Davy light at the end of a long corridor on a long decline. I feel along the walls and start to discern a skeleton of cold metal scaffolding keeping the earth above from collapsing in on me. I remember when this was a place that felt safe, how happy I felt knowing I could help my friends with what I brought up out of this place, the pride I had in the recognition of my superiors. But now I am here alone, resenting that I was born, and though the air is clearer in the corridor than it was in the hole, there's nothing to do but descend. I grasp along the wall, moving myself along, odd swellings in and out of the earth and the metal smooth against my fingertips, blood drying into a satisfyingly crackling texture as it drags. I can still hear all the other men talking about me—*Come on! You're just about there! Just a little closer! We believe in you!*—but the distance of their voices never seems to change.

Reaching the next Davy light, I snuff it out too to save on air. For a while, I move just in the darkness, until the tenor of the voices starts to change again. *Which way are you going? No, we're here! Up here! Come on!* I keep my hands to the wall and my eyes straight. They can't fool me, they are on the other side of the wall, following me down, and they don't even know it, the poor fools. Poor dead co-workers, poor dead Dad, poor dead Sam, not even aware of it, calling again and again, laughing amongst themselves, telling stories. *Yeah, I really loved her, but I had to cut it off. I still kind of feel fucked-up about it. She was just like really, really mentally ill, you know? And like, I totally get that, I get depressed too, but like, at some point I realized I had to recognize when somebody was drowning before they could pull me down with them. I just really hope she's able to get herself out of there someday.* I finally start to look up as I walk, hoping I might be able to get a glimpse of him, but it's the same black as elsewhere, no gap or ladder presents itself. I feel along the wall, descending ever farther, at a far steeper decline now. Yet another Davy light is out there in the distance. I think of my cozy hole, start wishing I had given up and died in it. Next to the Davy light is a figure shrouded in darkness. I stop in my tracks, feeling the weight of my own breath.

The body is in the shape of a gaunt girl about my own height, but her features are obscured in shadow, and shapes poking through the black surface suggest a face that's only beginning to emerge from a deep void. She picks at her fingernails, fidgeting in little jitters like she just remembered something embarrassing, a shudder through the shoulders, a bouncing leg, shaking head. Her hands seem delicate and tender. She sings under her breath, the old vocal jazz number. Her voice is light, wavering, pensive, like she's afraid to be heard. I sit and watch her, huddled in the shadows, hoping not to be seen. She does this routine again and again at increasing speeds until her movements are herky-jerky and her motions start to leave blurry, black light trails behind them. The weight in my chest becomes overbearing and I can no longer hear the cacophony of the noise outside. *I need to be back in the hole. Please let me back into the hole.* And then I'm doubling back the way I came, tripping over myself in sheer panic, feeling the ache in my calves, the incline working against my stride. I can hear the tittering footsteps of the shape behind me, and, running my hand along the wall, feeling out the distance between beams and the shape of the frame to guide me in the dark, I realize its shape seems to have changed, protrusions that I recalled from the way down missing now I'm scrambling in the opposite direction. I break into a full sprint. The noise of the footsteps echoes behind me, overlapping beyond comprehension, growing more and more overwhelming, drawing me in. My legs ache and my body is screaming at me to rest, but this is not a restful place, the hole is where I am going to rest, and it is going to be warm and beautiful and final. I look back to see my last bit of light before that warm sleep, barely able to make it out, and I see that the figure is gone. I feel a hand on my shoulder pulling me backwards into the light, and I gasp the last of my air supply into collapsed lungs.

I open my eyes again and I'm under a grey, clear sky, flecks of wet snow dripping down from my hair into my eyes.

I have a splitting headache and my hands hurt like hell. Rolling over to see them, I notice the dirt under my fingernails, and fresh blood on my hands.

I turn my head and see nothing but dirt. I can't help but feel like the whole dream cycle is about to begin again. Swallowing, I turn my head back towards the sky. I am lying in a two-by-six-by-one-foot hole I have dug in the park out back of the apartment building.

I can see the garbage area under a scaffold, with its awful buzzing, flickering automatic light, which turns on too slowly at night, and the bright plastic jungle gym, with kids in puffy coats playing and their moms watching them. It's a sharp pain to sit up and push myself off the ground, but I manage it, and I hobble inside.

11.

I have to at least try to be reasonable here. It's probably just a girl who looks like me who makes porn on the internet, plenty of those. If I can just try to find this girl's website, or her details or whatever, I can send her a message, clear everything up, and I might be able to focus on work again. Yeah, just a normal skinny white girl, blond hair, similar face, dick. It seemed like she was having an okay time, but I guess it's tough to tell. There's another reason it couldn't have been me—I can't pretend at all. People seem to know everything about me before I can deceive them, so I couldn't have pretended to have a good time. There we go, problem solved.

Padding the hallway between the elevator and my apartment, eyes locked forward, I shoulder into an old woman I've never seen before, nearly knocking her over, the hall too narrow for one person to walk beside another. She mutters something at me under her breath, but I don't catch it as I scurry through the door. I think of my father's warnings that people might want to do bad things to a kid like me when I'm in a vulnerable state, and a deep wave of nausea burns through my gullet, an urge to puke with nothing in my guts to draw from.

I lock the padlock behind me. My hands are covered in mud and blood, and as I trail them along the yellowed walls to steady myself, I leave long crimson stains. Finally, climbing over mounds of black bags, I get to the bathroom. Looking at myself in the mirror, I notice my deterioration seems to have escalated since the last time I really paid attention to myself: ribs jutting out from under my pyjamas, cheeks pitted inwards, eyes, always sunken but now vicious, conical, their white a stark contrast shining out from deep, dark valleys. Maybe it's just an effect of all the dirt, a thin, fine layer over my skin, with patches of smeared mud flecked across it. I focus on my hands and run some hot water over them. I can feel the cold breaking up inside my muscles, at first a pleasant release of tension but soon a piercing sensation of nerves overwhelmed by more change than they're accustomed to. My fingers itch, and I scratch them hard under the hot water, indulging the urge, before stopping myself. I've bled enough.

Turning the water off, I think for a moment of the anhedonia that's come to define this place, a lack of sensation that has become a terrible pain in and of itself, whenever awareness of it arises, and from which actual pain is now a reprieve. Part of me wants to take a hot bath, lie down, try to exist in myself for a few moments, but I think of how it'll feel once I get in, lying there, too tall for the tub, staring at my cramped limbs and weird little overhangs and crevices and bits of loose skin, nothing to do but stare at myself and consider everything that got me to this point, and try to motivate myself to get out for more punishment. Part of me thinks if I lay down for a second I wouldn't be able to get going again, and I can't kid myself with that kind of thing. The wounds are clean, back to work.

I push some shit out of the way to clear a space for the chair and pull into my desktop. The tower whirs like a plane preparing for takeoff, and I click back into the packet. I start clicking blind through a survey for some kind of military ration that claims to be stable for over a hundred years if kept dry. I can see the tab to Destiny K.'s livestream in the upper-right corner of the screen, but I try to focus on the questions.

19. If you had to rely on HARDWON to survive in an emergency situation, would that be a positive or a negative experience for you? 1 being most negative, 5 being most positive.

Okay, just one check. She's not online, it's the same grey screen as before. Is there another site? I click on the blue link to the account and find her page, its profile picture just a shot of her body, those pristine, porcelain arms, unmarked by the self-harm scars or rashes or bug bites. If this was me, it would have to have been prior to September. If the title of the video can be trusted, June 23 was prior to my tantrum the night Sam left, so the most visible scars wouldn't have been there yet. I don't know if my skin ever looked that good. I guess it wouldn't even have had to be this year, it could have been last year at a work party or something, high school even, maybe, back when I was taking better care of myself. Jesus.

I recall waking up at the foot of the hill out behind my school one time, bruised, covered in grass and dirt, seemingly having tumbled down in the night. Dad was on a business trip, but I could imagine how horrified he would have been. Mom made me promise to keep it a secret from him, which felt like a strange violation of trust. That was when I was initially prescribed sedatives, to prevent the need for any more secrets, and to keep the panic attacks at bay. It worked for a little while, too; there were a couple years without incident, and I was generally pretty capable of not abusing the sedatives, either, though I remember Sam and me overindulging together a couple times. I think about refilling my prescription then remember I'd probably just wind up eating them all again if I even had access to them anymore.

There are now six different Destiny K. account tabs crowding out the survey tab at the top of the screen. I have a notepad open in the bottom corner of the screen and I keep finding myself pecking away at my theories:

similar-looking girl
hallucinating the whole thing / dream
raped while sleepwalking
got too fucked-up at staff party or something?

Underneath the profile pic are a series of links to other websites, all paywalled, that claim to have more content. In another tab, I check my bank account. It's going to be tight. This week's packet is nearly at its end, so there's no way I can pull overtime to try to make it up. I've cut hormones from my budget every week for, god, like a month? Time was already passing slower and slower as Sam called less, and now that he never calls at all, the days are starting to blend together, sleep getting rarer, the nights never seeming to end. No appetite, no smokes. A little wine, but that's it. I tab back over to the survey.

47. Compared to competitor brands, how much does HARDWON's design and packaging remind you of your experience in combat? (1 if not applicable)

48. Generally, how do you feel about your experience in combat? (1 if not applicable)

49. Do you display symptoms of Post-Traumatic Stress Disorder?

1, 1, 4. I click back on the clip pages and put in the minimum subscription for each. For some of these, this is $1, for others $5, and by the end I've spent $35 dollars for access to all of Destiny's pages. I sift through these voraciously, scrolling through an endless wall of faceless, abstracted body, seeing Destiny's tits and ass and dick from every possible angle, but her face is framed out of everything. Multiple captions allude to the ability to go on private chat, and I send her a request, but there's no answer. The most recent video, dated around the end of August, shows Destiny in a latex nurse's uniform, stripping it slowly across her chest before pulling her dick out from just above the zipper and jerking off to completion directly into the camera. For months prior, she was posting dozens of these, every week, in different costumes, with different gimmicks. The consistency and degree of maintenance here doesn't seem like something I would have been able to pull off in a fugue. At the end of the video, she folds her leaking cock back into the dress, and speaks for the first time:

"Hey guys! Just taking a little time off to work on some personal stuff, but I promise I'll be back soon with more hot content!"

The voice is at a higher pitch than I attempt on my best days, but it's undoubtedly my own. The wave of nausea comes over me again. I feel light-headed. The room is sinking out from underneath me and the computer chair ceases to be a reliable counterbalance, sending me tumbling onto the floor, into the trash. I lie on the ground for a moment and stare into the last stand of the roaches nesting inside the radiator, a thin metal bar that runs along the baseboard. I'm inclined downwards, my face in the garbage, in the endless empty bottles of wine, cigarette packets, ramen wrappers, staring straight into my friends' beautiful home, their scattered egg casings, their black-pepper guano, the breeding piles of armoured monarchs, shells layered with microscopic children. I hope to myself that as the days get shorter and my friends dwindle away, they might crawl inside me and make me a world of their own. That I might be able to sustain them better than I've sustained myself. To become the landscape, more than just its overseer.

If the body in that video is my body, it has happened with this body's full participation, though not with mine. Or something has my body but I do not have its memories. Or someone has created an image of my body in such perfect detail that they know it better than I know it myself. Whichever it is, I was not meant to see it.

12.

I keep Destiny's livestream link open in a tab in the corner of my screen at all times, but it hasn't been active since the one time a couple months ago. Surveys go slower now that I'm clicking away from them every five or ten minutes, using every tiny slice of downtime I can catch while submissions are processing or while new packets are loading to keep absolutely certain that she hasn't come online to reveal herself to me even once.

There are still way too many possibilities for my mind to be able to follow. My familiar thought patterns are constantly clouded by that inactive tab at the corner of the screen. Why was the camera active with nobody onscreen? How did I time it up just right to catch her that one time? Why hasn't she been on since? Was there some kind of collaboration between her and the member of the Default Persona she sent to alert me to her presence? Or, worse yet, had the Default Persona itself become aware of me? *Destiny K.* feels like a tip-off: *Destiny K.*, *Destiny Knocks*, "(invitation) to one's (destiny)," "(sealing) one's (fate)." Was there some private chat log somewhere full of people collecting information on me, intent on driving me to suicide? Through some set of small details I'd given away through the posts, they'd figured out I was some horrible, poor shut-in, and they decided to build a little game for me to play, posting just infrequently enough to let me do the majority of the torture to myself. They had probably figured out where I live, filmed me, catching enough glimpses from when I would sleep-walk or when I stepped out to the balcony to create a database of images wide enough to make the deepfake porn that reeled me into this whole thing in the first place. And the best part is that they know there are no consequences, a shut-in has no self-defence until the boundary of the sanctuary is crossed, and until that point I'm helpless in the face of whatever they want to do with my name and to my image, with no real evidence that any organization was ever behind it.

The only thing I'm missing is motive. Was there a particularly mean post in my recent history? I usually just browse and don't post; the only thread I made with any real engagement was the porn thread, which went up way after this all started, so that's a dud. Is it literally just that I'm trans? But then how did I get visible enough to become a target? Since starting transition, I've figured somebody might have some set of issues they would want to take out on me the second I was "too perceived," but I've tried to keep my paper trail smaller than most, so they'd have to have really gone out of their way to find me. And there are so, so many trans girls on the internet, generally they'll at least have a reason when they pick one to mob.

The cold starts to get into my hands and I pull them back under the stack of blankets growing up for the floor that I am sitting inside. I hold them to my chest, I'm never quite able to get them back to normal temperature. Maybe the landlord is in on it too, nobody else in the building's been shut off and it's just me. They want to drive me out from where I have control, out onto their turf, to guide me towards this exact replica of myself to fool me into trying to kill myself again. If I can see through the ruse, they'll find another way eventually, and another, and another, until I succumb. Sam was an agent, I'm sure, and our conversation that night was the first of several approaches the Default Persona will take in order to murder me, followed by this demon clone. The sleepwalking itself was programmed in from childhood through subtle cues in speaking with them online, as they always knew what lay inside me and what their plans were, plans to make sure I felt too estranged from others to ask for help and to start me down the path of suggestibility that would make me delusional enough to comply with their goals.

One day, I'm certain, I'll wake up in a new place, quite far from the city. It'll be a quiet, soft, mossy-green place deep in the woods, a faerie's perch, settled between underbrush in a way that's invisible to everything, and extending up so many verdant ropes of undergrowth towards an endless night sky. Slowly, from behind bushes and from within shadows, every man I've ever spoken to on the internet will step out from behind his anonymity and introduce himself to me with his full name, tell me how I have wronged him, how I have made him feel small, and I will see a glint in the darkness from behind his back. He will produce his knife and he will pierce my ribs. I will bend over at an angle, not mortally injured, and breathe hard, and the next man will approach, and he will again explain how I have wronged him, and he will find a fresh unbroken spot, and he will show his blade, and he will show me how I made him feel. Man after man will visit me in this soft, quiet place, and each will have played a role in ensuring everything had built up towards this moment in exactly the way he needed it to.

Click click click click click, click click, click click click, click click click click click, click. Click click click, click click click click click click click click click click, click click, click click click click click click. Click click click click click click click click click click. Click, click click.

When compared to competitor brands, do you consider Kraft Singles sexually arousing?

1 2 3 4 5

I check the stream again.

Staring into the mirror of that grey screen, I go over in my mind every detail of my memory of the empty apartment it so briefly showed me. Where could the conspiracy have placed the camera in order to capture my being from enough angles to create this other self? The more I think about it, the less it seems to make sense. But what does anymore? With no information to go on, as I wait for stimulation that never seems to come, the fine details of the information I do have are magnified to immense proportions.

I begin to consider an alternative explanation: For my entire life, I've always been split in two, my body carrying me where it wants to at night. I've been sleepwalking into this other place and conducting another life, acting on desires and needs entirely beyond my own. Needs that constitute some ritual I am not aware of, but which holds the fabric of my life together in some way. This me on the screen is the *real me* that the *fake me* that I am is incapable of acknowledging. At some point, I still would expect some kind of physical evidence of this happening, but maybe the night self is extremely careful about ensuring that the day self remains undisturbed. Or is that too easy?

I still can't move, but as my gaze locks into the upper-left corner of the grey screen, I can feel myself crawling towards Destiny's apartment, as if there were an underground tunnel between the two. It hurts my knees to crawl, but I emerge from the tunnel standing, peering, it is entirely empty with the exception of a bed, that bed, from the background of the image that led me here. I shudder at the sight of it, but it starts to seem strangely inviting. The striplights above are on, coating the room in a soft pink fluorescence. The edges of things become soft and gauzy. I smell the empty room, its perfume and linen, its old smoke fried into the yellowed walls, the smoke of someone I'd had over, surreptitiously leaning over the windowsill with a cigarette while we talked. I can feel myself start to exist in the room, experiencing what it must be like to be me in this place. I can hear myself speaking to someone through the wall, laughing with words pouring out soft and smooth, without any distinct meaning. There's someone here with me, and I feel warmed by their presence.

I feel along the wall of the apartment. The floor plan is exactly the same: a hallway connecting to a kitchen, then around the corner into a barren living room, lingering empty with just a small table and chairs at its centre. A deep hum emanates through the room, and again I hear words through the wall that I can't seem to distinguish no matter how hard I try. I can feel myself interacting with the environment—pushing a chair an inch to the left, meandering towards the window, pulling the curtain forward. Seeing block apartments across the street, staring in windows to see if I can see myself there too, not seeing anything.

Now the other me through the wall and her friend are gone, but I can still sense myself experiencing through them, we are somewhere in public, surrounded by people, having a good time. I have someone to look after me while I'm out there. I begin to think very seriously about this other existence, happening somewhere else just out of reach. Maybe I can communicate with the other me telepathically, try to keep our paths from crossing. Maybe I could make some kind of agreement with her to stay chaste, to prevent any distortions of the type we've been experiencing and ensure that both of us can experience the same degree of comfort in this body we've been forced to share. I try, again, to place myself in her, to see something clearly in the mishmash of red and pink, the noise of the people she's surrounded herself with, but nothing comes.

It's still just me, in this empty, clean apartment, feeling along the edges of the white wall, listening for the edges of another experience. I begin to develop sense memories of how it might have felt to be fucked in this room. Destiny's sensations become a place that I can flick into at will, and I begin to ask myself if I was ever fully human, or if it was this duality within me that created the wall I experience between myself and others.

I place my hands on my knees and grasp hard at the computer desk, feeling the room change again, back into the garbage and the foul reeking. My eyes remain locked in on the dead stream, my mind focused on my memory of that clean, empty room, its clean, empty attached life, knowing its possibilities. The world is moving under me, my sense of control returning. I begin to test my ability to phase between the modes. Red, to white, to the grey of the CRT's fluorescence raining over me, and back again. Time passes faster. I keep my wrist clicking here for days, then weeks on end. I begin to attempt to collapse each of these streams of consciousness into a single self, a coherent being with a single set of memories. If I can get just a little bit more data, maybe I can build some kind of coherent narrative around their simultaneity. But the closer I come back to the computer chair, to the eye of the screen, to my "real" body, the more the other visions seem to slip from my mind completely.

I hope for her sake that maybe she gets to live without the wall, or can move beyond it. I've started to feel envious of her, travelling outside that place and leaving it empty for me to explore, while my only option seems to be endless recursion back into the same place I already am, but now stripped of its contents, stripped of my ability to claim dominion over even the smallest parts of my reality. Destiny is the real one, and I am the fake one. My physical body cannot die, but I know that I'm the one who will cease to exist when the collapse occurs. I must do everything I can to try to induce it as soon as possible.

13.

The bug with the horns in the trash is dead. I stand over him for a minute staring, not sure whether to cry for the fact he's gone or celebrate the fact he'd been here to present me with a novelty when I really needed it. It's quieter than normal. Where I would usually expect to overturn a pile of laundry and find a swarm, the nests lie unoccupied. There are maybe still a few roaches scattered, cannibalizing those they only recently shared with, but the hard-fought battle is over for most, and any and all flying critters long since bade farewell. I feel the welts along my neck and ribs, each a small goodbye kiss of acknowledgement from a guest who's now passed from this place. The red, barely visible discs lining the floor around the side of the mattress are no longer active, locked in nymphal stages. The only friends still present are the silverfish in my clothes, who, between their lack of sensitivity to temperature and their stable diet of dandruff and must, seem to have been minimally affected by the change of seasons. It's lonelier here than it was before, and the cold makes it harder to get out of bed in the morning.

It also smells worse than normal. It's been snowing and the heat is still off. When I turned the taps to set up for my coffee and ramen in the morning a few days ago, something thick and black spurted out, and it hasn't given me anything since. The bathroom sink worked for a couple days after that, then it did the same thing. I moved to the bathtub faucet and it did the same thing. I've been eating my ramen dry since then. I have to carry my sheets, sweat-sticky even when bone-dry, blood-stained several times over, around on my back or else frostbite starts to set in in my ears and fingers. Bathing was out of the question for several days even before the water went out, as attempting to dry off in some of these temperatures would be a gamble. I thought about calling the landlord, but if he came in and saw how I keep the place, I'm sure I'd be evicted.

I've been having a pretty tough time moving from room to room with the trash piled up and the blankets hanging off me. I find myself tripping and falling into and underneath the bags more and more often. I wonder whether it might be time for a cycling-over of the garbage, but there's too much work to do to get hung up on that, and every movement seems to pull from a very limited store of available energy.

It's sometime later. I'm staring at the base of the front door, and my neck feels like it's broken. Shocks run down my side when I try to bend upwards to look around and relocate myself. I can see the padlock facing me down from above. It looks like it's partially frozen, so I at least know I didn't get out. I didn't bring any blankets with me and it's burning hot in my extremities, like my flesh is melting. My neck isn't broken, but it's stiff from sleeping however long I've slept there half-cocked against the wall. I'm hardly able to get myself out of the corner I'd dug into with all the strength I could summon. Whatever energy I had left is now draining out of me like vapour, into the icy, nuclear-yellow light-pollution night. My will begs my body for some fuel to power itself out of this, but nothing comes.

I think back to the upper corner of the other apartment. Down the hallway, I can see a narrow slice of picture window between the wall and door. I start to crawl carefully around the bags, back to the window, to the darkness, the same route I have walked again and again in mirror image in that sterile room. Between the door and balcony bars I can now see a lit window across the street, a bedroom window, behind a balcony and beside a picture window. It is that apartment, the apartment in the grey apartment block that stands mirror to my own.

In that clean apartment across the street, the other apartment, two figures stumble through the door in silhouette, a man and then a woman, about the same height. He's pulling off his shoes without untying them, and she's fumbling with things on her vanity absent-mindedly as he sits on the bed. She walks to him, touches his hand, guiding him up from the bed and pressing him against the full-length mirror on the wall in a kiss. I slink forward across the detritus on the floor, pulling myself by one arm towards the balcony door. The angle is still wrong, and the girl's back is an obscure shape. My arms are wrist-deep in the warm, wet garbage, shaking, ready to give in as I keep myself propped up, and I can feel some surviving maggots slithering between my fingers in the moist carpet beneath. The farther I inch along the floor, the more details emerge: They are still in an embrace, now in the bed, now closer and under covers, shoulders bare from underneath. I roll forward, thighs pressed against the floor, numb and ripping themselves on and off each sticky patch of uncovered carpet. Finally I reach the frozen balcony door, but from this close the stacks of snow-covered trash bags on the balcony are higher than my line of vision. I can't see anything anymore. The perspective would be just right if not for the obstruction. Finally, pushing myself past an internal breaking point, I pull myself to my feet, dragging myself up with the door handle as a lever and my other arm jammed against the wall to stabilize me. I open the door. The fog and the snow are beating down sideways, rapping against my bare skin. I am no longer feeling anything. I push the bags over the edge of the balcony and hear them explode on the blue concrete seconds later. I am making myself a window.

What I can now see is Sam. It's Sam, face in full focus, making no noise and staring down at the girl's asshole. He's gained a little weight, pressing down on her from behind, forcing her shoulders into the bed. In front, the girl is me, I am staring at myself, a mirror reflection of my own face distorted into a mortified grin. Her jaw comes unhinged and mine follows, a sharp gasp escaping my mouth into the silent night air.

14.

I stare and stare and stare at her in the blue snow, sucked into her black eyes. She is showing me her teeth, and now the bones of her jaw. Slowly, the other me's expression morphs from a sickening pride into determination to begin the task at hand.

Sam is still pumping, eyes aimed downwards, dissociated in deep focus, as his tibia begin to twist out of their joints, ripping through fat and muscle, through his hairy thighs, to dig their way deep into my hips and ass. Hot, dark blood is running down my skin from the pin-tight perforations a polygonal lattice of bone is forming between bodies becoming one entity. Sam, his cock inside me, looking out from the picture window, is smiling, lifting his arms back over his head, extending his back, snapping his spine backwards, landing on his hands, extending his neck and sprawling backwards out onto the bed, his face hidden now as his cock delves far deeper than it should be able to into my asshole, his cock is at the centre of the polyhedron marking the point of connection, his legs slowly begin to lift backwards away from me, bending back towards his neck, moving in unison and revealing his thorax, folded in half, emerging from my spinal column, and now forming the silhouette of a great scorpion with my sneering visage as the head and Sam's broken body as the tail. The tail curls into a crescent moon, Sam's feet pointed forward as a stinger, and dual rib cages pile up across the back of the new animal. It begins to take on a pyramid-like shape, it gets taller and taller, and my smiling face at our bottom flattens its shoulders and my downwards-bent arms form front legs, elbows snapping and peeling through skin, its spine sticking out at a hard ninety degrees towards the central lattice, penis still pulsating in orgasmic tremor building towards the second face in the underbelly, Sam's face, locked in a sort of defeated sigh of embarrassment. As he comes, his arms are broken backwards, twisted past their sockets into half-length mandibles leaning forward on the radius, forming the set of middle legs between my front arms and the scorpion's tail, feet emerging from its back. The me-faced bug stops for a moment, still getting accustomed to the angle and to its new limbs' idiosyncrasies, then crawls down off the side of the bed. It must be in unimaginable pain just existing, but its movements are extremely fast, extremely precise, uncanny in its speed for something of its size. It preens back and forth, tottering on its little claws to give me a full view in profile, then starts to crawl slowly up the wall. My face at the front of the thing never breaks eye contact, it is imperious, it knows that it's got me stuck to this spot, regardless of how foul it becomes. As it maintains this eye contact, as it crawls all the way up the clean white wall, the me-face bends forty-five degrees from its neck, vertebrae breaking through translucent skin. The lights in the room across the street start to flicker. Now the thing is becoming more adjusted to its new body. It starts to skitter from wall to wall in little flashes, each movement barely perceptible, seeming to make greater strides with each shift back into light. Then it bares its bottom and twin stomachs against the glass of the balcony door, and puts its mandibles on the handle, fumbling for a second like a child unaccustomed to its own strength, before cracking the door and immediately slithering out into the snow. My terrible face sticks its neck back upwards to maintain its grinning eye contact as its six legs slither their way down the side of the building before disappearing into the fog below. I'll be back soon, I know, on the opposite end of the voyeur's divide. I step back inside and lock the balcony door.

I walk backwards, trembling, keeping my eye on the glass, but eventually stumble, falling helpless into the soft trash. It's then I start to hear the sound. It's a staccato tittering across the glass like a ticking clock. It's tough to tell from how far, but it's getting louder and higher in pitch. I pull myself up again and turn and run around the hallway wall and into the bedroom, locking the bedroom door behind me and diving across the room and over the desktop to hit the latch on the window as well. My face is hot and numb and my chest feels caved in. Sobs are coming every few seconds. Feeling is coming back now that I'm inside; I hate it, but it is alternately hot and freezing feeling shooting to the ends of each limb, ears and toes shrieking for release. I wrap myself in the sheet and wait to wake up, wait for all this to pass, but the moment seems to linger on forever, and the skittering keeps growing louder and more dissonant until I am sure I can hear scratching on the window next to my head. Something inside me shuts down entirely. This is sort of what I wanted, isn't it?

The sheet I am covered in is thin, not enough to hide in but enough to feel a little warmer, and it filters my vision piss-yellow as I see the first face in the window, the Sam face on the thing's belly, smirking like it's finally gotten off. It's scratching against thin glass, looking for a subtler solution than breaking the window, but not quite able to articulate its cracked wrist pincers enough to undo the locks directly. After a second it gives up and smashes itself straight through, face-first.

The violent wind and snow pour into the room. The Sam face pulls itself through the hole it's made, dragging the rest of itself through the broken glass around the edges of the frame. Long lacerations run all the way up its body, but it does not seem to notice or care about its injuries, keeping its singular focus on me as it bleeds all over the vinyl like an animal.

My face pulls forward from the back of the thing and, re-establishing eye contact, runs itself across the sheet, across my arms, my shoulder, my neck, until we're finally face to face.

I'm thinking nothing. The me-face's smile grows wider until only the top half retains any resemblance to me and the jaw is distended into a gaping maw, bits of broken neck jutting through the hole forming new teeth. Noises emanate from the red, like screams for help, masked and distorted through the drum-tight webbed tissues of its throat. It leans back against the scorpion's tail at its back, grabbing me through the sheet with the pincers, using its arms, my arms, lifting me into my new mouth, easing me in headfirst. As I'm covered in a first coat of saliva, I no longer feel a need to flee. Each layer of tissue takes a moment to break through as its muscles, still developing, push me on until I pass the foot of the throat and sit inside the stomach of the thing.

Someone is knocking on the door. At first pensive, nervous, a series of quick taps, then intensifying, louder pounds as knuckles turn into fists beating at the door. A familiar, higher voice, my own voice, is calling from the other side of the door over the beating growing more and more frenzied.

It's dark and warm and comfortable in the bug's belly. I wait patiently until I pass out.

II. LET'S TRY THAT ONE MORE TIME...

Time has come now to stop being human, time to find a new creature to be.

— *Thinking Fellers Union Local 282, "Noble Experiment"*

1.

Most nights when I go to bed, I remember the smell of that place: the old metal, the wood flooring soaked through from years of bleach cleans, the incense seeping in from upstairs. Sometimes, on worse nights: the smell of blood, the scraping noise, my mom screaming at me.

"WHAT DID YOU DO?"

I try not to think of these things.

Buzz in my ass.

Thank you so much, skylarrocks, for 500 coins. What am I doing this weekend? Oh, thanks for asking! You know, not much, making dinner, going to bed. Maybe going to drinks with the girls. Just the girls, but you never know. Haha, I can't tell you that. Tonight? No, just staying in, watching some Netflix, making nachos. Gaming. Gamer girrrllll, haha, yeah. Oh, I'm getting a DM.

Buzzbuzzbuzz.

Whoa! 100 coins! It looks like ozymandius_22 is taking me on private, guys, we're gonna go on a little break and I'll see you in five! Kisses!

Plonk.

Hi Ozzy! You've got five minutes on private. What would you like?

show face.

Oh no, I can't do that, I'm sorry. That's my one rule.

show face.

Clock's ticking, Ozzy. You've got a cute girl who will do whatever you want, except that, for four minutes and thirty seconds.

ass up at camera then.

I take a second to wait before I go. He's definitely got more.

ass worship mommy joi with countdown

Perfect!

Buzzbuzzbuzzbuzz.

I'm on the floor, bent over my laptop, and turn around to show my ass. I rest my elbows on the pillows I've set in the corner next to my desk and arch my back towards the camera, sticking my neck out under the desk. My neck hurts a little, but I stick to it to keep the angle. I check the screen from the mirror under the desk — the angle is perfect. I start wiggling my butt, gradually speeding up. It feels silly, but I still can't deny the little thrill that comes with knowing someone's whole brain is lit up looking at me.

Okay, you're going to be a good boy for Mommy, aren't you, and wait until I tell you to cum, right? Good boys come when Mommy tells them to. It's okay, you can look at my ass. Look at how it moves, doesn't it just make you want to grab it? Lick it? Grab Mommy's hips and fuck me? Cum in me? But you can't yet. Like I said, good boys only come when they're told to, and you have sooooo long. Four whole minutes? How are you ever gonna make it when Mommy moves her ass for you like this? Isn't it nice? Doesn't Mommy's big ass make baby feel safe? Look at how it moves. Do you want me to take my panties off? You've been really good, so I think I will. Look at it. Don't you just love staring at Mommy's big ass? Do you like the way it moves for you? Come a little closer. Smell it. Doesn't it smell all nice and clean and ready for my special boy?

Plonk. Buzzbuzz.

it smells disgusting. like sweat. you just got home from the gym.

Doesn't it smell so bad? Mommy loves her workouts so much, but then she gets home and she's all stinky and sweaty. All the guys at the gym stare at me but only my special boy gets to come and put his face in it. Come lick up Mommy's ass sweat. I need you to clean me off. Mommy's so filthy and she needs you to help her get clean. Stick your face right in there, yeah. Ahhhh, that feels so good, baby. You're so good.

Plonk, buzz.

i'm really bad at it actually. like, incompetent. let me suck your cock

Ahh, you're doing such a bad job. Mommy is so disappointed in you. Lick deeper, come on, I know you can do better than that. Eat me out and suck me off from the back. Let Mommy push it back for you, doesn't that feel good in your mouth? Letting Mommy feed you? Doesn't it make you feel better to have Mommy's ass and cock in your face? Doesn't she do everything around here, and you just take and take and take. You should be grateful I even let you do this to me anymore. My boy is supposed to grow out of this, but here he is, still licking my ass and cock at his age. Look at how I'm shaking it for you. Can you even begin to understand how hard it's been for me? The things I went through to bring you into this world?

please start countdown

10 ... Lick faster, come on, make sure Mommy gets off before you do... 9 ... I'm gonna be so mad at you if you come too soon ... 8 ... I can't believe how disgusting you are, doing this with your own mother ... 7 ... You'd better keep stroking fast or I'll yell at you ... 6 ... Look at how gross my butt Is ... 5 ... Do you really like this, or are you just trying to impress me? ... 4 ... You're gonna make such a mess on my nice clean carpet ... 3 ... I just had those washed and now they're gonna have cum all over them ... 2 ... You'd better not come yet ...

Plonkbuzz.

i'm done

I un-arch my back and un-stretch my neck. Spinning the pillow around in front of me, I slide onto my knees, neck at the edge of the frame. I make an exaggerated swallowing motion in my throat.

Pitiful. What a failure. I can't believe Mommy's gonna have to clean you up now. Can't you do anything right? Well, let me lick this up ... Mmmm, hmmmmm ...

There are still forty seconds left on his clock.

thank you

You'd better thank Mommy, she took such good care of you ...

Come on, are you really gonna take every second? Usually, if they come early, they dip right away, especially quiet guys like this. But nope, me and Ozzy sit it out in silence for another thirty seconds, me making little moans and nuzzling sounds to try to test if he's still there. He might have walked away from his computer to clean himself up and just left it idling. Checking the stream, most people in the public stream left during the break, just a couple weirdos sitting there staring at a blank screen for five minutes. I can't help but feel a little pissed. I perch my knees back on the pillow, keeping my head out of frame, hover my cursor over "End Stream" in the bottom-right corner of the screen.

Hey guys, it's starting to get late, so I think I'm gonna get going for the night, but love you lots, I'll see you tomorrow. Byeeee!

And *click*. I take a second to put my hair up, getting out of character. I try to keep my bedroom minimal: a matte-pink Ikea desk sitting in front of a window, a queen mattress on a wire frame facing it, kept tightly made with silk navy sheets, then the filming corner, with its fluffy pillows and sex toys. In the bathroom, I take the Lush out of my ass, forcing out a little lube-fart, which I quickly wipe off my hand with toilet paper. I spray down both the Lush and my hand with disinfectant and foam the spray into bubbles under the faucet. My hands get so dry when I'm working, but I hardly notice until I go to wash off the toys. I dry off the Lush with a towel and bring it back to the bedroom, laying my livelihood into its cute little box, placing the box into its silk carrying bag. I lay the package on top of a stack of similar boxes inside bags, all piled up next to my filming corner. I toss the dirty towel into the laundry basket, then come back to the bathroom to shower. I wind up spending longer than I'd meant to in there, fogging up the mirrors, applying cleansers, scrubs, exfoliating, applying a hair mask. I start dissociating after a while if I'm onstream too long, so it's really nice to just get to exist in my body for a while afterwards and take care of myself. I learned from an early age that no one else would take care of me, and little rituals are a nice way of honouring that.

My peace is broken when I look up at the wall and see a roach. I instinctively smash it with my palm. Last time I saw one, I set out traps and put all my open food into glass containers for a little while, then never saw one again. It looks like I'll need to set new traps and pull the containers back out. Swiftly wrapping a towel around myself, I dry enough not to make a mess on the floor and hop back over to the sink to wash the roach guts off my hand. I wash it twice to be sure, pull a roll of paper towel and a bottle of Lysol out from under the sink, and spray down the spot where its guts sat, stuck into the wall. I read online that they eat each other and that they're filled with diseases. I know you're not supposed to kill them, but I can't help it. I think about what you're supposed to do, letting them live, setting out traps, and letting them wipe themselves out in their own nests, and it gives me chills all over. Why should I have to suffer for my neighbours' laziness? I'm starting to really rile myself up about this when my phone starts to buzz.

I pick up. "Hey! What's up?"

"Where are you? We were supposed to meet at karaoke like twenty minutes ago."

"Sorry, work ran late. Be, like, thirty?"

"Fine, tardy bitch."

"Love you too. See you soon."

I catch myself doing the same little kissy sound I do constantly onstream and hang up.

I forgot about my plans with Vivian tonight. I have to admit I'm a little disappointed I have to do my makeup and get dressed. I was really looking forward to settling back into bed in cozy pyjamas and putting on some dumb YouTube video to fall asleep to. I open the bathroom door to air it out a little, it's too steamy in here even with the fan running.

2.

Vivian, a tall tan girl with a wild mop of brown hair, sits next to me nursing a screwdriver in one hand and a shot glass full of soju in the other, a cigarette tucked behind her ear, and we're watching Clara sing "Hungry Heart" on the public stage. The stage makes her eyes look even bigger than they are, and she's doing a goofy little mom-dance, swaying her arms as she sings.

We like to meet at this Korean karaoke place downtown sometimes, a red-lit joint hidden upstairs behind the Cactus Club and over the Shoppers. To get in, you have to walk through the dirty lobby of this really sketchy apartment building and go up one floor. The bar is filthy but somehow still cleaner than the lobby, its interior a series of sticky communal tables in rows faced towards the stage. Along the walls, TVs play music videos on silent. It's a Wednesday night, and the rest of the bar is empty except for an exceptionally hot bartender, Josh, whom I tried to make a pass at once and who acted like he was way too busy to talk, and a Filipino family of four who are there most nights we come, whose names I can never remember but who drove me home more than once when I was drunk. The family cheer Clara on like a pop star while Vivian and I talk.

"So, Montreal, huh?" Vivian is saying.

"It seems like Vancouver's kind of over? You can be a landlord, there's whatever's left of tech if you can get into that, or you can scrape by selling coffee and living with a zillion roommates, but there's no culture left. All the cool internet girls are either in Montreal or New York, but moving countries feels too big."

"It's pretty fucked," Vivian agrees. "I don't know if you're gonna do much better out there, though, tough to get a job if you don't speak any French. If you're sticking with Canada, I'd probably go back to the prairies, personally. Don't have to learn French, people *talk* to you, like, strangers on the street even. Rent's dirt cheap, and winter's a great excuse to stay in. It's not the worst."

"I do love the winter. But I can't go to a smaller city. I wanna shoot as big as possible for my career, you know?"

Vivian smirks a bit. "Your career in what? Are you, like, an actress now?"

"I don't know, I just want to make friends, and see people, and try to see as much and do as much as I can. Hopefully the money stuff'll just work itself out."

"Oh, for sure. Move to the opposite side of the country, no plan in mind, no education, no skills, always goes awesome. Still camming?"

"Yeah."

"You still owe me fifty bucks for topping you onstream, by the way."

"I'll get the next round. But yeah, still at it."

"No wonder you're broke. I'm telling you, you've got a car, you might as well put up an ad if you're that strapped for cash. It's hard fucking work, don't get me wrong, but the worst part's mostly just the driving. These guys are out on the edge of town and I'm stuck in morning commute traffic to suck some nasty, half-hard dick. You're better off, though, online's too much competition."

I must have made a face against my will, because Vivian sinks a little. Clara's really biting into that last verse about the Kingstown bar up there, she'd been quiet all night, so I could tell something was really wrong.

"Okay, well, maybe more than just the driving," Vivian says. "But it's way better money, and I have no doubt you could pull it off if you tried, angel."

"I just don't really want to. I like the distance, you know? The safety. Sitting on my own bed, with my own things. And anyway, if this corporate job pans out, who knows? Maybe I won't need to worry about it anymore."

"You mean the chatbox thing? I can't believe you'd trust people like that with your banking info. There's no way you're actually living alone off that, are you?"

I sink, embarrassed. "Well, my mom still sends me money sometimes."

Vivian stands up from her seat, hands flat against the table, incredulous. Clara floats down the stairs off the stage, fans going wild.

"Are you hearing this shit? She doesn't actually pay her own rent."

Clara chimes in, widening her brown eyes innocently with a smirk. "Oh, I don't either."

Vivian's taken even further aback. "I didn't realize I was surrounded by the idle rich. Never paying the tab again, just FYI."

"Mine's all student loans, though," Clara says. "Probably have to move back home once school's over, then it's gonna be pretty hard for probably a long time. Are you really getting covered, Amy?"

"I mean, partially. But Mom won't answer my texts or my calls, I don't know if she'll keep sending me money if I move. She hasn't even spoken to me since I moved out, but every month, right when I expect it to stop, the transfer comes in. I've been able to pay it without the help most of the time, but it still comes like clockwork. I just wish she'd acknowledge me instead of just throwing money at me, because it's starting to feel like a weird control thing. But yeah, I dunno, I try not to worry about it too much."

The three of us nod seriously for a second. I start to see that dreaminess again in Clara, her eyes drifting sadly towards the wall, preoccupied. I spot a chance to change the subject.

"Hey, what's up with you tonight, girl?"

"I broke up with Silas again."

Me and Vivian share a quick look.

"I think we're just kind of drifting, you know. I'm so busy right now, I think he was feeling underappreciated, and I snapped at him a little. He couldn't handle it. Said I was 'being unreasonable,' said some really weird stuff about how all my friends are trans girls and it made him feel insecure with me being around you guys all the time."

I put my hand on her arm. "Oh, god, I'm sorry."

Vivian pours Clara a shot from the jug. "Oh no, no more sermons from Silas. Who will save our souls now?"

Clara turns, hurt. "Hey, we might not be dating anymore, but I'm still going to mass with him."

Vivian scoffs. "Dude's hot, but he's so fucked-up. I couldn't date him."

Clara rests her cheek against her hands, elbows on the table. "Hey, don't talk that way, he's still my best friend. He basically saved my life when I was in a really dark place, and before this he's never been weird about the queer stuff before. I think he was just hurt and lashing out, but it was honestly so disappointing."

Vivian leans back in her chair. "Let me know when you invite him, so I can skip it."

"Yeah, it might be time to just move on," I say.

Clara turns up her nose as she takes her shot. "I can make my own choices, thank you."

I take Clara's hand, look her in her eyes. "We're totally supportive of you, we just think you're capable, and beautiful, and don't need some guy taking advantage of you. And I mean, I don't know about you, Vivian, but I grew up Catholic, so you getting all enthusiastic about it for your thesis definitely brings up some baggage for me."

Vivian bursts out laughing. "Talk to me when you get confirmed!"

Clara kicks her chair from across the table, laughing. "Confession is *scary,* okay! What am I supposed to say in there? I did a lot of bad shit!"

Vivian stands up, wobbling a little, and pulls me up out of my seat by the arm. "Come on, superstar, song's on."

We slur through "Only Happy When It Rains" to cheers.

3.

On the train home, I put on a podcast and scroll through Instagram. The voice in my ears is a man's voice, serious and stern.

Today, we're going to be examining the case of the Shinjuku Butcher, whose reign of terror from 1989 to 1991...

I am looking at photos and videos of people at cool parties, mostly other trans girls in dimly lit New York dive bars and apartments. Everyone is unemployed, and they are kept afloat by a million projects: podcasts, films, music, blogs, brand deals. They are all always asking for money and asking each other for money, and I wonder how someone could exist in that kind of barter economy. Maybe it's just the way I was brought up, but I feel like I would have such a hard time advocating for myself like that — a weird pride about having a job and being able to do it all on top of it, though I'd never look down on that life. Honestly, I'm jealous more than anything. They're the only people I know whose lives don't seem to revolve entirely around work.

Victims were girls, aged between twelve and fourteen, initially reported missing from the area around Nishishinjuku Junior High School in Tokyo...

I don't really know any of them, though they're friendly to me online. I'll reach out first, complimenting some project or commenting on a point they'd made on a podcast, and sometimes they reach back out to me. They're all so interesting and well-read and they message me way more than any of the people I know here do. Getting anybody out to do anything here is like pulling teeth; everything's too expensive and nobody has the money for anything, so you really have to be aggressive to put a party together or even go to a club. I haven't been to a club since faking my way into the gay bars as a teen, and I miss it so much. The connection on the dance floor, the openness with strangers, the sense of safety in community and the way that everyone seems cool in the dark. It seems like some people get to have that all the time.

A common thread between victims was that they commuted by train, and seemed to disappear somewhere between Shinjuku and Iwamotocho Stations, from middle-class families located in the outer-central industrial areas...

I guess it's a dream of living among artists, though I never really got into anything creative myself. I could sing as a little kid, and I performed in competitions and musical theatre and things like that, but by the time I was in high school, the pressure on my grades was too high to really take on any extracurriculars. Viv went to school for painting, and it really messes with my head seeing how little ambition she has with that kind of talent, something I would kill for. I write in a diary occasionally when I'm feeling bad, and I sometimes wonder if people would want to read it if I took some of that writing and edited it into personal essays, but I have to get myself stable before I can try that, basic needs first and all. I saw a guy for a little while who made beats, and he tried to get me back into singing, but I was really turned off by the people he introduced me to in the local music scene. It started to feel the same as camming, presenting a version of myself that was totally unlike who I really am to try to squeeze money and attention out of people. Anyways, I cut it off before we were ever able to release any of what we'd made. It seemed like the communication needed in a band and the communication needed in a relationship piled on top of each other, and it made working together impossible. We only got two songs finished; they're still on his hard drive somewhere.

By the fourth disappearance, police had identified a pattern between these crimes, and the community was severely shaken. A manhunt was held, with media calls to alert any suspicious activity, and police examining the area around these stations between April and August of 1991…

But there's still so much I wanna do. I want to be passionate about the life I'm living. That's why I opted not to go to school, to my mom's shame, even though I could have. I was thinking of going into psychology to try to help people who'd struggled with some of the things I'd struggled with, but I figured I needed to go out and experience life for myself first before I could really be qualified to advise anybody else on how they were living. Are you really accomplishing anything if you're just soaking up other people's problems all day? But even with my college fund paying my rent, it's been a constant struggle to get the money together to go anywhere or do anything.

Finally, a suspect was identified: Shinjiro Kawada, thirty-four, a local shut-in, or hikikomori, *living alone in a basement nearby…*

I'm really grateful that I've made any friends here at all. I met Vivian last year through a Facebook Queer Housing group, when my first lease was up. I came to see her place and it was a lot more chaotic than I could take: five girls (two cis and three trans) and one straight guy, stuffed in a bungalow with curtained-off sections marking "bedrooms," each one going for eight hundred dollars a month. I almost moved in just for the story, but it fell apart over unpaid debts and fights over chores before the end of the month. Vivian and I met for coffee after the dust settled and she filled in context for each of the people I'd met, all the accusations they'd thrown at each other, the night the cops finally got called. I'd started camming a few months earlier, and we bonded over our shared experiences in sex work: She had been targeted in her living situation for using her room, one of the few with a real door, to take incalls, and I was the only person she knew who took her side. I let her use my apartment for a little while, but I got a noise complaint from a neighbour and got too nervous to let her do it anymore. I still feel kind of bad about it, though it was scary for me sometimes, having strangers through at weird hours. She got really upset when I kicked her out, saying she didn't think I'd do this to her too. I didn't know what to say, I just need my space. We patched things up, though.

When they finally searched the basement, what they found was far more horrifying than they could possibly have imagined...

Clara was a weird find. We'd only met her and her boyfriend Silas at the karaoke bar a few months ago. They looked like movie stars, with sunken eyes and lots of little black tattoos, him towering over her. They sang "Total Eclipse of the Heart" on the public stage together sloppy-drunk, making eye contact so intense it looked like they were about to fuck onstage in front of everyone. Me and Vivian, who'd been meeting there for our girls nights for a little while, were instantly obsessed with them and moved over to their table. We learned very quickly they were grad students in philosophy, his focus in metaphysics and hers in theology, that they did a lot of cocaine and fought with each other a lot. At first, hanging out with them was an in-joke between Viv and me, but in time we figured out that, despite appearances, they were as lonely as we were, and liked us as much as we liked them. All of a sudden, that was the group.

But first, a message from our sponsor, BestTherapy dot org. Do you struggle with anxiety?

Stepping off the train into my neighbourhood, I feel the awful first wind of autumn cutting through the sky in the deep night. I am wearing a black cocktail dress and tights, and I'd thought open arms would be okay, but I guess they aren't by this point in the year. I've got goosebumps up and down my arms and just want to get inside. I take the shortcut through the park behind the apartment building across the street from mine, two identical brutalist concrete blocks staring at each other from either side of the street. They must be older than the rest of the buildings on the block, which are all sleek glass, mostly empty office space but with some apartments too. I guess I should be thankful they didn't tear them down and develop new ones, because I probably couldn't afford the rent in whatever they'd replace them with.

With promo code LETHAL, get 30 percent off your first session matched with one of our licensed therapists, completely confidential and in the comfort of your own home. Now, back to the show...

Getting in, I settle into the tub with some bubble bath and my journal. I send my mom a text:

hope you're doing good. just wanted to follow up on the move, would you be willing to send a little extra this month? i'm trying to get things settled but it's really expensive. let me know when you can, okay? love you lots.

I scroll up through the texts and feel myself tear up. It's just months and months of me asking for updates or asking for money to no reply. The last time she actually responded to me was two years ago, and the exchange was as follows:

are you okay? you seemed really shook up today. i promise i'll be back to visit as much as i can.

You can do whatever you want now.

I lay my head back against the plaster and let the scent of lavender take me away.

We warn you, this next section is extremely graphic, so please skip to the time stamp in the description if you are uncomfortable with detailed violence. Victims were handcuffed to a drainage pipe next to the mattress and beaten with a lead pipe. Then, this cowardly piece of shit would cut off their legs, so they couldn't resist...

4.

After my bath, I finally get into my pyjamas and put on a YouTube video on my laptop. I have a really hard time sleeping, and it's a little easier if I have something I can focus on. I have to lay off the true crime stuff when I'm falling asleep because it makes my dreams too bad, but videos about paranormal stuff, ghost encounters, cryptid sightings — that kind of thing really lulls me for some reason. My favourite of these channels is a guy called Nick Bessleman, a guy in his late thirties with a doofy frosted-tips hairdo who tells stories people send him about themselves. If he's really intrigued, he'll go on site and do a full-blown investigation into his viewers' hauntings. This one time he used EMF frequencies to detect that there was an actual rotting corpse inside the walls of someone's house.

It's a little embarrassing how much I feel attached to this guy who stands in front of a cardboard graveyard and mugs through his scripts in the exact same tone of voice no matter what he's reading, this *very serious* jump up and down in pitch that makes him sound like he doesn't even know what he's reading sometimes. Like, I try not to show anyone I know any of his videos, but if you spend enough time looking at someone, listening to their voice, hearing their opinions, you start to feel close to them, and I feel close with Nick. I can track different periods of my life through the changes in his segments, running jokes, and video quality. He used to do these really dumb skits where he would come out in a fake moustache and call the character "Dark Nick," and there was this whole running storyline, but he doesn't do that anymore. I kind of miss it, even though it was terrible. Most of the stories Nick reads are obvious fakes, but sometimes they feel real enough to make you wonder, and other times they're well-written enough that it doesn't matter that you can tell. Some of the most fun episodes are the ones where he gets an obvious lie from somebody and makes fun of it. It's a nice change of pace to get a lighter mood while still sticking to the subject matter.

I rub some moisturizer into my cheeks, slip my sleep mask on, turn the video up loud and roll onto my side, turning off the light.

Good evening, spookies and spookettes! This is Nick Bessleman, back just like every Wednesday, sharing your haunted stories. This week we have a terrifying ordeal that was shared with us via our email from Garth McKinsey of Des Moines, Iowa...

The story, from what I can tell, is about a guy who starts at a new job in a new town as a school janitor, who learns that he's replacing someone who died prematurely of emphysema, who had been beloved by the admin. Everyone treats him like he could never live up to the old janitor, criticizing his work and giving him the cold shoulder whenever he tries to reach out to any of the teachers or other staff. It's not really keeping my attention, even though Nick actually ended up going to see this one, met with the guy and talked to him about the heavy breathing he heard in the school's basement, met with the dead janitor's family and took them in to try to coax out the ghost's last messages. The hostility at the school ramps up more and more, peaking with a group of students throwing a boiling packet of Top Ramen at Garth, burning his face and hands, which leaves Nick on his own to lead the search. Ultimately, after a nighttime EMF scan and thermal reading, he decides that the dead man won't respond to them, and decides to consult with the dead man's wife. At first, she is unsure about bringing her husband's legacy into something sensational like this, but Nick makes the point to her that this might present her daughter with one last opportunity to talk with her dad, and finally she agrees. They bring a Ouija board to the school and they're able to trace him back to the spot where he took his smoke breaks, out by the back parking lot.

This must have been a place of respite for him.

I make sure that I stay focused on his voice so I can't hear anything else in the room. An old, clanging radiant heating system is a telltale sign of a ghost hoax, Nick says, as is a bad neighbourhood outside, an easy way to hear strange voices and calls for help through the walls without anything ever being there. He mentions gas leaks, high stress, substance abuse, drafts messing with the thermal cams. My eyes can't close tight enough to make my vision black. I can tell there's a peek of light getting through between the window and the blackout blinds. I get too angry to think and punch myself in the ribs a little.

Even behind the mask, I can see its shape still slide through that gap, over and across onto the carpeted floor. At first, I thought it wouldn't be as bad on a carpeted floor as it is on a wood floor, but it's way worse, because you can't hide the damage you leave behind.

The ghost of the dead janitor tells his wife and child that he loves them immensely and regrets cutting his own life short in such a wasteful way. As the story plays out, I hear the familiar grinding of metal against metal and the begging through tears ringing from what I know can only be my own vocal cords, what am I? Please just let me die between the words shared between Garth McKinsey of Des Moines and Nick Bessleman with the dead man's wife.

The ghost apologizes to Garth too, for scaring him and driving everyone against him, and says the burning was all his fault, that he won't do it again.

Remember, we have no evidence for the eternal soul, nor for the existence of poltergeists. But what we do have are our minds and our hearts. We know what we see. Even if there aren't apparitions living among us, we know that when something terrible happens, it leaves an echo. And sometimes, that can mean a reunion we never thought was possible.

I can now see the far edge of the claw emerging from the crack in the light of the curtain, the shape of the darkness forming into metal talons, bending as it crawls up the wall, skittering like a bug around the edges of my vision. Parts fold over and inwards to move like a slug, juts of steel cycling out of its body. It lands in an arcane shape across the bedroom floor, tempting. I shudder out of my sheets and hit the floor on my hands and knees. I scan for any sign of the thing, but I can't see it. Its presence seeps towards me from some impossible angle, tantalizing me to walk out into the dark to try to find it.

I am not going to get to sleep. The concrete under the carpet is etched deep with equations. I pull out my little wand and start working, measuring lines between the light and the shadow.

5.

I think I fell asleep for a while, then rolled into my other job. I log in on an old HTML site with a banner at the top reading Chariot Marketing Solutions, surrounded by stock photos of people in offices laughing at computers. My favourite is a lady in a power suit just doubling over in front of a boxy white desktop monitor, pointing at it. I have to imagine that whoever built this website did not know the context for which it was going to be used.

I still don't really know what Chariot does, but it pays minimum wage for three four-hour shifts a week watching over the customer service line, responding however I can, and it seems like a big enough company that there might be room for more serious employment somewhere down the line if I can stick to it.

There was very little training, but I did get an email with a huge PDF containing the employee handbook, which I was encouraged to repeat from as much as possible when answering questions. I use text-to-speech with the chatline, so I can keep watching my ghost videos while I work. It speaks to me in a funny robot voice that I made sound like a British lady, and I talk back to it.

help, says the British lady.

Thanks for contacting Chariot Marketing Solutions, how can I help you today?

employee number one nine four eight six six two, office number six, give tracking number for order # nine four five three one three eight seven seven, was not provided at arrival

Just one quick sec, let me check my system here for you!

thanks

CTRL+F on the handbook, "tracking number."

For on-site product orders, please check with your consulting manager!

we don't have one

According to the handbook, there should be a consulting manager on site!

he got moved. we don't know when he'll be back.

CTRL+F.

In the case where there is not a consulting manager on site, please refer to your immediate supervisor!

they don't have tracking number either. can i just not file

I feel a lump in my throat, knowing what the answer will be before I look it up.

Orders require order numbers in order to be filed. Loss of a tracking number can cause serious supply chain issues, and if not provided, the employee is liable to face serious consequences.

please give tracking number. no manager on site. contact corporate

My pay for the period of the thread is docked if a case goes to Escalations unless I'm being threatened by a client. I take a second to think here.

I do not have corporate available at the moment, but I can file a complaint for you?

how long will it take

When a complaint is filed, corporate processes it on a first-come, first-served basis. I cannot advise exactly how long the process will take.

will it be before consequences

I cannot advise exactly how long the process will take.

i will only file if timeline can be advised

CTRL+F, scrambling for an answer. Part of me genuinely wants to help this guy, but part of me just wants him gone. The YouTube video loops over itself.

Good evening, spookies and spookettes! This is Nick Bessleman, back just like every Wednesday, sharing your haunted stories. This week we're gonna be doing something a little bit different. We're gonna be responding to a video from Cryptid Cassette that I found really interesting, about the drama that's been going on recently in the paranormal community...

I zone out a little, panicking.

i'm not leaving until you get me that number

Please let me check my system.

So, I'm sure you probably saw this video, titled "The End of Skepticism." Here, Crypty kind of gets into, I don't wanna say a problem in our community, but just something they've noticed about a lot of content creators faking evidence while on investigations...

My hands are shaking. Every resource keeps pointing me back to refer to on-site manager, but I know there's gotta be some way to help him out here. They should just be able to reprint the tracking number, or it should have been affixed to the package in the first place, but it seems like it's a cultural difference office-to-office, because there are no references to it in any of the official documents. On-site stuff like this gets really hard because it's so rare in comparison with the online services support — usually they don't end up having to come to us. I wonder where this person is that corporate would relocate their manager without replacing them first.

thank you for your help. i am really not trying to make this hard for you

Absolutely! Just one more minute and I'll be right back with you.

CTRL+F again. Shit, okay, nothing left I can do.

And you know, a lot of what she's saying here's true about ghost hunting equipment, how much of it is about exaggerating the importance of pretty minor evidence, but there's nothing wrong with adding some flair or production value to your show. It's when false proof starts getting presented as real, with absolutely no critical analysis, that you get into some real problems...

Unfortunately, due to a shortage of staff, we will not be able to file a complaint for you.

there's a shortage of staff here too

Please provide the tracking number now, or you will be liable to be terminated.

no way that's allowed

I type Y and delete it to make sure that the little dots showing that I'm typing are bubbling away. I decide to let this hang for a couple minutes.

So much of contemporary spiritualism traces its origins back to the late nineteenth century. Even Blavatsky's Theosophical Society, which rejected spiritualism in favour of the Eastern occult, while still a religious movement at heart, was devoted to the same Enlightenment values that govern Western scientific skepticism...

Loss of a tracking number can cause serious supply chain issues, and if not provided, the employee is liable to face serious consequences. Please check with your consulting manager.

youre gonna get me fired for this

i know they have it

come on just ask corporate

Please sir, report to the support team on site. It should have been received properly. Please be honest so that I can report this behaviour as negligence.

dude please

Ma'am. You can file a complaint here.

I send the link to "Contact us."

thats the link i clicked to get here

what the fuck

And you know, that's the whole point of this channel, and why I love reading you guys' personal submissions so much. Sometimes we get a great investigation out of it, and other times we can really break down the details to figure out the facts from the fiction. And that's what this stuff is all about, keeping an open mind to the evidence, while maintaining a keen eye for, well, there's no nicer way to say it than the bullshit, that's out there...

Sir, please refrain from using profanity in the support chat, or I will be forced to report you to your direct supervisor.

you know what

i dont even care anymore

go ahead and report me

dumb bitch

I right-click on the top corner and forward the thread to Escalations.

My email reads as follows:

Hello!

I hate to do this, but please look over this thread. I have a customer who is making active threats of violence and using slurs against me in a dispute over their missed data inputs. It has made me feel incredibly unsafe and I feel that the Escalations team may be better equipped to handle an unpredictable employee of this kind. Please call him and advise options to resolve his situation.

Employee #1948662

I feel an immediate sigh of relief, then the guilt. I only got to talk to the lady who works at Escalations once while transferring a call, and she sounded miserable. She spoke in euphemisms about how, you know, we have some pretty tough cases. She said it was rare a call crossed her table that went under an hour, where she didn't have to raise her voice at the person. It seems like there's not a lot more she can do for anybody than I can, she's just allowed to be meaner to them.

6.

After my shift, still in my pyjamas, I look up a yoga video on YouTube and sit in my feathery pink cam corner, surrounded by velvet boxes and moving along to the lady on the screen's instructions. The yoga instructor is the kind of ultra-put-together cis girl I can't help but feel jealous of, her edges all impossibly smoothed out and made even smoother by the ultra-high-def footage.

Starting in our mountain pose pranamasana, we're going to inhale deep, na namaste, letting in that beautiful bright light from outside. It's a nice warm sixty-eight degrees here, feeling that warmth running through you as you climb up that mountain, and out into Sun Salutation A...

Pressing my palms into my thighs, I let go of any judgment I feel towards myself. I remember a hot fall day like this with my mom, checking all the spots I'd missed while cleaning the bathroom while she was at work. She asked me if I *really cared* if it was clean, or if I was *just trying to call it finished so I could go back to my toys*. I said sorry and went back down to scrubbing.

I remember that Vivian's exhibition is the week after next. She hasn't been too active with her art since I've known her, she says she's just too busy for it between survival and keeping an active social life. I think about how much I love her for her pragmatism, how many important lessons she taught me when we met — not only to avoid queer collective housing situations, but to cope with the world in general. I remember she sounded like my mom: *There's no point in wondering how people see you, you're still you no matter what other people say about it.* I remember almost believing that stuff when I heard it from her.

We used to cam together sometimes, but it started muddling things in our friendship, which we agreed was too important to take risks with. I don't think I could date another woman in a serious way, like, I would feel too competitive with her or something.

Okay, now dropping back down into Sun Salutation B, building up that tension. I know it's hard, but you've got the power to pull through this...

This is always the part where the burning really kicks in, the pain waking me up from the last bit of grogginess that hangs on after work. As excited as I am for Viv to be back into her creative process, it means we can't hang out until she's done, which means it's just me and the clients for a couple weeks. I could reach out to Clara, but honestly, I'm sick of the complaining, the constant breakups, the passive-aggressive critiques of Silas's thesis, her asking if I've heard anything from him in the last few days because he's off the map again. Both of them get way too drunk every time, too. Like, they'll tell you they want to hang out as if they're actually interested in your life, but the whole thing's just an excuse to make a show of themselves. I can tell Vivian's ready to drop them outright, but I'm not quite sure. Part of me really does feel bad for her. One night I broke down drunk after Clara read my tarot and I told them about the claw, everything I could recall, and I remember a look in her eyes like recognition. And I love Viv, but she's a little too grounded to give me that. Maybe I should head over there later.

Okay, we're gonna spread wide, out into padangusthasana, reaching our hands deep up and out then dooooown into the earth, spreading our toes...

I can feel my hamstrings pull and I want to quit, and I remind myself this is all for the body, for the product. I think about the shower I'm going to take after this, about my skin care routine and the time spent applying makeup that the audience won't ever see. Hardening myself in order to later be soft, pliable, welcoming. It's become my artistic practice to set things up, to look nice, to get to connect with people in such an intense way, even if they mostly don't see it that way. I feel myself heat up and it turns for a second into an overwhelming anger that no one will ever appreciate this work, that they'll only notice the seams if I fuck something up and break the illusion.

Finally, into our triangle poses, starting in utthita trikonasana...

I remember Viv telling me I was going to have to show my face at some point if I wanted to cam seriously, if I wanted to survive the slump that would come once my "New User" pin came off and I no longer smelled like fresh blood. I wanted to punch her, because she was right. Recently, the well has started to dry up. More and more, it's guys with grey profiles making promises they can't keep, asking for payment after service, trying to pretend they have money to throw around. And I've felt obligated to fall for it, taking less and less to push further and further, because at least there I have some kind of power. Unlike the chatbox, where any kind of boundary setting would lead to disciplinary action from my managers, onstream I at least have the power to push back, to kick guys from the chat, to chew somebody out and make it look sexy, to turn the crowd against anybody I feel is taking things too far.

Finally, let it all go, and rest down into savasana...

Realizing it's already two, I leave the hot woman on the screen smiling blissfully as I get into the shower and start putting myself together. I can hear her breathing, and the soft New Age music sounds even nicer through the wall. Steam enters my pores and the noise of the water overtakes the video. I shave slowly and savour the feeling of the lather on my skin, scrubbing deep and hard like I'm trying to take my skin off. I can hear that the video is still playing in the other room, something else on autoplay humming through the wall. I douche, gently and shallowly, giving it a minute before I get out, careful not to create more of a problem than I have to. The feed has autoplayed into the new Nick Bessleman video.

Hello spookies and spookettes! This is Nick Bessleman, here with another one of your Wednesday ghost reports. This comes courtesy of news footage in Vancouver, British Columbia. It's security footage of a ghoulish, pale figure, appearing to be a male wearing women's pyjamas, who emerged from under the rails at a subway station just this morning. After delaying the morning commute for upwards of five minutes, standing facing the wall in a stupor, this individual bit the conductor's hand when offered a hand up onto the platform, then sprinted off into the bustling downtown commuter traffic. In their email, our source described the figure as "gaunt, barely human" and "covered in blood and wounds," informing us that they had placed a public call for information about the incident.

I haphazardly wrap a towel around myself to get back to the computer, dripping water onto the carpet. I lean over the computer chair. That person he's talking about looks exactly like me.

The ghoul seemed to be last spotted heading southeast, in a park near a group of low-cost block apartments.

I pause the video on the girl's face and take a screenshot.

Lying on my back on the floor, I stare at the popcorn ceiling. It starts to look like mountains, and I feel too much all at once. I had wondered for a long time if one day she was going to show her face, but I just didn't know how I was going to be able to contact her. Now, though, it seems like all I have to do is figure out where she is. I notice, belatedly, that I'm crying.

She's there in every second of everything I do. I resent her, and that makes me resent myself. I hate letting myself feel it. I hate the way my vision goes out and it makes me want to do stupid things that would get me in trouble. I hate getting so fucking angry when I have no power to do anything about it.

This is a great example of something I've wanted to call attention to for a while in your submissions, which is the stigmatization of mental health and substance abuse issues in the supernatural community. With just a little research, you can see that the area surrounding the station is famous for its high density of unhoused people, especially those suffering from substance abuse issues, and this is clearly someone in desperate need of care, likely in some kind of drug- or sleep-deprivation-induced psychosis. You wouldn't believe the number of submissions I receive for this channel which are just people pointing cameras at the unhoused or the mentally ill and declaring them to be cryptids, or who believe signs of squatting to be evidence of dark forces from beyond this world. In my opinion, this is absolutely inappropriate, and it really demonstrates the depths some people will sink to just to try to get some online clout. Look at this person. Look into his eyes, see the fear and panic and desperation that would put someone into his position, obviously this is a human being and not some kind of monster, and while I don't feel great platforming this kind of image of real human suffering, it's a huge disappointment to me that I've fostered the kind of community on this channel where someone would even think to send this to me.

I go back to the bathroom to fix my makeup before the time I posted I'd be online.

7.

I put some soft music on, carefully slip the Lush out of its velvet slip, lube it up and slide it into myself. It slides out at first, and I have to give it a more serious shove to actually fit it in. It hurts a little then settles comfortably. I pull one of the panty sets I keep aside to stream out of the closet, a high-waisted two-piece with a dramatic CALVIN KLEIN across the waistband, pull it high and tuck deep into it. I slip a pink silk mask over my eyes, with holes to see. I pull out my little trick wheel, with slots reading SLAP ASS, BRA OFF, SUCK DILDO, and so on, and set a Hitachi wand onto one of the pink fluffy pillows in my corner nest, set the angle up right and hit Start on stream.

I keep an eye out for the little number in the bottom-right corner at 0. Usually it takes a minute for anybody to hop in, and I sit passively, taking the second to just sit. I'm struggling to get settled, still thinking about the vision of my double on the screen. God, I hope none of these people saw that. There's an odd kind of relief, too. I had thought something like this might happen for a long, long time, and now I've got something to look for. Very quickly, the number jumps from zero to two and my posture changes.

Helloo, it's Destiny! Thank you so much for joining me today.

how are you

Aw, you know how it is austin8633. Just got my workout in, got some work done this morning. Felt great!

Buzz, plink.

u are beautiful sexy girl hello from turkey <3

Thank you so much! So, today we're gonna be spinning the wheel for five hundred coins a pop, plus regular rates in the chat for Lush and private sessions. Be good, okay?

The number isn't going up as quickly as I thought it would.

Buzz.

Are you guys shy today? Doesn't anybody want to pay for treats?

beautiful lovely girl

No money.

come on man it's a dude lol

I reach back down and over, blocking the account. The username is all just numbers. The number goes down by one.

Fuck off, dude. Some people are just so mean, right, chat?

hahahahaha

Buzz, plonk.

I get a private DM from another account with a long string of numbers as a username.

come on dude

be honest with me

youre just gay right

I hit Block without reply.

You guys, he's literally still sending me DMs. Isn't this shit just embarrassing?

Buzz.

Thank you rsj543 for your gift! We're gonna spin the wheel!

I built this thing myself and I'm really proud of it. The signs are written in neat handwriting in thick Sharpie, laminated and hot-glued onto the wood. It's a little rickety, but it makes a nice satisfying sound like spokes on a bicycle as it spins. I wonder for a second if I've trained myself to associate the sound of the wheel with the pay that comes right before it. The wheel lands on PULL PANTIES DOWN. I lean myself forward onto the pillow, arching my back, and put the Hitachi against my clit, easing the waistband slowly over my ass.

Okay, you get two minutes here. Mmmm ... I'm getting so wet ... You know, I haven't been fucked in a while ... It's nice coming onstream all pent-up like this.

Buzz buzz buzzbuzzbuzzbuzz.

Okay, there's the pickup I've been wanting to see. You can't give them anything before they pay for it, but I know these guys are floating their mice over the thumbnails of thousands of girls online right now, and I know a thumbnail of my ass is going to bring more guys in than a sitting-in-bed thumbnail. Momentum on here builds on itself in that way. I moan and yelp like I'm cumming, though I'm closer than I'd like to be this early on, as the alarm hits two minutes. I flip back around and come back to chat to find there are way more messages than before.

priv for 20000? dm me

spin wheel again

buzz buzz buzz.

degenerate.

Another one of those fucking numbers accounts. I don't care if this is what he wants.

Whoever you are with the million burner accounts, please back off, seriously. I don't have admins set up because I like keeping the control over things myself, but I know there are plenty of people here who would do it if I wanted them to.

ok then block me again faggot

I hit the Block button before I can engage.

You just know that guy's gonna be in my DMs. Anybody who wants negative attention like that is always getting off on it, you know? Does anybody want a promotion to admin?

spin wheel again

wait r u a guy

beautiful hot sexy would love to bbq with you

It's really not that much responsibility, just somebody to take over dealing with the asshole in here. Just somebody to hit Block if a username that's just numbers pops up.

take off top

Priv for 50K? DM for details.

hahahahahahaha

The number of viewers has dropped precipitously. I feel myself heat up.

Okay, fine. I'm available for the next hour for privates only, payment up front. You've lost public chat privileges.

I pull the Lush out. The mommy-kink JOI guy comes back into my DMs and apologizes for how I was being treated, then we do our thing, and it's nice enough. Why can't everyone be as consistent and easy to please as the mommy-kink JOI guy? Then, as I expected, a message from another numbers account:

hahahaha i reported you fag

Fed up, I finally just send him a DM back:

is there anything i can do for you?

A longer gap between messages.

are you crying?

would you like me to be?

Thirty thousand coins appear in my wallet from the anonymous account.

go on priv.

This guy just fucked up my whole stream just to get me alone, and I definitely could've made more than the measly $300 he's offering if I hadn't gone off stream. I can't reward that behaviour, especially with no idea what he's got for me in exchange for that $300. On the other hand, I'm otherwise only making my Chariot paycheque today, which is nothing. I consider it for a second before accepting the invite.

Immediately, I can hear him speak to me through a voice-changer that lowers his clearly already frog-like, guttural voice.

did you cry?

no.

can you cry?

uh, it'd be a little tough. I'm not a great actor.

didn't I hurt you? didn't I take money out of your pocket?

i mean, i guess...

the answer is Yes, Sir.

Yes, Sir.

is the little sissy bitch-boy going to cry for his daddy now?

Yes, Sir.

Get a hanky or, like, a cloth or something. I want you to cry a faceful of makeup into it.

Laughing a little under my breath, I search through the boxes for one of the toys' velvet slips. It's red and should be able to stain the way he wants it to. I cover my face with the bag and scooch myself over into frame. I make a soft noise, pretending to sob, and start wiping the makeup on my face off onto it.

i can tell when you're faking it, sissy. make it real. you're nothing. your life is nothing. i'm the boss, and i want you to cry.

This is pissing me off. This guy paid for seven more minutes, so I start faking even harder, mewling and whining and rubbing. I can hear him start screaming, digitally mangled from the other end.

I TOLD YOU I CAN TELL WHEN YOU'RE FAKING IT FREAK. I WILL COME TO WHERE YOU ARE, AND I WILL TAKE YOU AS I WANT YOU, AND IT WILL HURT AND YOU WILL LOVE IT, AND I WILL TAKE YOU APART LIMB BY LIMB, AND SEND THE PARTS OF YOU TO YOUR FRIENDS AND TO YOUR MOM AND I WILL STREW THE STREETS WITH YOUR ENTRAILS, EVERYONE WILL SEE YOUR MALE BONES, A BITCH BOY WHO WANTS NOTHING MORE THAN TO—

I hang up on him. I sit there breathing hard for a second. The rage passes through me like a wave, heat moving through my eyes, through my spine and down into my feet, out through the pillows into the carpet. I try to slow my breathing and laugh a little to myself, like what did I think I was getting myself into here?

I get a DM from the numbers account:

i'm sorry. extra $500 if you send me the hanky.

He includes his home address. He lives in the suburbs pretty close by, something that shouldn't be possible with location protection on. Another wave hits my eyes. I slam the laptop closed.

8.

I climb up from the pillows on the floor onto my bed and roll over on my side to give my body a rest. I can feel my breaths deep, shudders through my arms, my chest, into my toes. I check my phone. Lots of likes on today's promo, a handful of clip buys. I should be able to order some food.

I think again about what Vivian said about showing my face. I get that she was being glib, but I really want to try to keep my job at arm's length from my life. It feels like there's so much pressure to let everything blend into one and let it consume me, to make my life and my sexuality and my personality and my online presence all one and the same, and I feel dissociated enough from my body already without adding all those extra layers of meaning onto it.

I send Viv a text.

hey! still working?

I take a second, wrapping my fingers over my phone, then send Clara a text too.

hey! free for a coffee? feeling shitty lol

I take another second, listening to cars pass out on the street below from the cracked window in my bedroom, facing onto the bed. I hear the buzz back straight away. It's Clara.

Oh yeah, I just got back from class. Come over whenever!

Soon after, another:

Vivian's still off the grid, yes?

seems like. see you in like, 30min?

Clara's place is in the bougie part of town up near campus, and I always put a little more effort in when I go to see her than I do with Viv. The train ride is really quick between us, with just a quick stroll in the rain in a nice neighbourhood full of sushi restaurants and head shops between the station and her building. Her apartment is on the thirty-fourth out of forty floors, with a wide view of the city and the ocean. It always wigs me out a little bit being that high up, like once you go in, you're stuck in there.

She buzzes me in, and as I crack the door, I see her hunched on the couch ripping a bong then waving her hand to break up the smoke. Her walls are lined with crosses and prayer candles, and the massive flatscreen in front of her is playing some girly anime with the sound off.

She says this, choking a little on the smoke, and gets up off the couch to come give me a hug. She's wearing oversized grey sweatpants and a black crop with straps, her five-foot-four frame swimming in the cozy terry cloth. She's extremely soft and smells sweet under the sour weed stink. I pull her in tight, and we settle back onto the couch together, the bong still streaming off towards the high ceiling.

"It's good to see you, girl!"

There's an echo in the room. She draws her hand across my back and we settle down onto the couch, her back in her gremlin-hunch posture and me crossing my legs at the end, keeping my distance.

"How's it going?"

"Pretty good, just got out of my seminar presentation. *Hermeneutics and Eroticism in Augustine and Theresa.* Hot, right?"

"Totally."

"Went awful, though. Critiques were brutal. I just don't think people get what I'm going for yet."

"Aw, that sucks." I never really have a reference point for this stuff, so I just try to act supportive.

"Yeah, I don't know if I'm gonna see the program through at this point. I really like what I'm doing, but my mom's getting really down on me about how much money it's costing me. She wants me to move back home, to fucking Fort Mac. You been?"

"No, never."

"Pretty sad vibes. Like, really sad vibes, actually. I'd probably end up in my mom's place for a while. Have to learn to drive. Oh, do you want some chai? I made some the traditional way, with the fennel and stuff."

She gestures towards a pot on the stove. I nod and she hops up and over to it, pouring out a little of the steaming, milky mixture into a goofy vintage coffee mug with the comic strip character Cathy on it. She settles back in, knees up on the couch.

"But yeah. I'd probably end up just working another town over, marrying some guy, buying a house, getting fucked up on the deck. It's not like there's anything keeping me from reading or writing if I ended up somewhere like that, I guess, but the idea of, like, contributing to some greater body of knowledge keeps me going, you know? Even if it's a totally meaningless contribution."

I sigh, despite myself. "It's cool to know yourself like that," I say. "I've always kind of just been trying to keep my head above water. I really want to start trying to figure out how to have some kind of purpose in my life. Like you with your studies, or Viv with her art. Something that makes the pain of just staying alive worth it."

"Girl, you're like twenty, right? I didn't have half as much figured out as you do by that point."

I always forget that my friends are all so much older than me. I look at them and I still just see kids, especially Clara since the rest of us all tower over her. Clara leans in earnestly, making deep eye contact.

"Most people don't even have their heads above water by then. Keep your head up. You transitioned, you're cool as fuck, you're running a business, you've got an apartment and a life in a big city. That's way more than most people can claim. More than I'm gonna have by thirty."

She sounds wistful, trailing off. I feel that familiar survivor's guilt and shrink into the couch.

"Anyways, are you still planning on moving? That might be good for all that feeling-through, working-out-your-shit stuff."

"I still can't get a hold of my mom. I need her to release more of my college fund instead of just parcelling it out like this if I'm gonna do something that expensive."

"She's just not getting back to you?"

"Yeah, she took me coming out really badly. I thought I was gonna get cut off, but then she just started sending me money and doesn't talk to me at all anymore. I keep, like, begging her, like hey, I really wanna do this, and she's just not answering."

"Did you guys have a good relationship?"

"Not really, no. She's, uh, pretty intense. Really religious. Never really liked that I was gay, then *really* didn't like that I was trans."

"Ah, yeah. Same. I mean, not the trans stuff, but uh, yeah. Hard. I'm sorry."

I can feel her zone out a little, and I follow suit. On the TV, it's all pink-and-blue noise, huge super-deformed eyes and fancy dresses shifting and shrieking in gaudy colours. Was she actually watching this? It makes me feel kind of ill. Clara takes another long hit off the bong and passes it my way.

"Want?"

"Sure."

I don't really do drugs except when I'm with Clara, who seems to need a pretty elaborate cocktail to stay upright. Viv mostly just likes getting drunk. Taking up the purple bong, all blackened inside with resin, I pull and choke nearly instantly, hacking. I can taste some of the cold, bitter water flick up onto my tongue as I recoil. Clara puts her hand softly on my shoulder.

"You good?"

Still coughing, it comes out as barely words. "Huh, yeah."

I feel a little warmth in my guts, and lean back onto the couch, staring into the screen, the pixels burning into me. The internet keeps going in and out and the resolution keeps changing between hyper-smooth ultra-HD and blocky 480p. I feel a desperate need for fresh air all of a sudden, like the smoke in the air is blocking my ability to breathe. I hold tight and just keep staring ahead. Clara whips a baggie out from the coffee table's drawer and cuts a line into the well-marked glass with a prepaid credit card that was already sitting out, dotted with flecks.

"Do you want some?" she chirps.

"No, that's okay."

She bends over the table and I can see her shoulder blades poking through the sweatshirt. She really is beautiful.

"Do you wanna know this ridiculous shit Silas did the other day?"

"Uh, sure."

"So, we were planning on moving in together since I've been having so much trouble keeping the rent up on this place. Even though we're broken up right now, you know, he really got me through a lot of really hard times. Kind of saved my life, so, y'know, even if he does his kinda edgelord routine, I know there's a really sweet guy in there and I was ready to try to give him a chance. But he starts waffling on about how long it'll be until he can actually start helping split the rent, and I'm like, dude, we're not even dating anymore, I'm not gonna let you tool me around like this."

"Uh-huh."

I can't stop looking at one bloody Christ on the wall, lit up pink by the backlight of the screen. It reminds me of home in the worst way.

"But I mean, like, you wouldn't put up with that, would you?"

"I think you're just lucky to have somebody that loves you."

Clara curls up on her side of the couch again, plaintive. “Yeah. It just sucks.”

She scoots over to the middle of the futon towards me and wraps her arm around my shoulder, rubbing deep into the tissue. She’s murmuring under her breath, nothing in particular. I keep looking for words in it, but none seem to really materialize. She moves her hand up into my hair and starts drifting her fingers through it.

“I’m just so grateful I’ve got you guys,” she’s saying. “More than anything, that’s why I can’t go. I’d miss you, and Viv, and, I mean, Silas goes back and forth between a reason to stay and a reason to go, but…”

“Yeah.”

I feel overwhelmed by the sensation of her hand, reaching deeper and deeper, fucking up the hair I’d pretty carefully arranged to come here and see her. I like it, but something feels wrong, not because she’s in a relationship or anything, I have no issue with cheating, but it’s just like, why does everybody act like I’m gay? And, like, really? The reason you would put tens of thousands more dollars into something you’re clearly not very successful at is to be around two transsexuals who laugh at you behind your back? People you see once a week, maybe, and get too wasted to really talk to every time you do? Do you know anything about us? I find myself getting riled up, first at her, but then at myself. Is that how I think of my friends? It’s sweet that she cares so much. Who cares that she’s a freak? I’m sure I’m a freak to her, too. I edge backwards, but she follows me, keeping her slow undulation of the hand through the hair going while I start to tense up.

“You two are just… so beautiful. It’s amazing to, like, know what you want and take it like that.”

“Yeah.”

I gotta get out of here. I bat her arm down with my hand, almost involuntary. She gives me such an offended look; her big brown deer eyes hurt at the idea of needing distance. I let my arm back down and she reaches back in, that same gradual shuddering sensation again through my scalp. I feel myself sinking into the couch again, staring at the screen burning its image into itself.

God, I miss Viv. I didn't think one week without her would start to feel like such a gap, but after such a hard day at work I miss the way she minimizes things, the way she'd one-up my story of a bad client with one of her own. She never seems to lose her cool or let it get to her. Sometimes it bothers me, but I think of what life would be like without it and I can feel my eyes watering. I don't know if it's tears at the thought or if I'm just stoned, and I don't know how long I've been sitting here in silence with Clara, still running her fingers over my scalp, one at a time, slowly, tenderly.

"Hey, I, uh, think I gotta go."

Clara sinks a little again and shoots me that begging look another time. "Oh, okay. I thought maybe we could, like, read tarot or something."

"That sounds awesome, uh, sometime. Sorry, I think I just feel cramped in here with the smoke."

"We could go for a walk or something?" She hops up to her knees, excited.

"Oh, no, I think I have to be alone."

She sinks again. "Okay, well, if you change your mind, just give me a call or a text or something. I'm really glad you came over."

"Yeah, thanks for the chai."

I gesture towards the cup, still mostly full. She takes it to the sink and pours it out, then looks back as I'm nearly past the door.

"Hey, remember, two lefts to the elevator, one right out at the bottom!"

Two lefts to the elevator, one right out at the bottom. The walls of the hallway are disorientingly textured eggshell, broken up by a broad window with a full view of the skyline. It gives me a little vertigo from thirty-floor floors up. The sky's all black now, earlier than I was expecting, and I check the time to find it's much later than I had suspected. I'm running my hand along the wall now to try to keep myself steady, scared I'll lose balance on the turns as I shuffle towards the elevator. The elevator's chrome doors close with a dull thud, knocking me off balance again. I put my hands on the tight metal railings to either side of me, clinging for dear life as I can feel in my stomach the depth of the descent. I stare into the elevator's wood panelling, wondering how many people have made this same trip today and if any of them were as afraid of it as I am right now.

The cold night air is only a partial relief after the stuffy apartment, too damp to properly break up the weight I feel in my lungs. When I look up, all I can see are the glass sides of buildings blocking out the sky, and I feel as enclosed as I did indoors. I hurry to the train.

9.

Arriving home, I see from the end of the apartment hallway one door hanging wide open into darkness inside. It's mine, I realize.

Approaching the doorway, I feel unreal, hoping what I'm seeing isn't true. I stare into the black void of my own apartment, broken up only by the LEDs on a couple chargers in the bedroom. How long has it been open?

I check my coat pockets for my keys, and they're there. I don't think of myself as the kind of fucking idiot who would just waltz out with the door hanging open behind me, especially knowing what I know now about the ways entities can enter places that are left unbound. Nick talks about the spiritual entries and exits of places, ways to ensure that the mind and soul are as secure as the physical boundaries of the world.

My barriers have all been broken now.

The hallway seems longer and darker than it ever has before. I can sense something in there, ready to jump once I move farther in.

"Hello? Is anyone there? I'll call the cops!"

No answer. I start to feel my way along the hallway wall, inching step by step through the door, feeling between the two walls. The mirror to one side of the entry reveals nothing as it reflects the darkened kitchen. I tuck my hand around the corner of the wall and flick the light on, bringing about a third of the floor space into view under dim bluish fluorescence. Dishes still in the sink, another roach in a Tupperware container eating a congealed hunk of leftover curry from last night. It skitters away before I can kill it.

I know that whatever's in here isn't going to answer me when I call. It prefers to watch and wait. But in some faint hope a human being is what wandered in, I call again.

"It's okay! You can go! I'm home, you can just leave if you want!"

And nothing again, as expected.

Turning the corner, I flip on the overhead light, and the room stretches out towards the picture window, towards the street. Nothing seems to have changed, though I can't stop scanning the edges of my vision for anyone, anything, lurking just outside what I can perceive, ready to spring.

My life is so fragile. Locks can be broken and jobs can be lost, friends can leave without warning, and there's very little I can do about it if they do.

I realize that the door is still hanging open, and I jog back to lock it. I quickly turn the corner and flip the light on in the bathroom as well, revealing nothing, and finally reach my hand into the slightly open bedroom door. The corner is still set up where it was, the hanky with its lines of black mascara sitting out on the pile of pillows in the corner, the laptop still closed on the floor.

I stay at the precipice of the bedroom door, scanning around, too worried to move in any particular direction. Everything feels suddenly out of place, the kitchen table and chairs seeming a few inches away from where they had been sitting prior to my coming home. I wonder if I really left the hanky out, or if I put it away before I left. The disquiet of the empty space discourages me from looking much more deeply, and I rush to bed, in my jacket and clothes, wrapping the blanket around my head.

Has she been here? I can feel her indent in the bed next to me. The thought occurs, lit in only soft pink through the sheets, and I start to feel comforted by it.

I can hear the noise of that other place louder than I can most nights, the walls turning dark with echoing screams, all distinct. Down into that place she calls me into. Even with my head covered, the shape emerges, skittering across the floor and preparing to take her from me. The indent in the bed seems to flatten itself out. I refuse to look, and I wait until the sun rises again.

10.

I spent a long time getting ready for Vivian's exhibition and left early. I wanted to meet up with her beforehand, but she said she'd been on site all day setting things up and that she didn't want me to see the piece until she got it up and running. But when I arrived at the little warehouse space on the East Side, converted into a series of small art studios with sloppily nailed-in boards of plywood breaking them up, I couldn't find her. I walked into the room where her piece was set up, looking for her, but she wasn't there.

It was a video art installation titled *Animal Mask*. On four walls, strobing primary colours flashed between footage of Vivian wearing a series of different papier mâché masks: a tiger, a bear, a donkey, a pig. They were all cheaply built, with visible seams, and had oddly large, cartoonish eyes, with a black hole in the centre through which you could make out just a little bit of Vivian's own eyes. Through a loudspeaker overhead, audio samples from old cartoons alternate with wild sub-bass blasts in what I can tell is a looping rhythm but I can't quite place the loop point. The whole thing is really overstimulating and creepy, which I know is her intention with it, but I'm not totally sure if all the pieces fit together into anything. After a couple minutes of this, I start to feel myself overtaken with a sweaty kind of sadness and feel the need to dip out.

I look around the space, empty save for a few people milling around in the back. I really wish I could find her, not just to cool the awkwardness of standing alone in a gallery, but to ask her about it too. I'm realizing I might not ask enough questions in general, or maybe don't listen as closely as I should when I do. I walk across, a little self-conscious, and poke my head out of the door to see if she might be smoking with someone outside, but she's not. I drift over to a little stand at the back serving drinks with a few people standing around it and join in with the hope that somebody will know where she is. I stand behind a tattooed girl with a buzz cut in a home-cropped T and loose jeans while waiting my turn, looking at the skin on her back and feeling overdressed in my long blue cloth dress and heels. I look at the ground for a second so she can't see me looking.

"Hey! Thanks for coming out tonight. What can I grab ya?"

The man at the till is tall, bearded, wearing a four-sided orange long-sleeve with a logo I can't read, probably for some metal band. There's a little cardboard menu that reads "BEER $5, WINE $6, POP $1, WATER JUST ASK."

"Hey. Uh, red?"

"Got it."

I pull out my wallet and reach for my debit card. "Do you guys have tap?"

"Oh, uh, no, cash only."

"Shit, sorry. Is there, like, an ATM nearby?"

"Not really. Don't worry about it."

He shoots me a toothy, yellowed grin and hands me a solo cup full of bottom-shelf box wine. He's extremely lanky, staring down over me with goofy cherub cheeks that make him look like a kid next to deep crow's feet.

"Who are you here with tonight?"

"Oh, uh, Vivian. Have you seen her?"

"Oh, yeah. She was, like, stalking around here for a while, trying to get her sound mix right. You know that look she gets when she's focused on something? The one where, like, she'll kill you if you talk to her?"

"Sure."

"Yeah, it was like that. I didn't really wanna ask where she was going."

The girl with the tattoos chimes in from across the room. "She went for pizza, I think."

"Yeah, there's a by-the-slice place next door," Pat adds.

"Priya, by the way," the girl calls from across the room.

"Thanks. I'll be back in a minute! Do you want me to leave this here?"

"Nah, it's all good."

Spilling a bit of the wine on my dress, I run back out into the summer dusk, solo cup in hand.

The pizza place is a tiny, rundown spot on the corner with white trim along the edges of huge windows, and there's Vivian, sitting under the neon Open sign nursing an orange soda. Her hair is in its regular messy bun, and she's wearing a purple corset top, the kind of thing I always kind of envy her for wearing with the confidence she does.

"What's up?" I say. "I thought we were meeting at the venue a half-hour early."

"Must have lost track of time." She's got that intense look of focus again.

"I saw your piece," I say.

"What'd you think?"

"It's interesting! Not gonna lie, Viv, I didn't really get it. It felt difficult."

"It's supposed to be." She's being oddly cool.

"If you don't mind, what inspired it? It's clearly a really developed piece, I just, uh, didn't really know where you were coming from with it."

She seems off, but maybe if I can get her on a tear about her work, she might open up a bit. Vivian plays with the straw in her drink as she speaks. "I guess sort of, like, identity and the way you can never really be sure who you are until somebody defines you for you? Like kind of a parody of the rapid shifts you're forced to undergo all the time just to try to be a person in the world when everyone has different expectations of you."

"That makes sense."

"And honestly, I had one really bad time at a furry convention, way before we met, before I even came out. Did a ton of speed and ended up fucking a lot of people I don't remember at a hotel. Makes you sorta start thinking about that stuff."

"I didn't think it'd be that obvious."

"Usually is."

"Jeez, I'm sorry. Guess there's a lot more drugs in that scene than you'd think?"

"Oh, trust."

"So, like, people defining you and stuff, I guess that's why you haven't done art stuff in a while?"

She's still not looking at me. "Yeah, I guess I just get self-conscious when I'm showing my work. It's like it's the only thing that I have to offer outside of sex work, and I don't know if I'm even any good at it. And I fucking hate every other artist. Like, thanks for putting me on in this empty warehouse for no money, guy with rich parents who does this full-time, I really feel like a vital part of my community. You know?"

"I guess so, yeah. I don't know, though, the guy who was running the show seemed nice."

"His name's Pat. I don't like him, but I don't really know him, either. You still trying to lodge a move to go be with your people, wherever they are?"

"I dunno. I haven't been making as much money on cam the last little while. I might be here longer than I thought."

"Aww, that's too bad. I guess you'll have to slum it here with me for a little while longer."

"Is that what you're mad about? You thought I was moving?"

"I don't know," she says, looking directly at me now. "I guess I've just been feeling a little abandoned lately. Like, I want a community, people I can actually rely on, you know? You're trying to find an escape route, and Clara, bless her heart, is not somebody I'd trust with anything. They're not coming tonight, right?"

"Uh, I don't know if they are. I'm sorry. And if I do leave, I'd way rather you come with me than doing it alone."

"You know what, I don't even wanna get into this with you right now. Are you getting anything?"

"Nah."

"All right, let's get going, it's hot as shit in here."

11.

As the sun sets back at the warehouse, a couple dozen more people pool in, mostly other alumni from Vivian's program. There are three exhibits: Priya's, a set of enormous papier-mâché sculptures of game pieces from Monopoly, Vivian's *Animal Mask*, and Pat's, a set of paintings of crying women in wartime backdrops with a shimmery gold layer over them. He's the only one not hovering over his pieces — he's at the back of the house, bartending and DJing with a friend, another lanky, bearded guy with tattoos, who looks like a palette-swapped version of Pat with black hair instead of red. Jungle tracks blast from a set of speakers with their rental stickers clearly visible, echoing on the high metal ceiling of the warehouse.

Priya is clearly the star of the night. She is still in school, and has managed to get a lot of the younger classes to come admire and try to network. She talks a lot about the origins of *Monopoly* as a feminist-socialist satire, about how her practice is built around taking materials and styles of sculpture that have been historically dismissed as crafting, women's work, and putting them in a gallery. The younger students she'd invited are awed by her, and I have to admit her confidence feels like a relief after working through Vivian's anxiety with her.

I don't really know anyone here, and mostly no one notices me as I drift from conversation to conversation. Priya is really nice, but I find myself at the edge of the conversation zoning out, worrying if Vivian is okay. I notice one boy in the crowd wearing a mustard-coloured hoodie who keeps sneaking glances at me from eyes with deep bags, but he always seems to position himself on the opposite side of the room, like he expects me to come talk to him. I try my best to ignore it. Most people who came to the show go into the curtained room with *Animal Mask*, but nobody really talks to Vivian. She sits for a long time next to the entrance playing on her phone, putting out that same intense energy. After a while, I decide to check in on her.

"Hey, pretty lady. Feeling a little better?"

"I'm fine." She makes a little grumbling noise and looks back down at her phone.

"Come on, so many people are here seeing your work! Isn't it exciting?"

"Nobody who knows me, they're all just walking in and out, just like you did. Nobody's even talking to me."

"Hey, it's an intense piece. I mean, I think maybe the same reason people can't take it for too long is the same reason it's got you in such a mood."

"What do you mean?"

"You're working through a lot of trauma there. I know you cringe whenever I bring this up, but that YouTuber I like —"

"The muggy ghost guy?"

"Yeah, the ghost guy. Nick always says that trauma leaves an echo. Maybe people are just feeling that echo a little too heavily when they go in that room, and that's why they're turning away from it."

Vivian sits quietly with this for a second. "I guess that makes sense. Still bullshit."

"Totally. Some people just can't take it. Do you want another drink?"

"Yeah."

She smiles for the first time all night. I go get in line at the back and walk up to Pat, still manning the booth. I brighten my voice and push my chest out a little.

"Hey."

"Oh, hey. More red?"

"Two this time. Actually, three."

"Still no cash?"

"Yep."

"Tut tut." He mimes slapping me on the wrist and pours three glasses. "Here ya are. Hey, uh, do you smoke?"

"No, why?"

"Do you wanna come outside for a minute with me?"

"Sure."

"Just a sec, lemme grab my jacket. You go ahead."

I smirk. I forgot how nice attention from boys feels when the boy isn't a scary stranger through a screen. As I brush by Vivian, I hand her a drink.

"Here you are, my girl."

"Thanks."

"Just a minute, I'm just gonna join Pat for a smoke."

She gives me a look she's given me before, the one that says, *Really, this guy?* I give her pleading puppy-dog eyes back.

"Heard he's a bad lay."

"It's just a smoke, come on. We're not getting married or anything."

I can't help it, but I giggle a little, running a finger over her shoulder as I flit by her and out the door.

It's pitch-black out now, the gravel parking lot lit with only one hanging bulb off the side of the warehouse, casting a broad yellow spotlight onto the rocks. It's gotten chillier already and it feels like it might rain, and Pat comes out in a big, thick brown peacoat over his doofy metal T. He bounces down the stairs and out into the circle, lighting a cig. He offers me one and I take it, coming in close to get a light. He smells so good, like the dust in the warehouse and the rotted wood and the varnish. I trade him the second glass of wine in my other hand for it.

"Hey! Having a good time?"

"Yeah."

"That's so sweet. So, are you just Vivian's friend, or do you do art stuff too, or . . . ?"

"I'm definitely interested in getting into it. Vivian and I just met through, like, housing drama, and I'm kinda just getting started figuring out what I wanna do, you know, working. But this is my first show, and it's been a great time. How about you?"

"That's awesome. But yeah, I've been mainly just painting for a while now. It's still not making me a ton of money, but I lucked out with some investments I made a few years ago, so now I mostly just live on passive income."

"Wow, that's crazy. Like, stocks and stuff?"

"I guess so. Honestly, I don't even understand a lot of it myself, the money just seems to come in on its own."

"I get that." I think about Mom for a second, and zone out until Pat interjects:

"So, like, as far as being interested, what are you working on right now?"

I feel a burst of panic, and for a second I try to figure out something less risky, knowing how weird some guys can be, but can't help but tell the truth.

"I'm a camgirl. Yeah, it was something I picked up to fill in the gap until I found a job after school, but now the gap's gone on for a couple years and it's kind of just my regular gig."

I try to read his response. He's unfazed, hands in his pockets, grinning. "That's so sick. I mean, not to be weird, but you're definitely hot enough for it."

I feel flattered even if I probably shouldn't, then choke on my smoke, coughing and gasping. I fold myself back upright and compose myself quickly. He laughs a little, but brushes it off gracefully.

"That must be a super hard job, though, right?"

"I do like it a lot of the time. It can be frustrating some days, there are a lot of creeps, but it gives me some freedom other jobs wouldn't."

"And I mean, you talk about not being an artist, but, like, you're basically a filmmaker. You've gotta manage your lighting, your hair, makeup, your angles and your performance. You've probably got more applicable skills than I do just from doing that."

This is just a line, but it's nice to hear it said. I play along. "It's true! Part of me wanted to get into acting for a while, and you learn so much about putting on a character and about people, mostly men's, perceptions of you doing that job."

"That's actually so fucking cool. Your, like, job is to make people cum. That's so much power. To tap into those, like, visceral, core parts of people that they don't want to show in public. Of course you'd make a good actress. Yo, we should write a script."

I was already pretty sure he wanted to fuck, but now I'm sure. I move a little closer to him, staring wide-eyed. "I noticed that in your paintings, too," I say. "They all have these very, like, public displays of tears and emotion and violence, a lot of, like, explosive feelings. I really liked the one of the hooded lady in the ruins, especially, like, the textures of the gold over it, it feels so ironic and so mean. What inspired that one?"

"Oh, I, uh, used a reference photo."

"Okay! What was the reference photo? Like, where was it from?"

"I dunno. I just found it."

"Did you see it online or something?"

"I'm sorry, I genuinely don't remember. I gotta get in."

Huh. He pulls the last of his cig down to the filter and tosses it on the ground, stamping it out with his black leather boot. I put out my half-smoked cigarette and gulp down the rest of my wine, following him back to the bar for another.

12.

People start to leave around midnight, including Priya and her crowd, and eventually it's just me, Vivian, Pat, the friend and the boy in the mustard sweater, who remains on the opposite side of the room, drink in hand, staring. I get a text from Clara: *hey girrrrrl! how's the show????*

I take a second to think about it. Vivian would be pissed if Clara showed up too late to see the piece, and even more so if she brought Silas. On the other hand, didn't she say all she wanted was community? Why would she cut herself off from people who like her, who want to know her, even if they are a little intense? Viv and I are intense in our own ways too. It'd be nice to see them, even if it's just to get some new updates on the gossip. I reply:

hey! it's good but it's winding down. me and viv are probably gonna head home soon. :(

I put my phone back in my purse and hope that's that for the night. I head back towards Vivian, only to get cut off by another buzz, Clara again:

oh just wanted to let you know we're almost there. don't leave without us!

Just then Vivian comes up behind me and taps me on the shoulder. "Hey, we should probably get going soon, right? Pat said he'd take everything down and lock it up, and the pieces are gonna be here all week, so there's no real point in hanging around babysitting them anymore."

"Yeah, totally."

I'm going a mile a minute trying to figure out a way not to make anybody mad at me here.

"Just let me go to the bathroom, then we can go home. You wanna stay over tonight?"

"Yeah." Vivian seems warmer, both with the offer of an exit from the show and the offer to spend the night.

I rush back to the bathroom in the back, dodging eye contact from Pat and feeling my phone buzz in my purse. Too much is coming at me from too many directions, I just want everyone to be able to hang out and not be so lonely and pissed off at each other anymore. Honestly, after that client earlier, I don't want to be alone. No, I need to be around people — I need people to tell me that I'm not just a slut or a sissy or a mommy or a hunk of dead meat. I can't let myself get lured in again, I can't let any more of myself be stolen away. I need to be surrounded, to sink into others, and I don't care who anymore. My phone keeps buzzing and I keep just not checking it, hoping Clara and Silas aren't out there starting some shit right now. Washing my hands, I feel the wine seeping into my bones, my vision blurring, and for a second, when I look up at the mirror, I see myself the way I feel other people see me, and I feel seasick.

Back in the gallery, I see Patrick staring at me from the far end, silhouetted in orange light.

"Hey! I heard you and Vivian were heading out?"

"Oh, uh, yeah. I think we were gonna get going soon."

"I was gonna throw an afterparty back at my place if you're interested. Just, you know, drinks, spin some records, get to know each other a little better."

"Oh, well, let me ask Viv."

He pushes me back against the hallway wall, holding the back of my head, and I feel my arms fold back, clearing the way for his hands to run up my dress onto my thighs. He kisses me, using a little too much tongue, and speaks slightly muffled into my mouth.

"I just think you're really cool." He pulls my hair back, looking in my eyes with a flat, drunk focus.

"And it might have been nice to spend some more time with you tonight."

That flattered feeling comes rushing back all over again. I feel myself get hard, then self-conscious, pushing my thighs together to try to avoid any weird conversations before they need to be had. He immediately pulls them back apart, laying a big, calloused hand against my clit through my panties.

"It's okay, it's okay. Don't worry. I know, it's fine. I'm bi anyways."

This pisses me off, but not enough to care. I wrap my arm around his waist, swaying back a bit, and kiss him on the cheek, pulling into his ear to whisper:

"I guess we'll have to try to make it, then."

I'm trying to rearrange myself and hide any wet spots on the dress when we come around the corner to a disappointing sight: Clara and Silas standing over Vivian's apple box she's been set up at all night, chatting with her as Pat's friend takes down the bar. Vivian looks pissed. Out of the corner of my eye, the mustard-sweatered boy is folding tables down, still staring at me, and now at Pat too. He has an unreadable, intense expression. I tap Pat on the shoulder and whisper:

"Hey Pat, do you know who that guy is?"

"Oh, don't worry about him. He's cool, he's just a little intense right now. He might actually come tonight, if that's okay."

"Can he not? He's been staring at me really weirdly all night and it's making me really uncomfortable."

"Oh, uh, sure, yeah."

Pat seems a little disappointed, but before we can really get into it, Clara notices me from across the room and zooms her tiny self over to me, Silas in tow, looking like James Dean as always. He speaks first, in his gravelly voice, which may have started as an affectation but now is very much real.

"Good to see you."

Clara chimes in, chipper as ever. "Hey! I'm so sorry we were late. Silas had a night lecture and couldn't miss it for his grade. It sucks that they turned Vivian's piece off so early in the night."

"It's one a.m. We're supposed to be out of here by now."

"Don't be so mean, this is important to us too. We love you guys, and Viv seems happy that we at least made it."

"That's good." I look over at Viv, sitting blankly in silence, no longer staring at her phone but out into the middle distance.

Clara's looking around the deserted space. "So, is there like an afters, or . . . ?"

Pat brightens up and chimes in. "Yeah, my place, I'm gonna get a cab if you wanna tag along."

Clara shoots him a bright-eyed smile, her dark eyes glowing huge at him. "That sounds perfect."

Silas is here, so I doubt Clara would do anything, but I can't help but feel jealous seeing them interact. I turn to Vivian:

"Hey! I think we're all gonna go to Patrick's and hang out a little later, if you wanna join."

"What about us going home?"

"It just, uh, seems like everybody wants to keep the party going."

She raises her eyebrows at me in a way that wrinkles her forehead. "Fine, whatever. I'll come. But, can I talk to you outside for a second?"

"Awesome! And yeah, totally. Just a second, guys."

Vivian pulls me by the arm outside, and swings through the door, talking quickly as soon as it shuts.

"I just told you I don't feel comfortable at these kinds of things! Why would you just turn your back on me like that?"

"I'm sorry! I just — Patrick wanted to hang out, and we were really hitting it off, and I really didn't know you had so many issues with Clara and Silas, and —"

"I just thought that you'd recognize tonight was *my* night. Like, I did something I haven't done in years, put this work out there and made myself really vulnerable, and you were really good! You were helping me through it! But the second some guy starts drooling over you, you throw me under the bus, try to drag me out to some party to watch you suck him off."

"Whoa!" I take a step back from her. "Not everything is about you, Viv. If I want to go to a party, I should be able to go to a party without it being a big deal, even if you don't wanna go. I feel like sometimes you act like we're in a relationship, just because we're such close friends, but we're not. I'm not even really into girls that way."

"Oh, really? So, all the times we hooked up, that was all just, like, gal pals? Bullshit. Honestly, the more we hang out, the more I get the feeling that you look down on me."

"What the fuck, Viv?"

"No, listen. You're so afraid of being the wrong kind of girl that you just do whatever anybody asks of you, and as long as you think that way, your whole life is gonna be this weird, fucked-up game of shaping yourself into whatever you think *one of the good ones* looks like. Honestly, I see the way you look at me! Half the time you look like you're embarrassed to be seen with me."

"I'm really not! You're being cruel."

I start stepping back from her, flinching. I can see in her eyes it's only offending her more that my instincts are kicking in like this. Vivian starts gradually drifting away from me and towards the street, talking with her hands.

"Is it just because I'm older than you? Is it escorting? I know that's why you kicked me out of your house, but, like, I just want to know why. I'm sorry for not having a rich mommy who pays my bills. Even tonight, I said I was having a hard time, and you just pranced off to go kiss ass instead of sitting with your supposed best friend at her first gallery premiere in a decade."

"Viv, go home. You're fucked-up, you're saying stuff you don't mean. We should try to talk this through in the morning, when you're feeling a little better. I love you a lot, and I really don't think it means I'm some kind of traitor if I want to get out there and meet other people."

Vivian's crying a little, slurring her words. "You're gonna have to let go of the superiority complex at some point. I don't even wanna stay over."

I can feel my face contort and my voice crack. "What fucking complex?"

"Bye, Amy."

She wanders off towards the bus stop as the car pulls up, a silver minivan. I see Clara, Silas, Pat and his friend, and the boy in the mustard hoodie piling out in their jackets, marching towards it. The boy in the mustard hoodie finally approaches me, faster than I expected. He grabs me by the shoulders and looks into my eyes.

"So, *he* was worth leaving the house for, huh?" he says.

"What are you talking about?"

"Don't lie to me, Annie."

"That's not my name."

"If it's not, then what's your name now?"

I don't know how to process this right now, still shaking with nerves from Vivian's exit. I can't wrap my head around what this guy's saying. I put my hands over my face and start to back away from him.

"Please, just give me a second."

Before I can say anything else, Pat grabs the boy's shoulder and gives him a little tug backwards. His whole fun-guy affect drops instantly. "Come on. I don't know what you're trying for here, but now's not the time."

The boy rips his hood back, keeping his eye squarely on me. "Look at me. You don't leave the house for a year and you're immediately out with this asshole. You can't even look at me now. What did I do to make you do this to me? Like, seriously!"

"Dude, please. I'm heading home, can I just go?"

"Congrats on your fucking recovery, I guess."

I'm shaking as I get into the back of the cab with Clara and Silas. The boy who thinks he knows me looks at me with wide, pleading eyes as Pat and his friend talk him down outside, giving Patrick a shove then getting a shove back that knocks him to the ground. Pat and his friend get in as well in a hurry, and the van takes off.

Clara immediately starts quietly dipping her key into a baggie in her purse. "What was up with Vivian?" she's saying.

"I dunno, I think she was just a little drunk and feeling insecure about the show. She lashed out. She'll probably be better in the morning. We'll patch things up."

I say this knowing full well I'm too pissed off to want to resolve it right now. As much as I love her, and as much as I need her as a friend, if Vivian's going to freak out when she can't have me all to herself, that's not somebody I want around.

"And that guy?"

Patrick cuts me off before I can reply. "Sounds like he thought you were his ex?"

"Fucking weird," I say. "Was he, like, really fucked-up, or like can't tell us apart, or what?"

"I dunno. I never met his last girlfriend, but he talks about her a lot."

13.

In Patrick's loft, Silas is holding court, standing tall over the rest of us hunched over the wood coffee table.

"I mean, like, the thing about Nietzsche, right, is, it's really more kind of like a pre-postmodernism than it is any kind of, like, right-wing ideology. Like, he's basically advocating for, like, the rejection of all values, as opposed to like the strength and domination that he's constantly sort of using as, like, a rhetorical tool, this like example of the like amoral good, so he doesn't have to say good to prove his point, but like ultimately he's still sort of talking about the good, just in terms of, like, the free rather than the good. It's like an entire world of just, like, freak shit. Everybody trying to create a completely new set of their own laws that they're trying to wield over everybody else all the time, to try to meet their own needs and create their own happiness on no terms except their own, faking at having a free will that they never really had in the first place, because it's all just coming from the affects, right? That place beyond where your ability to, like, express what you're feeling in words ends and where the gut kicks in, that kinda instinctual sense that you gotta do what you gotta do at the end of the day, that's at least what it feels like it means to me, and such a big part of it too, in terms of that kind of, like, proto-postmodern thing, is like that sense of uninterpretability, like, speaking simply but in ways that resist easy interpretation."

He's rapping on the table rapidly with one hand, twirling his wrist with the other, each one just out of rhythm.

Clara hands me the straw and I bend back down to the table, bored. Pulling up, I look at her, staring rapt at Silas, then Pat, who smiles at me then stands up to interject.

"Wait, weren't you just talking about being Catholic all night, dude? Isn't Nietzsche, like, very atheist?"

Pat pronounces it like *nee-chee* versus Silas's overemphasized German pronunciation. I think it's very sweet.

"Well, yeah, Pat, but you see, it's, like, dialectics. I'm absorbing the parts of the stories that serve me best and acknowledging the, like, parts that cancel each other out, trying to, like, look ahead to the future of what the conversation might be by absorbing pieces of everything. It goes back to that thing of being misunderstood, being the outsider, making yourself impossible to recognize so that future historians are forced to figure out who you are and what you were doing because you were trying to synthesize everything you had, like obviously I'm gonna look dumb in the future, but so are you, right? At least I'm trying."

Patrick lies back on his elbows, slack on the opposite end of the coffee table. He speaks at half the speed Silas does. "Sure, but that's just a fancy way of saying it doesn't work, though, right? With, like, faith? You know, like, unironic belief in a God that exists, who, like, created everything, in real life, who controls everything, and who has, like, moral positions that are passed down through a church?"

I've taken a bump off Clara at karaoke a time or two, but I've never really done coke, not like this. I feel like my muscles are going to slough off my bones and I want to announce to everyone how numb I feel, but I don't want to either, so I just grind my teeth. I sort of wish I'd just gone home with Vivian, and then I remember how mean she was being to me and I start to want to cry, but I can't feel feelings anymore, so I just get mad at myself again.

I pull my head back down and back up and back down. Clara jumps up too now.

"That's a really reductionist perspective on what faith means," Clara says. "You know, there has to be some separation between the political structure that is *a religion* versus the cultural position of that same thing, versus *faith*, which is like the sorta inner relationship you have to it. I feel like there's basically no, like, moral problem or even any, like, core-metaphysical claim attached with participating in a religion based on an internal notion of a faith, or, like, based on a cultural positioning of where you're at in a place or time, right?"

"All claims are metaphysical claims," Silas says, "but continue."

Pat bursts out laughing at this, and he looks at me like he's totally lost too.

Clara looks up into the corner of the room before continuing. "And I mean, it comes down to that first question, the question of the political institution, is it justified to turn that sense of, like, *one*-ness, connection to the One, into something that has the right to use state funds, or to exact violence? And, like, you know, I think we all have our doubts about that sometimes, but that to me is what's so valuable about like *religion* versus *faith* in the first place, like that ability to, like, come together, make something, shape the world in your image. Actual *community*, you know?"

Pulling my head back up, I look square at Silas and the words escape my mouth before I can think them through. "So, Silas, like, what was that thing you said about Clara hanging out with trans girls?"

Everybody stops and looks at me.

"The what?"

"I don't know, she said you had a fight about something where you said you were insecure about how her friends were trans girls, and, uh, I was just curious about what that meant."

Silas turns to Clara and gets in close, like no one else is in the room. "Why would you tell them that?"

"Oh, no, I'm sorry, baby, I didn't realize it was such a —"

He starts to raise his voice gradually, turning back towards me. "What did you hear, like specifically, what did you hear?"

I'm shrinking to the side of the table with Pat and his friend, not realizing what I've started here. Silas turns back to me and starts hand-talking wildly towards my face.

"So, like, I guess what I meant was, like, you know we're open, right, and that we're both bisexual, and that's something that I was always kinda just, like, cool with, you know? And like, for me the whole idea of being open was kind of this, like, ability for us to still have access to our bisexuality, you know, where it was like a lot easier to not feel constrained by the choice to, like, only have one partner of the same sex, or of the opposite sex, or whatever. So like, I've seen some guys on the side, and Clara's been cool with that, and —"

"You've been seeing guys?" Clara says, taken aback.

"Yeah, like we said we would?"

"Okay."

"Sure, sure, yeah. But like, outside partners not of the gender that we each, uh, are, or like the sex? I don't know. But like when she said she'd met some new girlfriends, I was like, oh this is awesome, like you know Clara's really been missing that kind of, like, feminine essence thing in her life for a while, so I thought that'd be really good for her, and, like, you know, maybe good people to, like, hook up with, I don't know. And she'd said stuff about you, like how you guys maybe have like a little bit of a crush thing going?"

Clara gives me that wide-eyed look like the one she'd given me at her apartment, pretending like I didn't already know. I scoot away from her, creating a little distance. I really don't want any of this attention.

"But, I mean, then I started to kind of wonder about it," Silas continues, getting more frantically animated, "because I realized, like, you're a woman, I totally fully recognize your womanhood, but like, I don't care if my girl fucks another girl, but, like, you could give her dick, which means you might be able to give her better dick than me. And that just kind of got me feeling like I was small, you know, or like I'd failed somehow for her even wanting that? Then I started to get kinda turned on thinking about it, but then that just made me feel bad too, so I kinda freaked out. But then I came to her and said I was sorry about it, and we had a whole, like, really beautiful night where we were holding each other and crying and I thought we actually made a lot of progress, but apparently she just went and told you I was the bad guy again right after, like she always does. Is that why Vivian was all fucked-up too, because she hates me now?"

I sigh and throw up my hands. "I don't know, man, please."

"Wait, you guys were fighting because of me?" Silas says. "She was pissed at you because you're even, like, associating with me? Oh my god, this is just like my last ex all over again. It's such darvo bullshit, people love to lie about you while they say that you're lying to them. I can't fucking believe how much people talk shit here."

Clara puts her arm around his shoulder and starts pulling him down to the pillows around the table. "Hey, you know we all know that. It's not a big deal. Amy forgives you, right, Amy?" Clara shoots me an encouraging look.

Trying not to show panic, I nod and smile warmly with my lips closed tight, teeth still grinding inside. "No, you're a really great friend, Silas," I hear myself saying. "I've always thought you were just so cool and so interesting."

Silas is a really, really hot guy: his deep eyes and ruffled shirts, his coiffed hair and his ridiculous jawline and his beautiful olive skin. He's right to see me as a threat to his relationship, just not to the side he thinks. But Clara's eyes are giving me a big thumbs-up as she pours him a cup of Scotch and cuts him a line, settling him into his spot at the table.

As Clara tucks a strand of hair behind his ear and moves in to kiss him, I feel Pat's hand creeping up my thigh again. God, it's nice. But it's also a little too out in the open, and I push him back a bit. I turn to Pat's friend, who has slightly deeper bags under his eyes. I'm a little unnerved by the fact that he seems like he hasn't done any of the coke. I give him an awkward half wave, and he gives me one back and starts to speak, the only one not slurring by this point.

"This is a sick party. You guys are so cool, we gotta hang out more often."

"Yeah."

"So, uh, Pat was telling me you're, like, a porn star or something."

I give Pat a look but decide not to pursue it any further with the amount of chaos already in the room.

"That's actually, like, so cool, man," he's saying.

"Okay."

I stop trying to talk to Pat's friend. Desperate to change the subject, I gesture broadly towards Clara. "So, uh, how's your program going?"

"Not good," she sighs. "Gonna get kicked out in the fall, I think. My adviser's out to get me. I dunno."

"Sorry to hear that..."

"It's okay, what was I gonna do with a master's anyway? Probably just end up moving back to that shitty town either way."

Silas leans up from his stupor. "Don't say that, baby."

"Of course not, baby." She gives him a little peck on the nose, and he reacts to it with a sort of offended double take, starting to stand up again. She looks back at me. "Maybe we should just start heading home," she says suddenly. "I feel like maybe we've all gotta just, like, cool down a little bit, you know?"

A spike of panic jumps up my throat. I really don't know how to ask Clara and Silas and the friend to just leave. And I really don't want to spend the night alone. I really don't think I could stand the shadow in the doorway and the scratching and the etching, it's like I'd wear out my wrists right through the bone until they started jutting out through my skin, so much scraping and scratching that'd happen if they left me alone right now—

"I mean, you guys could go," I say. "And, uh, you, uh..."

I'm looking squarely at Pat's friend, but he's not getting the hint.

"Or we could all get a cab together?" Clara says. "Like, stop midway at your place on the way to ours?"

Panic is rising in my chest. "No, really, you don't have to do that, it's okay, I can just get my own after you go."

"It's really no fuss," Clara says, undeterred. "I heard you complaining about how little money you were making to Viv the other night, and I'm just ripping through the last of my debt before the rest of my life starts, whenever they decide to dump me from the program, so let me take care of you."

"Clara, no..."

She grabs my hands and leans over the table, staring deep into my eyes with her huge brown deer eyes, even bigger than normal now, dilated like a bat's. "*Let me take care of you.*"

I want to shake her, and just scream in her face, *Stop being weird! Take your weird boyfriend, and this other weird guy, and get out so I can fuck this other, less weird guy! It should be clear to you what's happening here and please, in the spirit of sisterhood, just fuck off!* What happens instead is I crack under the pressure of the eye contact and feel myself start tearing up.

"Aww, you really weren't ready to hear that, were you? It's okay."

I try to speak, but I can't feel anything come out, like it's all just stuck. I feel my throat start to close, hyperventilating, a thin trail of blood running from my nose down into my mouth.

"Oh, sweetie, let me get that for you."

Clara waddles out of the room, holding the edges of her loose little plaid dress around her thighs. I'm still trying to speak, but there's nothing coming out and I'm looking up at the high ceiling of the loft with its concrete walls and unfinished hardwood as I taste iron. Everything looks like it's being viewed through a fish-eye lens. She sits down right in front of me with those huge eyes in my face again, handing me a tissue.

"Oh my god, wait," she says suddenly. "You just don't wanna be alone tonight, do you? Is your ghost back?"

The boys, who had lost all attention by this point, all jerk up on hearing this, especially Silas. I feel like a toddler, everyone trying to guess what I'm getting at, mouth running with snot and blood and tears, and feeling like language is going to keep failing me, I just nod my head.

"*Ohhhhhh* my god, baby, I'm sorry. That's probably what's made all the vibes so weird lately, huh?"

Silas lifts himself from his incline next to the coffee table. "She has a ghost?"

"Yeah, uh, is it okay if I tell them?"

I take a deep gulp from one of the cups on the table and choke trying to clear my throat, Scotch burning my sinuses. I try to cough out a word, but it just comes out like *GHRAWK* from the bottom of my throat. I can tell it's lower and more guttural than any other noise I've ever made to any of these people; they all look concerned but like they're waiting for someone else to help.

She's speaking for me, cautiously and then speeding up. "So, uh, she had this nightmare when she was a kid..."

I'm looking into the floor at the dirt and crumbs of food accumulating on the wood's edges. I jerk my head up at the upper level of Pat's loft, with more paintings of veiled women screaming in flames.

"And this, like, spider thing, it took her down to a dark basement and it, uh, cut off all her arms and legs?"

I give her a *comme ci, comme ça* hand gesture. I blow the blood-snot out of my nose and a little bit of it bursts out of the tissue onto my hand, and I'm sweeping it up as quickly as I can and trying to hide the mess away on the floor.

"And she had to do math on the floor to stop it?"

I do another line. I close my eyes and try to pretend I'm not here while she does this. Pat does one too. His friend is still sober, ominous, smiling politely at Clara's story.

"And now she's scared of sleeping or being alone because, like, anywhere she lives, it follows her and it settles in. That's kind of it, right?"

Finally, I feel a breath reach the back of my throat. "Sure, uh, yeah. It never really went away."

Pat moves his hand from my thigh to my shoulder. I guess his curiosity has been sated enough for him to finally step in. I wish he'd moved to take me home earlier, but I'm so, so relieved that he finally is now. He gives me that same kindly look he did at the art show.

"Hey, don't worry about it. I think if you do want to get going, that might actually be great."

Silas, still rapt, dilated eyes in tight focus on me, has a smile crack across his face. "I could exorcize your apartment," he's saying. "I know the rites, and we've got enough people to do it."

Patrick pulls my head into his shoulder, protective. "Come on, man, she's exhausted, I'm exhausted, we can't just keep jumping from place to place, I'd rather just, like, settle in here, put on a movie, keep things chill. Maybe put the coke away, you know, just ride it out."

Silas seems to not hear him. "Amy, you're not the kind of girl who just sits there and takes it, are you? If I can help you get rid of this thing, we may as well do it as soon as we can, then you can move on with your life, you know? Not feel so fucked-up all the time. We had some ill spirits in our place, and I had some people over, read the rites, and there haven't been any issues since, right?" He gestures to Clara, who's still smiling at me warmly.

"Yeah!" Clara says. "Honestly, if you do want to keep going tonight, it's really healing, I think you would get something out of it."

The room is spinning and they're all looking at me with expectation in their eyes. Clara wants to keep Silas happy, Pat wants to get me into bed, Silas wants to keep getting more and more fucked-up and try to go to whatever outer limit he's trying to reach through this whole exorcism bit, and Pat's friend, always there, always silent, seeming pleasant if zoned out, I can't read at all.

I lift my glass from the table, take a deep sip to try to keep my throat clear, and feel myself settle a little. "Fuck it, yeah, let's go."

Silas pumps his fists. "Let's do it! I'll call the next cab. Baby, do you have my phone?"

"Oh, yeah, it's somewhere in my purse here..."

As Clara scoops up the rest of the baggie and the two of them put their coats on, Pat scoots me aside, framing out the friend. "Are you sure you wanna do this? This seems like a bad idea."

I feel completely numb now. "It's fine. We just give him what he wants and he'll leave."

Patrick seems visibly concerned by my tone. "Okay, I mean... is he okay? Something is, like, really off here, right?"

I try to put a little more life into it. "Yeah, they're fun. They get into all sorts of shit like this, it's why we're friends." I hear myself slurring my words and start over-enunciating to make up for it. "And anyways," I say, making my voice softer, "don't you wanna see my bedroom? You could see my studio too, you know, the place where I cam? Once the party settles down and stuff, we could, you know, have some fun with it, maybe make a little money."

Pat seems to shake awake at the idea of this. "Oh, uh, yeah, that would be cool."

Silas, now fully dressed in his long cream coat, jogs back over to the table, bouncing a little. "It came quick. Come on, the car's outside."

Out into pouring rain, shocking against bare skin, into another car. The movement of the streets past the window of the car makes me feel ill, as the wooziness of the drunk starts to overtake the numbness of the coke, the spinning getting faster as red lights zip by outside through the layer of rain, realizing just how far I have travelled from home, how bad it's going to be when I get there. Everybody's silent in the cab, with this weird air of seriousness. I feel like I'm locked onto a track towards something that the sober, reasoned part of me would never agree to but that needs to happen for some unspoken reason, and everyone here seems to be in that exact same energy.

I look over to Silas in the passenger seat, still bouncing, and see in his eyes this deep, unhinged longing for something he can't begin to understand. I feel like I understand him, just trying to push things further and further to try to hit the point where it all breaks, your mind cracks open, and you find some permanent truth, some keen emotional awareness that doesn't leave when you come down. I get that longing for God too. I look back in the side mirror at Pat's friend. *What are you doing here? How are you awake? What time is it, even? Why weren't you doing drugs with everybody?*

I start to feel puke rise at the back of my throat and swallow it back down, tasting sour bile, my stomach burning from taking back in the poison it had already rejected. I really don't want to be the girl who makes the cab pull over three times on the way to the afterparty to the afterparty, and nobody else seems to notice how sick I am.

"Hey, Clara."

"Yes, dear?"

"Can I, uh, you know?"

"Oh, yeah, just, I'm running a little low."

She leans over with the key, and I take it. I make eye contact with the cab driver as I do. He looks put off but not quite ready to make a fuss about it, as the numbness hits again and I feel better about being in the car. I can already feel myself ache, a preview of what I have to look forward to in the morning. Handing it back to Clara, I spill a little on my lap.

"What the fuck, girl? I told you to be careful."

"I'm sorry."

I sound like a foghorn. Clara lightens up a little, but I'm starting to feel that edginess cross over the whole car, everyone waiting to park so they can get into my place and keep the party going. Maybe we'll be too loud and I'll finally just get kicked out of there, might give me the motivation to move that I was missing, though I'm still waiting on Mom to get back to me on whether the payments will still keep coming. Fuck, *Mom*. Probably wouldn't be surprised. *This is exactly what I thought would happen, you start calling yourself a woman and then all of a sudden you're making your living masturbating on camera and doing hard drugs with grad students.* Fuck her, whatever. I mean, not fuck her, I don't mean that, or at least I'd hope I don't mean that in case she can still hear my thoughts. I feel like I can still hear hers, like a cold chill every time she remembers me or says something to one of her friends. She'd better text back soon.

The car pulls up. It's gotten way colder and still raining hard, and I'm shivering trying to get the keys out of my purse as Silas and Pat shield me with their arms huddled over the apartment door. It's nice to feel small under the little space they create for me. I finally get the key in, fighting my shaky hands to slide it through. The hallway is too small to really fit five people, and we're cramming through it like a clown car, everyone in a hurry to get upstairs and settle in, then into the elevator, and through the last stretch onto the eleventh floor. As soon as I get the door open, everyone piles their jackets on the floor and goes to the table to immediately start cutting more lines. Frustrated, I start neatly shaking out each jacket and hanging them in the front closet, one by one. I can see Clara starting to get stingier, cutting less and less for me and Pat and more and more for herself. Silas is in the process of speedily lighting candles he found in the emergency kit I keep in the kitchen cabinet above the stove. This, too, is left out in pieces, Band-Aids scattered across the counter, and I rush to put it all back together and put it away before things really begin. Clara pours me another cup of her Scotch as I land at the table, and the boat-fuel burn isn't happening for me at all now, it flows as easy as water.

Silas runs his hands through his hair, pushing it back as he turns up his beautiful nose and starts to recite.

"This is directed to the spirit that's followed Amy for her whole life now, whatever entity you are that's made it so hard for her to sleep for years. Right?"

I look up to the overhead light and to the popcorn ceiling. The claw won't come if anybody else is around, but I'd rather let Silas have this than try to explain any further.

"Yes."

"Okay. Now, repeat each line after me. *God, Creator and defender of the human race . . .*"

Silas chants these first words, but after a second becomes self-conscious and slides back to something closer to his usual portentous monotone. Something immediately starts to shift in the room. The faces of my friends, people it seemed I could trust, begin to turn into reflections of that disconnection from myself and from everything that seemed before to only run through me when I was alone. I've never felt the presence like this when there were people around to watch over me. I shrink into myself, hoping not to be noticed.

". . . who made man in your own image, look down in pity on this your servant, Amy, now in the toils of the unclean spirit . . ."

I start to feel the thing enter the room. I see Silas's eyes start to widen, too. I'm seeing someone really witness it and not believe what he's seeing. Some mirror image of myself in him. His voice shakes as he continues, his heavy breaths moving the candles' flames around him as the sound of the rain beats down outside.

". . . now caught up in the fearsome threats of man's ancient enemy, sworn foe of our race, who befuddles and stupefies the human mind . . ."

I look back at Silas and his eyes have gone fully bloodshot and he's staring at me in disbelief, then in the same direction that I can feel her there, my lost part across the street, looking in at me.

". . . throws it into terror, overwhelms it with fear and panic."

After this one, Silas immediately bends over to have another line. He sits up in shock, gripping onto the edge of the wood kitchen table to try to keep himself upright. Everyone else's eyes are closed, but his and mine are locked into one another in a full stare, eyes bugging into one another, summoning something inside one another.

"Repel, O Lord, the devil's power, break asunder his snares and traps, put the unholy tempter to flight."

He's screaming the rites now, trying to hold in grunts of pain. Clara and Pat have opened their eyes now and are starting to ask him questions like *are you okay* and saying things like *oh God, please stop*, *Silas, you're scaring me*, shaking his arms and trying to pull him out of his seat, but neither he nor I acknowledge them as the fingers spread across the floor.

"By the sign of your name, let your servant be protected in mind and body. Keep watch over the inmost recesses of her heart; rule over her emotions; strengthen her will."

Silas stands as he's saying this and begins to take off his belt, moving methodically and mechanically towards the picture window at the end of the open living room and unlocking the balcony door. Clara is pulling on him to move back into the room, but there's nothing she can do now, he's on rails, just like I am, a puppet on a string of something far bigger than he can understand. Clara looks back at me, pleading, but I'm frozen to the spot, an empty shell.

"Let vanish from her soul the temptings of the mighty adversary."

He wraps the belt around his neck, face beaten by the autumn rain, and continues to recite as he's trying to tie the other end of the skinny belt to the thin metal bars covering the side of the balcony. Clara has nothing but his shirt sleeves as he keeps climbing over the edge of the railing, shrieking the end of the rites out into the night sky.

"GRACIOUSLY GRANT, O LORD, AS WE CALL ON YOUR HOLY NAME, THAT THE EVIL SPIRIT, WHO HITHERTO TERRORIZED OVER US, MAY HIMSELF RETREAT IN TERROR AND DEFEAT, SO THAT THIS SERVANT OF YOURS MAY SINCERELY AND STEADFASTLY RENDER YOU THE SERVICE WHICH IS YOUR DUE; THROUGH CHRIST OUR LORD."

He jumps from the balcony, hoping to fall, but Clara, Patrick and the friend have all grabbed him by then, pulling and pulling him back up against the side of the balcony and refusing to let the belt tighten. I am sitting, dull-eyed, letting the forces take me too, quietly, in place, the way they always have.

I am the only one who says *Amen* before Silas starts yelling again:

"It's me! The demon is me!"

I faintly wonder if his and my experiences of the thing were really alike at all. He's still trying to speak, but he's bawling too hard for anyone to make anything out, as they pull him back up to the edge. He flops over the side, the metal divider cutting into his belly, as Patrick pulls a box cutter from his belt and chews slowly through the thin belt leather, letting him free, falling back into the balcony limp. Clara is crying like crazy now too, hyperventilating as she drags him on the ground through the door back into the apartment.

"I love you so much, baby, let's get you inside, okay?"

Everything is quiet and still now. I'm in the chair, staring at the wall, shaking, as everyone else is looking at Silas, tending to Silas, wondering about what happened to Silas and what Silas's needs at this moment are, Silas who is crying like a baby into Clara's lap as she's running her fingers through his hair. He asks softly, under his breath, something about whether they can go home, and Clara lifts him by the arm and starts to call another cab. She comes over to me, Silas, dull-eyed, resting over her shoulder.

"Well, thanks for having us over, I guess," she says.

"Yeah."

I can't even inflect my voice one way or the other, everything coming out in a low monotone. I would like to tell her that I am sorry for what happened.

I would like to cry with her and hold her and help her with what's definitely still going to be a long, hard night to come for her, but there's nothing left in me. Clara's looking at me like I'm the lowest of the low.

"You really didn't help at all, did you?"

"No. Sorry." I'm still looking at the wall.

"I was having such a good time."

"Sorry."

"Have a good night, I guess."

And she drags him back out the door.

I stand up with the last of what I have left in me and walk over to the bedroom, lie down on the bed. As I start to feel myself go limp, Patrick cracks the door open with a creak and looks in at me.

"Hey, can I come in?"

"Yeah."

He sits a little ways away from me on the bed. "Crazy party, huh?"

"Yeah."

"So, uh... I was thinking, just, um, about the offer you made earlier?"

"Yeah."

"Is that something you, uh... still might be up for? I know it's late, it's like five a.m. or something, but I still think it could be fun?"

"Yeah."

"Okay, uh, awesome. What's the password on your laptop?"

I stare into the wall even deeper, trying to get a word for a minute. "Cantaloupe1999."

"Thank you." He turns his head back. "She's down! Dude, get in here."

Patrick turns on the camera as the friend enters, unzipping his pants.

14.

When I wake up, the sun is already setting again and it's started to snow. They're gone. Everything hurts. My ass is bruised blue outside and in, my ribs covered in green-and-purple marks too. They really worked me over. I remember loving this feeling: the lingering hurt of a lover's souvenir, keeping them with me through the day. I don't want to remember this.

My brain feels like it's going to explode. My sinuses burning, the booze drilling on the back side of my head. The burn rises up at the back of my throat again and I run to the toilet and puke for a couple minutes. It's mostly water, but thick, with a mix of red from the wine and yellow from the whisky. Everything exiting me as it had come in. My face is cold next to the porcelain and the silence is becoming palpable. I can feel the air starting to get colder around me.

I'm well and truly alone for the first time in months. Even the claw is silent, curled up in some corner where it waits for deeper night to fall, and the double hangs in the air, a non-presence. There really is no one left to look out for me but myself.

I crawl back from the bathroom to the bedroom around the corner, over the pillows, now scattered around the room in a mess, the camera still pointed down from the desk, the light still on, unblinking. I pull the blankets up over myself and grab my phone, plugged in on a side table. I send Vivian a text:

hey. good call on getting out of there. rough night, let's catch up and talk soon, k?

I send it, open Instagram for a second and don't really look at anything, then tab back over to texts. I send a second one to Viv:

love you lots <3

I copy-paste the same text and send it to Mom.

I notice the hanky sitting next to the side of the bed with some of the old makeup still on it from my attempt to wipe it off. Still on my back, I unfold it carefully over my head, and sob last night's face deep into it. Tomorrow I'll print the mail label and send it to the man with the numbers account.

15.

As the days got shorter and shorter, I could start to hear the walls talk again, louder now, louder than when I could shut them out with the noise from the computer.

Staring up at the fairy lights and the LEDs glued up to make the place look nice on camera, I started to notice that my neighbour, night in and night out, screams at his TV. *Goddammit! Fucking no! Jesus Christ! Fuck!* It seemed to be around the same time every night, around 8 p.m., then going for a few hours. Always this same set of screams again and again. One time I saw him standing half poking out of his doorway, staring towards mine. He was a big guy, maybe six foot four, maybe forty-five years old, with a beer gut and a little bit of stubble on his chin. He was just standing there, arms at his sides, not seeming to have any particular business being in the hallway. I waved at him and gave him a nervous smile, said hi, but he just kept staring at me, didn't say anything at all, seeming to freeze tighter to his position. I got a little more cautious in the hallway after that.

His shouting started to become a transition point between the awful quiet of the days and the nights, which were getting worse than I thought they ever could. The noise became unbearable, the shrieks of a million voices in unison calling to me through that crack of light through the curtains.

I stayed up late every night, posting old pics to my accounts, repeating old posts on new platforms, struggling to write captions that could try to apply some story to the same, blank images on repeat: my cock, folded up in panties or out cumming in a Fleshlight, my ass, pointed straight up at the camera at the top of my dresser; my chin and tits looking up from on my knees demurely in a set of thigh-highs with little bows at the top. I had to use old pictures because my ass and thighs were covered in bloody lumps somewhere halfway between pimples and scabs that I couldn't stop ripping open. I'd tried to ignore the constant irritation, but I still found myself passively peeling them off and letting them bleed. Looking at them made me think of early attempts at shaving my legs, cuts and ingrown hairs growing back as aggressively as they'd come. I thought about finding somebody on an app to keep me company for a night, make me feel useful, drown out the noise, but no one could ever want me like this.

I kept the stream running but wouldn't appear in it directly, hoping people might want to go on priv, but those dried up quickly too. Only one viewer seemed to linger, another numbers account, but they never posted anything in the chat or interacted at all, just watched and waited as the others dwindled away.

After the first couple weeks of this, I texted my mom asking for more money. I told her I had found a job, a temporary position, that things were slowing down right now, and it'd really really help if I could get just a couple hundred more per month to help with the rent. I got the usual expected silence, next to the apology texts I had sent to Vivian and Clara weeks earlier, which I had read and reread so many times at this point I couldn't bring myself to open them in the faint hope of finally getting a response. Shifts on the Chariot chatbox stayed consistent, but more and more I found myself checked out, brick-walling clients intentionally on their problems to try to get them to go away, anything to get them off the line so I could go back to refreshing the same few apps again and again, getting a little rush from the notifications, but which, like the cam audiences, dwindled more and more as time went on. Each buzz I'd hoped would be Mom, or Viv, or Clara, but always just the audience: everywhere, hungry, both disappointed and desperate for more.

Then back to bed, the claw gradually getting closer, farther and farther across, its scrapes cutting through the noise of the voices, on the floor in the dark, trying to measure it out, trying to carve in the correct angle that could prove it all away once and for all, hours of scraping and scratching, tearing at the skin on my thighs and the blisters building up on my hands like little pimples, bleeding and getting infected in a wax and wane as the weeks passed.

Lying in bed one long autumn afternoon, my mom's lawyer reached out to let me know she'd died some months ago. Nothing changed at all. I asked about my inheritance and he said that she had asked them to continue the payments at the same rate until the estate ran out, and to deny me a lump sum if I asked for one. I thanked him.

It's getting harder to keep the apartment clean now that I'm in it all the time. I notice things pass me by that I would have immediately caught when I was more in my routine — small spills and crumbs from cooking left to rot and attracting bugs to the kitchen, clothes left on the floor for days on end, usually the same couple sets of pyjamas worn again and again until they stink — days lost spent playing video games or checking for money coming in. I stopped exercising because when I do, it hurts and it makes me feel ill because I'm not eating enough anymore to make up the caloric debt. I'm noticing that I've become nervous about other people, I find myself thinking that maybe all I can do is hurt them or embarrass myself, and I start to wonder if I'd be better off just keeping to myself.

And I can feel the constant presence of the one watching me, the echo, who seems to hold all the secrets somewhere just out of view. I pored over

Nick's video on her again and again, went to her station every morning hoping for a recurrence, through the playground across the street, attempting over and over to retrace her steps each day, to see if anything changed. Back down the hill, across the bridge, through the bad part of town, seeking out each of the places she appeared in the security footage. I eventually sent Nick an email about it, asking where he had gotten the footage from, who had shared it with him. In a mailbag episode a week later, he posted my message and chastised me, said that he'd received an undue number of emails and messages about this piece and was planning to pull the video. He said he felt a lot of regret for even making the video.

All of a sudden, mixed into those fewer and fewer horny notifications, there were more and more angry ones. Nick hadn't done a great job of blurring my email address. People started telling me I was a bad fan and a worse person. I had to turn the notifications off at some point, and Nick never replied to me when I got back to him letting him know that this was happening.

I went back to that video's comments section and noticed a running thread of people who claimed to have seen the figure. I DM'd some of them and the majority didn't get back to me, but the few who did were located all over the place: some in Europe, some in the USA, some in South America, others who told me that they believed it was their face as well. This made me lose hope again. We were all just having some sort of mirroring effect off a set of muddled pixels stolen off some city hard drive somewhere and leaked anonymously, almost certainly just to create an online dogpile on me, in some other shape. Alive, somewhere, acting as me.

I had almost given up until the day I found the hole. Some early morning in this fog of weeks, a light snow drifting overhead, I went on my daily walk to the station and felt the echo in a more pronounced way than I had in a long time. I hadn't gone far, just to the playground behind the identical apartment building across the street. I could faintly see a lone set of tracks in the snow leading back from the playground to the street, and looking more closely, I observed dots of blood following them. The footprints blended together on the sidewalk, so the trail cut off before the street, but following it backwards led me to a small clearing in the grass by the playground. An indent had been made in the earth, a rectangular box carved out exactly my height. At the foot of the hole was a little puddle of her blood.

I looked up at the sky again for a second, a continuous grey breaking into pieces and blowing sideways. I lay down in the hole, and felt the still-warm blood where my hands rested. It smelled like home. I felt my feet landing where hers had sat at the hole's edge, and pushed my hands down into the soil, feeling out the places her hands had been, losing myself in the sensation of her. Somewhere in the back of my mind, I hoped nobody was watching me, but I didn't care anymore. I wasn't meant to be looked at, and if anyone did, it didn't matter. I had her.

I lingered there, face wet and hot and freezing, staring up into the sky, full of gratitude, reaching a sudden sense of clarity. I wasn't afraid anymore.

16.

I stare at my phone for the rest of the afternoon, disgusted that I'm doing this. I feel awful about myself for hours on end thinking about it, but by 4 p.m. I can feel the time slipping away from me. The sun is starting to set by the time I finally reach out to Patrick.

Hey :) do you know who that guy you beat up at the party was?

The read receipt and the "…" indicator pop immediately.

hi! how's it been? ;')

Dots pop up instantly again.

and, uh, i beat somebody up?

other than u ofc lol <3

Disgusting. I try to play along:

hehe, yeah. there was that weird kid in the yellow who thought i was his gf

A minute before dots this time.

o shit, yeah, sam

dude's a creep

I take a second to figure out the right approach here, drafting a couple ways of flattering him before just going for the direct approach.

do you have his number?

i mean he rsvp'd. why?

he said something weird i wanted to ask him about

yeah, he fuckin does that lol

you sure? bad vibes on that guy

pretty please? :3

okkkkkkk fine. shoot again soon? <3

totally <3

The next text contains Sam's contact. I save it and block Patrick's number. Immediately, and without thinking, I shoot Sam a message.

hey sam. i'm really sorry, i admit it now, i saw you at the party the other night. i wasn't ready to face things yet, but now i am. but i'm ready to make up. new number, just wanted to make sure this was still you.

Instant response.

what the fuck do you want from me annie.

i just wanted to apologize. i didn't know what to do at the party but i'm ready to talk things through. i know things have been really hard for you, and i've been really struggling too, but i wanted to meet, clear the air, really just get some closure for both of us. i think i still had some shirts of yours i wanted to bring back too

from what, like a year ago? sure you're not getting me confused with that asshole you sicced on me at the party?

idk, i just really need you right now

There are a few minutes of him typing.

fine. wanna just meet at the old place on campus?

sure, what's the address again?

you know, roxboro hall?

of course

I tab over to a browser and start scrambling for directions. Seems to be some pub on campus, I haven't spent much time out there, but clearly she has. I feel dirty, but it feels oddly familiar. I always sort of feel like I'm someone else on a first date, that's nothing new, and I've certainly played the proxy to a man's ex enough times to know how that feels. But despite the fact that he's pissed off at her, there's an odd warmth to him I'm not really familiar with. I feel like he really cares about me.

Outside, the snow is starting to whip into a storm, and my map's telling me it's gonna be an hour-plus on transit. I don't really have money for a cab at the moment, so let's see how much he really cares.

can you come over, like right now?

I sent the address.

really? you never had me over.

i'm ready to change, sam

Another minute typing. I like that he takes a minute to think these things through.

i guess. but just for closure, right? i'm not going back on what i said in september

of course :))))

ok. i'll call a cab, be like 30min

perfect. thank you.

Overcome with a sense of panic, I run to the washroom, strip off and shower. I try not to set the water too hot, so as not to irritate the rash, but hot enough to help with shaving. I rush through this too, and nick my inner thigh, sending a hot wave up my leg and a slow stream of blood down the drain.

I tuck myself halfway over to shave my balls and ass, and I wonder what I've eaten in the last twenty-four hours. Last night, in a depressive haze, I'd walked to the gas station and gotten a bag of chips, then gobbled the whole thing down, not expecting anything like this to come up. Was that going to fuck this up for me now? Why do I even think I'm going to fuck this guy? He just said he wanted to maintain boundaries. I guess I'm just settled into the rhythm of these things at this point, the rush to prep after sending an address for the first time. Tearful reunion with the ex, held at the apartment, to say yes to that kind of invite implies a level of desire the guy might not be ready to admit to. It's definitely wrong to do that under the false pretence of being this other person. But am I another person? Have I loved this man? As much as he scared the shit out of me at the party, something about him feels oddly familiar. I have to admit there's something relieving about being treated with the weight of a long-term relationship — I've never sought that out. I'm twenty years old, I've been at this a while, I get that nobody's getting married until they're a little more settled in. I mean, I'm still wiling my inheritance away piece by piece; maybe once I get to be a grown-up at all, I can chase some great love, but for the time being, sex is okay. Most sex, at least. I admit I've been on a break lately after the Patrick thing. I still really don't know how to process or to talk about that shit, I've sort of just shut my libido off for the last little while. But something about the desperation of this guy, the way my sudden reappearance seems to be some kind of fantasy coming to life for him, makes it easier to at least pretend again, and for the first time in a while, I'm kind of hoping something happens. Isn't that wrong of me, given I set this up under false pretences? I should probably tell him before anything happens, that I'm not her, right? Either way, he's going to be able to tell me at least something about her. I'm going to need to play my cards close to my chest.

I rush through putting on makeup, toss my hair up into a bun, and throw on an outfit I'd worn on dates before: tight skirt, larger silk blouse tucked out and over, a leather jacket on top keeping it in silhouette. Pulling the jacket down around my waist, I get another text message.

outside, i think? did you give me the right address?

Shitshitshitshit—

yesssssssss, just buzz in. 1104.

My phone rings immediately, and I hit the button before I can hear his voice chime through.

As I unlock the door, I'm suddenly aware of how barren the apartment around me is. I've still hardly decorated in a year of living here, with the exception of the bedroom, to make it look good on camera. There's nothing but a wooden kitchen table and a few chairs out here. A moment passes in this quiet barrenness, standing at the end of the hallway trying to look at the space as if I were a stranger coming in. My back is turned when I hear the door squeak reluctantly, then glide open.

There he is, shorter than me, light-brown eyes glowing from under his furrowed brow, one eye darkened with bruises on the left side, in the same mustard hoodie, with a friendly cloud of dark hair. He looks wounded, quivering like he's going to have to put me out of my misery, but readjusts himself quickly once our eyes meet.

"Annie?"

"Yes."

A wave of nausea comes over me. Am I really going to do this?

"Oh my god, I missed you."

He sets his bag down quickly and moves fast, not knowing his own strength, embracing me hard. I'm still tense, but as he takes me into his arms, I loosen my muscles. He's breathing hard into my neck. I can feel the depth of his care for her. I can feel it for myself, and despite some efforts, I start to accept it as my own. It's intoxicating. I pull myself back for a moment, kissing him on the cheek.

"How are you?" I say.

"A lot better."

"I'm glad to hear that."

"Annie, uh..." He immediately starts pulling the hoodie off, revealing a grease-stained black dress shirt. "You really broke me, you know."

"What do you mean?"

"Well, uh, I guess I just don't get along with people. Most of the time, at least. I really didn't think anybody could ever love me. Uh..." He trails off for a second, reaching for the next word. "Then you came, and it was like, oh my god, perfect, right? Like, I have to hold on to this as tight as I can. It really felt like we built a perfect little place there for a while, that first summer, right?"

"Yeah."

"So, why did you get so miserable? I mean, things were going so good."

"What do you mean?"

"What? The depression, the lashing out, the locking yourself in. I hated myself for letting you get that bad."

"I guess it just happened. It wasn't your fault."

He presses his face into my neck and breathes out harder. I can smell cheap rye whiskey on his breaths. He really took a lot of hyping up to come here.

"I, uh, really just wanted to keep it together, and I just couldn't. It felt like you were avoiding me, and at the same time were asking for all these calls, all this attention, and work, and late nights, days off work just for me to sit there and tell you that you were okay, to stay on the phone to keep you on suicide watch. And the whole time, I was sitting there and I was thinking, you know, this is what you have to do for somebody you love."

Her name is Annie and she doesn't go outside. She dated this guy, and he dumped her a couple months ago. I step back a little and he peels off me, oddly wet. He walks through the kitchen and slumps down at the table.

"And it fucked me up. I mean, I've never even been to your place. Pretty clean for a girl who doesn't go out, huh?"

I laugh weakly, imagining the way someone being confronted about the worst period of their life might laugh weakly and trying to re-create that.

"So, did you just, like, get over it? You seemed pretty certain the last time, on the phone."

"Yeah, you know, I was having a really hard time, but I guess I realized at some point, you have to just get out there, exist, be the person you are and move on."

"That's, uh, great. New, but great. Are you sure you're okay?"

"I moved on."

"Clearly." He turns away from me slightly and I see his eyes unfocus a little. "I don't see you for half of our fucking relationship, and then as soon as I finally admit to myself you were a lost cause, as soon as I stop putting myself through your shit, you're just out and about and having a good time at a party like anybody else with some fucking rich kid, like none of it ever happened. How is that supposed to make me feel? I wanted to fucking kill myself, Annie. I was, like, still going in for shifts, looking at the knife rack and going, I could just put that in my neck right now if I wanted to. That guy kicked the shit out of me, and you didn't do anything! Your friends were laughing at me! How can you say you still care about me at all, then look at that and just stand by? What the fuck did you say to them?"

I become aware that there is a strange man in my apartment, whom I have invited in, and wonder if this was a mistake.

"I didn't say anything. I'm sorry. I was overwhelmed and I froze."

"You can't just say your social anxiety is so bad that you have to have a long-distance relationship and then just go out with some guy like it's totally normal. It just doesn't make any sense to me."

I strain to keep my tone pleasant. "Try to think about it another way. Maybe our relationship was a way of keeping myself in a safe place, and maybe I had gotten attached to safe places so much that I was too scared to take any risks anymore. Maybe you dumping me was what made me finally look at myself, and realize that if I was going to live, I was going to need to value myself. To be willing to take those risks again if I ever wanted to be happy. So maybe, while I'm still working on those parts of myself, maybe I've taken that time to get to a better place."

"That doesn't sound like you at all."

Sam pushes himself back in the chair, making an awful low-pitched scraping noise on the floor. He leans his elbows down on the table and steeples his fingers, pressing his mouth against them to hide his face.

His voice is strained. "I guess I still just ask myself, why couldn't it be with me? Why didn't you care enough about me to be able to do that work while we were still together? It still makes me feel like you never really gave a shit. I always wondered if you'd lied, if you weren't really some basket case, if you were just trying to sneak around. Figure out a way to let me down easy. And I thought I was being paranoid, but when I saw you out with Patrick, it was like my worst nightmares had come to life."

"Do you want it to be with me? You were the one who ended it."

He stands from his chair and comes across the table, wrapping an arm around my shoulder and pressing his face into my hair. "I'm sorry. I just missed you so much..."

He seems like he wants to cry, but he's breathing too hard to get anything out. I'm trying to piece this together as he goes. We look and feel enough alike that he's fully convinced I'm her, even now, close up, facing each other head-on. This is her, I know it now, but who is she? Who am I? What's my or her bearing on any of this stuff? She doesn't go out? Was she actually cheating on this guy? How do I incorporate this all into my performance?

"There, there..." I run my fingers through his hair. I pull him back a little. "Wait, I thought you came over before."

"Not since you moved."

His eyes are squinting-to-closed, blissed-out, melancholy. I'm really straining to not break character here.

"Moved from where?"

His eyes open wider and he looks at me for a second like I'm crazy, then eases himself back down into my palm. "From your old place. Can I go down on you?"

Stupid. I'm panicking a little as I push his head down into my thigh, feeling his breath up my skirt, but at least for the first time in a while I'm not at all scared of a man. It's nice watching him grovel, to get to have his impossible dream realized while I watch from the dissociative distance of being someone else. I lean back and stare at the ceiling as he pulls my tights down around my thighs, past the rash, which goes totally unnoticed. What does it mean to be loved by someone so intensely? I don't think I've ever seen someone make themselves so vulnerable before. I'm terrified of what I've just made myself responsible for.

"I missed the smell of you..."

"I missed you, too, Sam."

He rips the tights the rest of the way off, haphazardly, one leg at a time, taking the panties with them and throwing them on the floor, standing up and starting to undo his belt in a manic sprint, hands tripping over themselves. He pushes me back in the chair and kisses me, and I can taste that booze more vividly now. He must have needed to get pretty fucked-up to come see me. I put my arm between us as he closes his distance towards me on the chair.

"Can we go to the bedroom?"

"Oh, sure. Uh, yeah."

I slip between him and the wall, trying not to touch him as I lead forward. He waddles behind, half-hard cock in hand poking out from under his T-shirt. It's a pretty average length but thin and needle-nosed, flecked with jet-black hair. He seems to become aware of how ridiculous he looks and rips the shirt off as he follows. In the bedroom, I flick on the mood lights in their purple ambient glow, and he's taken aback for a second looking around the place. He stares especially at the cam corner, the feathery pillows and the camera and the toys kept in their boxes.

"You sure have a lot of nice stuff now..."

He gives me a judgmental look and I shrug at him, staring up from the bed. "Yeah, I do. Come here."

I toss myself back on the bed spread-eagled, giving him an expectant eye, and grabbing some lube from the bedside table.

He looks back at me, confused. "Come on, you already forgot? Present to Daddy like I like."

Before I can stop myself, I recoil a little and shoot him a look like *what the fuck, dude*. He catches it and gives me a confused look back, before deflating completely. His dick softens a bit and his posture slumps.

"Come on… You know I need this."

I flip over and arch my back in the desperate hope this doesn't take too many guesses. "Like this, Daddy?"

I feel him on my ass. "Good girl."

Ugh. I'm reaching back to lube up and I can feel him grabbing me, lining me up. He spits on his hand and rubs it on, putting a finger in me. I let out an involuntary noise.

"*Wuh!*"

"You fuck one other guy and you're all sensitive now, huh?"

Shuddering, I put on a baby voice and try to buy myself a second here. "Yeah, I guess I did, Daddy. You can show me who I really belong to."

He leans over me and kisses my neck. "Good."

I'm finally able to get some lube on him and he immediately starts pounding me, pushing my face forward into the bed. It hurts at first, but eventually I start to feel very little from it at all. At first I do my porn moans for him to try to help him along, but eventually, as things settle in, I realize he doesn't care and I just go silent, craning my neck around to see Sam staring intently at my ass before eventually closing his eyes, pace fast, constant. I notice I've left the curtains open, and for a second feel self-conscious, but preferably this'll just end soon and I won't have to take the indignity of saying pause, pushing him off and walking across the room to close the blinds before returning to this exact same position. You can hardly see anything between all that white, anyway. I start scanning neighbours' windows to see if anybody might be able to see me like this. I start to get into it despite myself, staring into squares of drawn blinds, reflective black, blowing white, sideways from the street lights, yellow light-pollution glow against the December sky. I feel myself straining, trying to shift position slightly under Sam's weight, to be met with grunts and shoves back into position. I shove a little back, and relent, still scanning, the room starting to spin. Finally, in defeat once again, I look straight ahead.

Bathed in blue light in the unit across the street, there I am, worse than in the video. Hooded in ratty rags, rail-thin, pale, empty-eyed, hostile, completely horrified at the sight of myself. Bad skin, not just on the legs but all over.

The snow spins between us. We disappear into each other, the echo and I. I can't feel anything anymore. She stares at me harder than I've ever been stared at, saucer eyes a black view into her skull, yellow enough teeth to tell from this far they're gritted tight to the point of breaking. I try to communicate with her telepathically.

I always knew you were here.

I always knew you were watching.

I always knew I would find you.

Thank you for showing yourself to me.

I hear nothing back. Her eyes somehow open yet wider, and she flicks the blue light off. I watch her shape scurry through the darkness and out into the unit.

I need to get her before she gets away. I push my back up and turn to throw Sam off me and onto the bed. A splatter of lube drips out of me as I push him off. He screams:

"*What the fuck?*"

He follows after me as I start getting my things from off the floor.

"Sorry. Just, like, Jesus! What the fuck was that? Did I freak you out or something? Why the fuck are you so weird now?"

I am not paying attention to him, just to getting dressed. I am moving with purpose, directly across the apartment, to each place I was when each piece of clothing was removed. He's right behind me.

"Do you want me back or not? You're not making a great case for yourself here, Annie!"

Pulling my jacket back on at the table, I turn to him flatly. "What was my old unit number?"

"What the fuck are you talking about?"

I shove him, harder than I intend, and knock him over onto the bed. I put a knee on his chest and apply pressure, screaming, towering over him now, hair hanging down between us.

"*What was my old unit number*?"

His voice is shaking. "Uhh, I think it's the same as this one! 1104! I thought it was funny that you moved so close! Why are you *so fucking weird*?"

"Please never speak to me again."

"*What*?"

He looks like his mind's been shattered completely, lying there naked. I lock the door behind me and float down the hallway, ecstatic.

Out into the snow, I feel lighter than I ever have. My life has changed.

Around the back of the building across the street, past the hole she left for me to let me know she was there, I wait in the orange light by the dumpsters for what must be an hour, keeping an eye out for either door to see if she'd make her escape. I am relieved when someone finally comes down — she hasn't been out, and I won't have to chase her. I hold the door open for the little old lady who's come down with her trash, and she wishes me a Merry Christmas as I slip inside.

III. REBIRTH

(...) the universe of our unbearable personal vision was certain to be replaced by the pure stars, fully unrelated to any external gazes (...)

— *Georges Bataille,* Story of the Eye

1.

Crack.

The girl inside the apartment freezes like an animal as soon as the first knock rings out. Huddled in the garbage in the hallway, she stands tense, blank-faced. She feels her way around the wall in the dark towards the kitchen and pulls herself over the geological configurations of black bags, shifting them unpredictably.

The girl outside the apartment with the same face is still knocking, and saying things like:

"Hello?"

"Can you let me in?"

"I just want to ask you some questions!"

The girl inside the apartment is not worried about anything the girl outside the apartment with the same face is saying. She is too focused on hunting through drawers, around the cutlery, around the dice and cards and empty cigarette cartons, scrabbling around and trying not to make a sound as she looks across the counter to find her serrated breadknife, caked with blood, wine and months of built-up grease and dust. She finds the handle in the faint darkness and holds it upwards, pressed back against the scars it produced on her wrist. She floats purposefully towards the door and pauses for a moment before undoing the padlocks and turning the handle.

The girl outside the apartment is face to face with herself, several days unshaven, twitching, twig arms covered in deep gashes sticking from the ends of soiled cloth wrapped loosely, staring directly into bugged dinner plate pupils, holding a long blade. Her skin is sallow and marked with bug bites, her eyes sunken and empty. The walls are yellowed from months of smoke and moist from mould and undergrowth.

They stand like this for a split second. The girl inside is realizing how much joy it will bring her to end the life of someone exactly like herself without sacrificing the continuity of her own mind and body, and the girl outside is realizing that the girl inside is standing in front of a mound of garbage up to nearly her knees that extends down the hallway and into the bedroom. The girl inside lifts the knife, exposing herself, and, without thinking, the girl outside tackles her over the trash pile and rolls them both backwards halfway down the hallway.

Doubling backwards, the girls are both gripping the knife handle now, diving into the mound of garbage, nearly submerged as they wrestle each other back and forth across the hallway. The girl who was outside rips the sheet off the girl who was inside, retching at the sour smell of it and leaving the girl who was inside nude. The nude girl finds an opening and bites the clothed girl's neck, deep, latching on like a dog and pressing hard, trying to break skin. The clothed girl screams. This thing gripping her is her, she knows it: the part she hates, that doesn't know how to take care of itself, that's shrunk away to almost nothing but that hate. She hasn't lost her grip on the knife, pressing it inwards towards the nude girl's chest and trying to get an angle where she can force it forward. It now seems that she's going to need to kill her before she gets to talk with her, but that's beside the point. The clothed girl is losing track of her own boundaries in the pile of limbs on the floor, and her grip hurts, the nude girl is not giving way to let her press it back into her, and the nude girl crawls on top of the clothed girl and bashes the top of her head, then her face, and the clothed girl has gone limp, still screaming, but the nude girl still doesn't understand any of the words she's saying, and the nude girl has gotten her arms underneath the clothed girl and is sitting on her back, pressing her face against the floor, the clothed girl's face sticking to the fungal underbelly of the nude girl's apartment, her nose burning with the omnipresent decay of the nude girl's past year, and the nude girl stands taking the clothed girl by the hair, lifting her head, slamming it, again and again, into the wet floor until her grip lets up enough to take the knife from her, and the nude girl takes the clothed girl by the feet and drags her down the hallway through a desire line in the debris.

The orange light from the hallway outside the apartment hangs over them as she drags her past the open door, the clothed girl saying, "why? why? why? why? why? why?" with a little more force, in hope there might be some world outside this place, some other being who might want to prevent whatever agony awaits her once the nude girl slams the door behind her.

And once she does, dragging her up onto the bed, they're in stasis again. They are looking each other in the face now. Their eyes are locked.

The clothed girl chokes out words through sobs:

"What's your name?"

The nude girl stands back, knife still clenched in her hand, her eyes darting nervously around the room.

"We're the same," she says. "I know you. I know your name. You're the bug."

"My name is Amy," says the clothed girl.

"No. You're me. We're the same."

Amy slowly reaches out and places a hand on Annie's hip. The inside girl flinches at the touch, but doesn't resist.

"Is your name Amy?"

"No. Look at me. I'm you. That's all."

"How do you know that?"

"You're that me that's been acting on my behalf, and I need you gone."

"You that's been acting on your... What do you mean?"

"You showed everyone my body. You took Sam from me. I didn't want to do any of those things, you made me do them. You're the part of me I hate the most."

"Wait, fuck, oh my god, okay. I'm not going to do anything. If you want, I can tell you everything, or I can just leave if you want to. I'm sorry I came in here. I just wanted to know if you were real."

"Are you real?"

"Yes! You just almost killed me."

The nude girl thinks it through for a second.

"I won't trust you unless you make yourself different."

"Sure. Whatever you say, I'll do it. I just need to know you."

The nude girl drops the knife on the bed and shuffles back slightly.

"Make yourself look different from me."

"Okay."

Amy lifts the knife, eyeing the bits of material caught in its teeth. She bends her elbow to where the blade is parallel to her cheek. She presses in one tooth and drags it across her cheekbone, opening a wound following the line of her contouring, as small as she could apply with such a primitive tool but still a wide-open gash past the fat on the upper end of her cheek, the muscle just visible underneath. Amy writhes as she applies the cut, looking at the nude girl, who's shifting uncomfortably on the other end of the bed. There's bile in Amy's throat. She folds over and hacks a little up, burning, before looking back up at the nude girl.

"Is that good enough for you?"

"Yes, thank you."

"Once I get this patched up, can I tell you why I came here?"

"Sure."

In the silence, they both hear a heavy knock in the walls. For the first time in weeks, the heat is back on. The nude girl sifts through some of the stuff on the floor and pulls pink, fuzzy pyjamas from under a trash bag, slipping them on. Amy is still crying a little bit on the bed. The girl in pyjamas mutters:

"Annie. My name's Annie. By the way."

2.

Amy showers to try to clean the wound. She doesn't manage to find any bandages, and all the clothes Annie offers seem too filthy to do much, but she finds some hydrogen peroxide. She folds a piece of toilet paper, applies it, and it produces a layer of stinging red foam nearly twice the size of the cut.

"You wanted to tell me why you came here?" Annie says. Annie's legs are crossed and back hunched over towards Amy, her frail frame swallowed by the oversized pyjamas. The bed is the only clearing among the trash, so Amy sits down beside her.

"I'll try. Have you ever seen, like..."

"What?"

"Like, you know how, when you're a kid, everything seems really meaningful, but, like, the specific meaning isn't clear yet, you know? You start looking for patterns, drawing connections between things, but you don't really understand what any of it means."

Annie thinks about this. The thought seems fractured, like there's something she's not quite getting at.

"Not really, no."

"Like, okay, at some point, you start to notice weird coincidences in things, right?"

Annie's eyes stay locked on the floor as she speaks. "I don't remember much. Flashes here and there. Mostly boredom. I miss it."

"You might not remember it, but it's there. It's gotta be."

"Uh."

"No, wait. Let me try again. I can explain everything."

Amy crosses her legs, takes a deep breath. She hasn't tried to explain this stuff to anyone since that night in the apartment, and it's been a long time since she's wanted to.

"Do you believe in ghosts? When I was a kid, I always felt like there was something watching me. Like, there was this shadow on the far end of my bed, from this radiator in front of the window. We lived in a really old apartment, right, like from the 1910s or something, and we didn't have a ton of money, so it had one of those awful old clanking ones, with the long bars. During the day, the shadows that came off of it would look like these long, stringy human limbs, with these razor-sharp fingers. It was bad enough to look at during the day, but at night the limbs would extend and move across the room with their fingers forming this ring in the centre of where the moonlight fell on my bedroom floor. They'd place themselves in ways that were totally impossible to still be shadows if you tried to figure out the angle of the moonlight and the little juts that made the shadow. For a few years, when I was a little kid, I'd just stare at them frozen every night, waiting for when the dark, circular figure they'd made on the floor of my room would pull me up into its centre, snap together, and do whatever awful thing they seemed like they'd promised to do, pull me down into the dark.

"I spent so long staring at them and letting them fuck with my dreams. I'd wake up and fall asleep and have the same dream, where the limbs would snap closed on me. Then I'd wake up, then fall asleep and have the same dream, again and again, and sometimes I'd wake up to find the limbs still snapping closed, still in the dream. Eventually, I decided I would prove that they weren't there so I could sleep again. I stole a ruler and a protractor from school and thought I would figure out the directions the moonlight hit it over the course of the night, to try and figure out those impossible shapes. You know, basic geometry. For the next couple years, I would get out of bed with the lights off and go into the middle of the room for a couple hours after bedtime every night, between the grasping fingers of the shadow, where it had snapped together and collected me into its world so many times before. I couldn't bear it, sitting in there, but I just had to know.

"So I figured out the angles where the light would hit the window over the course of a night relative to where the radiator was, and mapped the lines where the shadows fell along the floor with pencil, figuring out which ways it *should* land and which ways it *was* landing, trying to find the discrepancy. I was pretty good at math as a kid, so I figured I'd be able to learn the trick my brain was pulling on me eventually. It never quite worked, and the math was harder than I thought, and I kept rethinking the problem, and it kept getting more complicated and less certain.

"As the years went on, my floor became completely covered in chicken-scratch notes and calculations. The nightmares got worse and worse, the circle mocking me and the fingers drawing me in, dragging the ruler back and forth across the ground like a cat toy, teasing me, knowing I'd come into the circle. Then the ring of twisted shadows would slowly close and take me up into its world, and I'd wake up. It happened enough times and it became such a constant part of my life that I started to feel like whatever shadow, dream-self, whatever, some part of me was gone, never coming back. Every morning, I would wake up with a little bit less of myself.

"By the time I was in high school, my grades had gotten worse, and I started doing a lot of stupid shit, you know, shoplifting, bingeing and purging, doing drugs if anybody had any, though that wasn't often. I was a weird kid. I didn't wanna talk to anybody about the ghost because I didn't want to look crazy, and I didn't want to say what I wanted to say, which was

Mom, my room is haunted, it's stealing my soul piece by piece, and we need to move, until I really, really had the evidence to back it up, you know? Anyways, one night, I crawl down into the circle like I usually do, I look at the ways the shadows break from the lines in the floor, and I start carving my pencil into the hardwood, not just writing on the floor but scratching grooves into it, and I felt something really awful. Right as I'd gotten my line down, the shadow moved. Just for a second, I saw it pull inwards and stop right at the edge of where I was sitting. I looked back at the other side as the circle had narrowed there too. Both of the shadows had, in *seconds*, moved millimetres narrower than the narrowest lines I'd recorded in months prior to that. I ran back into bed, covered my head with the sheets and curled up. When I woke up the next day, my ribs were covered in deep bruises, like I'd been crushed in a massive vise."

"Whoa."

"Yeah. So the dreams got worse for years after that, and I felt like I couldn't tell anybody once I'd given up on proving that what I was feeling was real. I started to just walk into the circle and stand there, to try to bait it into taking me away, to reunite my body and my soul after feeling so fucked-up for so long, but I was never able to get it to manifest in person like that again. When I was sixteen, I tried to hang myself with a belt, right in the centre of the circle. I'd given up, and I was ready for it to take my body the rest of the way. I'd nailed the end of it into the ceiling from a few places, made sure it was sturdy, and kicked my chair out from under me. I almost lost consciousness but never did. I hung for about thirty seconds before the belt broke. The claw wouldn't let me die."

"I'm sorry."

"Whatever. When we finally did move out of there, my mom and I got into a huge screaming match because the landlord spotted the lines on the floor during the inspection, and it kept her from collecting the damage deposit. Nobody'd ever noticed the lines before then. Why would they? Only time she ever hit me, as far as I remember."

"Jesus. Did the dreams ever stop?"

"Only once I moved out. I never *saw* the fingers again, but whatever they belong to followed me out of there. It got worse when I moved into the place across the street from here. I could — I don't know how to explain it, but I could *feel*, or sense, the parts of me that I'd lost near me, like this profound, constant grief for all the parts of that kid that had gotten stolen away by those hands, and I knew something was really wrong again, but I couldn't pinpoint it.

"By that point I was thinking, like, not fair! I transitioned, I put myself through the bullshit, the self-scrutiny, the medical poking and prodding and passive aggression, just to have an identity again, and that was supposed to bring the rest of me back. It did bring some of it back, but the parts that were still missing hurt so, so much, constantly. So I floated and fucked around however I could in my spare time, trying to avoid coming home to that haunted room every night, hearing the voice of that little kid, begging for help from some place I could never reach. I'd almost distracted myself, but it all got a lot less fun a few months ago, when I first saw you for real, knew you were really there."

"You saw me?"

"You were on the news. They said a vagrant had caused a scene downtown stopping a train and biting the conductor. It wasn't clear if they wanted to arrest you or if they wanted to help you, but they had some blurry footage of the incident and were putting out calls to search for you. I saw you and it was like all my worst nightmares had come to life: me, penniless, out on the streets, not passing — oh yeah, the report said 'male, with long blond hair, in his mid-twenties, wearing women's pyjamas,' which stung — but, you know, out of luck, close to death."

Annie mutters, seething, her leg bouncing staccato against the edge of the bed. "I'm your worst-case scenario, then. Makes sense."

Amy dodges eye contact. "I'm sure you felt the same seeing that video, how the world sees me."

"I guess."

Amy inhales hard, putting her hands to her temples, steeling herself. She turns back to Annie and looks in her eyes.

"All I could think when I saw you was, *that's the missing piece of me.* That's everything the world took away. That's every piece of my soul that the hands ripped out, in dream after dream after dream when I was a kid, all compressed into one body. I needed to save you. I needed to save you and to heal you and to tell you that because things turned out okay for me, they're going to turn out okay for you too.

"I became obsessed with finding you. I'd been trying to find a job, but nothing was calling back, so I just kind of committed myself to looking for you. I'd go walking around that train station in the early evening every day, hoping you'd trail by again, but you never did. After a few weeks, I'd given up on you. I didn't really know if I wanted to go back to school or if I wanted to go back to camming, but there didn't really seem to be any point to any of it."

"So how'd you find me, then?"

Amy looks startled. "Uh, I managed to find somebody who knew you."

"Sam."

Amy tenses up a little. "Uh, yeah. Sam."

"Was that really you? In the window."

"Yeah."

Annie stands up. She looks a little more the way she did when she first opened the door. "So, how the fuck did that happen?"

"Uh…" Amy stares into the wall of orange-lit snow for a second, thinking. "I was, uh, scrolling on a dating app, and it was really such a crazy coincidence, like, he came up on there, and he was acting all overfamiliar and weird when I messaged him, like he already knew me. And I told him no, I'm somebody else, not the person you're imagining. And then it hit me, and I asked him if he'd known anything about the train incident. He hadn't, but he said that you lived here before, and he pointed across the street. But I looked over, and there you were. The lights were on for a second, then you flicked them off as soon as I looked. The second he said it, I knew it was you, and I knew I had to come here. I literally ran out on him. He's literally probably still sitting in there now, thinking *oh no, another crazy trans girl, what have I gotten myself into*, jacking it maybe. Sorry."

Annie looks hollow, face red, in a different world.

"I know the circumstances are weird," Amy offers.

"Yeah. Still really wish you didn't fuck my ex."

"Yeah. I'm sorry. But, like, it brought us together, right? Now we can finally figure out what's really going on."

"I guess."

"I needed this, Annie. I needed you. I needed to come here so I could ask you if you're real, or if you're just the ghost of me. Either way, I love you."

Annie looks at Amy. This stranger, herself, with a fresh wound and a complete alternate history. She wonders if any of what Amy said was true. She briefly considers reaching back for the knife and ending the bad dream here for both of them, but she can't bring herself to do it. Faced with a version of herself with a real life, who might have a chance at happiness, Annie gives in. She puts her head on Amy's shoulder.

"Okay."

3.

The lights are still on in Amy's apartment across the street. Snow emerges sideways from the street lights in a teeming mass. The heating is back on, the pipes' banging echoing through the room, but the insulation was never really built for these conditions; this kind of weather was a freak occurrence in this part of the country until the past few years. Annie and Amy are huddled together for warmth in bed.

Amy was resistant to putting on the filthy sheet at first, but eventually accepted it, knowing she couldn't convince Annie to let her wash it. The gaping wound on her cheek is still bleeding, and she tries to position herself to keep it off the pillow, but she sleeps on her side, so she smears blood all over the pillow and stings herself every time she shifts even slightly. The pillow has seen worse.

Amy almost immediately passes out, having been up for nearly thirty hours. Annie is rolling back and forth between positions, trying to get comfortable, trying not to bother Amy while still staying in her arms. It's the first well-meaning touch she's felt in a year, and it feels like a lifeline back into the world outside. It's like Amy is holding her spirit down to the bed, holding her mind inside her body again.

She presses the full length of her body up against Amy. She shifts a little, then, against her better judgment, shifts with intention, forward and back, feeling Amy get hard in her sleep. Annie falls into a rhythm, feeling a thrill in the shame of it. Amy starts to stir, moving in tandem for god knows how long. Once Amy is fully awake, they pretend they're playing the original game for a little while longer, until Amy pulls her arm around Annie's side.

Amy slides her hand in long, dragging motions, first over Annie's breasts, across her ribs, slowly back up, slowly back down, across the waist of her panties, eventually reaching a little lower, feeling her cock. They reach a stalemate, spooned with Amy stroking Annie's cock, with Annie pressing her butt against Amy's, both not quite sure whether proceeding from here is a great idea. Staying there, both of them unsure and hesitating, seems better than any of the other options could possibly be.

Amy pushes Annie back for a second, sensing where this is going, and feels around in the dark for her purse, which had fallen off in the struggle. Amy briefly wonders if she's up to this, but she's way too deep in the moment by this point. She looks back and sees Annie writhing, desperate in her slow, unsubtle scoot towards her, as she recognizes her own movements, her own need for warmth. She finds the bag quickly, thank god, and pulls a slim bottle from it, lubricating herself slowly, shocking and cold. Amy slides back into her spot in the dirty bed and finally allows it: Annie pulls her in with her legs and wraps around her.

The blood from Amy's wound drips onto Annie's face, slow and viscous, landing on the same spot on Annie's cheekbone where it's sourced from Amy's face and running down in a single rivulet to Annie's open mouth. The iron and salt make her salivate.

Annie feels in Amy deep in her that her loneliness is over. An all-encompassing warmth runs through her entire body, a complete and total acceptance as she watches this beautiful version of herself over her. Annie pulls Amy's head down to kiss her deep, tonguing haphazardly into her mouth, murmuring *IloveyouIloveyouIloveyou* when finally pulled back. Annie wants to climb inside Amy's skin, learn her secrets, be held in the self-assurance she told her to have.

Amy's dick kind of hurts, this being the second time she's fucked tonight, but it still feels good to see herself getting fucked, even this filthy, ragged version.

Under the sound of the storm through the walls, both girls sort-of come.

4.

The overcast sky in the window glows a sickly yellow, the pre-dawn light at the midpoint between the light pollution of the city and the beginning of sunrise. They're both nestled together under the filthy sheet.

"So, uh, are you my ghost?" Amy is saying.

"Been trying to be."

Annie laughs a little and gasps through restricted airways. Her voice is low and raspy from months of disuse.

"Where did you come from before that? Do you remember at all?"

"Not much to remember, I think. You know. Suburbs, parents made okay money, played a lot of video games."

Amy chews on her cuticles as she speaks, preoccupied. She pulls Annie in with her legs.

"So, like, was that a good relationship? I mean, I never really knew my dad, and my mom, Jesus, that whole thing is a nightmare."

"You mentioned. They're fine. I really wanted to get away from them, but not because of anything they did. They loved me a lot, as far as I can tell."

"You left because you just felt like you needed the space, or... ?"

"I guess I just didn't want them to see me like this."

"Like, the way you live, closing yourself off and everything. Did you think you'd disappoint them?"

"Sort of? I guess the same reasons I don't want anyone to, whatever those are." Annie buries her head in Amy's chest, so like her own. "Why are you asking me all this?" she mumbles.

"I just want to know everything I can about you. That's how you're gonna get past your shit, you know, you gotta open up. So, anyways, parents. Suburbs."

Annie puts herself back upright on her elbows. "I guess. Well, yeah. I just felt stuck. Even when I was a kid, I thought about running away a lot. I'd freak out and have these tantrums, get really embarrassed. But I could pretty much just exist in my head. Junior high was when it got bad. I felt this urgency, like, I have to be useful, I can't just be myself anymore."

"Like, feeling a need to impress people? I think that's pretty normal. You've gotta stop beating yourself up over this stuff."

"I just felt, like, unsafe. I'd never really felt unsafe before. I didn't realize how much I'd have to plan everything in advance. How cautious I'd have to be. Getting away from it – getting away from everything – felt like the only way to get out of that loop. I felt like otherwise I'd be stuck, from primary to secondary to uni and back to the suburbs again, nothing ever really changing until I die. I thought about that future a lot, but I don't think I'm welcome there anymore, if it exists at all." She trails off.

Amy shuffles a bit, still folded over and around Annie. "How old are you now, by the way?"

"I'm twenty."

"Okay, same. So when you're talking about this need to be super vigilant or whatever, you're talking about figuring out you're trans, right?"

"Maybe. Like, you want to make yourself known, but don't know who you are, and the desire gets in the way of figuring it out. I had this feeling that everybody else was complete, like in a way I could never be, then realizing I already was complete in the eyes of others, in ways I could never control. Envy for people who could control it. I never really connected that envy to anything about myself until I figured it out. What about you?"

"I never really thought about it that way. You are who you are, other people are who they are, you make the best of it. I took a lot of shit for it, but having the words made it easier."

Amy separates herself and sits up cross-legged on her side of the bed, expectant for Annie to continue.

Annie, still supine on her elbows, stares at Amy's unscarred arms. "Were you pretty popular?"

"Not really. Why?"

"I dunno. I'm just wondering how bad the cycle I've gotten myself into is. You know, fail, feel like a failure, don't try, and then I know I'm not wrong to think that. Did you ever fail? Like, were you ever just ignored by people?"

"Of course. My mom fucking hated me for being gay, and then didn't even speak to me once I was out as trans. I got kicked out of the house at sixteen, and I had to figure stuff out for myself. I never had the opportunity to ask myself who I was because I always had to stand firm against all the shit I was getting. Still seems like a waste of time to me to think that much about it."

"Maybe. Either way, I don't remember anything about radiators or screaming moms or spindly hands dragging me into some black abyss, so that shadow self, child ghost, whatever called you into my apartment, isn't me. You can close your case."

Amy pulls her legs back and leaps off Annie, taking the sheet with her and circling the room, hands up in front of her face, bursting with nervous energy.

"You don't know that! We could both be lucid dreaming, or maybe, when I crossed this street, I entered into some other world and now I have to pull you back out. Maybe you've been given false memories to hold us back from coming together. And, like, growing up in different places doesn't explain our faces, our bodies."

Annie's covering herself with a pillow, shivering, and looks up at Amy. "I mean, I dunno. We've, like, confirmed we're two distinct people with distinct personalities, by some massive genetic accident we have very similar faces, and we both wound up trans, living across the street from one another."

Amy sits on the side of the bed, slides back in and takes Annie's face in her hands. "I don't know yet. But I knew it all needed to happen, so I need to stay with you for as long as I can. Keep this weird energy going and see if it evokes anything."

"I mean, this is nice, I don't mind it. But I really don't get what the overarching goal is here."

"Just trust me, okay?"

"Fine."

Amy runs her fingers through Annie's hair. Annie lays her head on Amy's chest again, listens to her fast heartbeat.

"Sorry, where were we? You turned eighteen and immediately shut yourself in?"

"If you wanna put it that way," Annie mumbles. "I was doing okay for a little while, but I got stuck in my habits, I guess. It got the best of me."

"How long were you actually out before you did it? I guess, how long did you make it, like, actually transitioning, where other people could see it?"

Annie tenses, tightens her face. "Didn't you just say we're always who we are?"

"Okay, you know what I mean, though."

"I mean, I stopped going out after a year working, because it wasn't worth it anymore. If you had the opportunity to stop dealing with people's shit, you would too, wouldn't you?"

"Not at all!"

Annie scoots backwards on the bed and looks away from Amy. "You said that before, too," she says. "Like I'm the worst-case scenario, or I haven't actually been trans this whole time, and that's just not true. It's *because of* the shit I've been through that

I am the way I am. Like, if I wasn't *really* trans, I could just stop taking hormones, and go along with what was asked of me, but I can't. Just because I don't put a ton of effort into how I look doesn't mean I'm not a woman, not any less than you are."

Amy starts to slow her speech and stutter a bit, trying very carefully to figure out how to word this. "No, I get that. And I'm sorry, I really don't mean to make a bad situation worse for you. But I just . . . What good are you doing for yourself by *being trans* without *being*? If, like, the goal of transition is to shift the way you're perceived in society, isn't not letting yourself be perceived kind of admitting that you don't really want that? Like, are you sure this is working for you? And, like, it's a lot easier to get somebody to get rid of themselves than it is to actually take them out. No, seriously! You know, go ahead, live your degenerate lifestyle, just do it in secret, drive yourself further and further into the margins until you may as well not exist. So why not just take the stares, take the passive aggression, thank god you were born white and with a little money, you're not in any *real* danger, just live your life. Even if people were out to get you, wouldn't you want to die with some self-respect?"

They sit up from each other on the bed, their little island surrounded by trash. Annie is a little unnerved that Amy has acclimatized so well to her domain, feeling some loss of control. The boiler pipes rattle inside the wall.

"I know that. Whatever the reasons are for it, it's not a choice anymore. If I could just go pick up a normal life that easily, do you think I wouldn't have done that by now? It's not like I'm trying to make some kind of statement by not going out. I just want to be safe. So what if I die in this place? It's my call to make at the end of the day."

"All I'm saying is that as long as you stay inside, you make yourself less real. Like, has anything ever *really* happened to you? You went to school, you dated this one boy, you got this job, and what? Were you like this as a kid too? Did you have any extra-curricular activities or anything? It seems just as likely you materialized into existence in this spot as anything else, as far as I can tell."

Annie sighs and stares at the wall for a while with tired eyes. She stands up, looking down at Amy. "You're right. I've never done anything in my life. I'm going to die alone, forgotten, and it will be like I'd never been here. My parents will grieve, but it'll make no substantial change to their routines. You win. I'm you, but already dead. You can have your closure."

Annie walks out into the hallway, stumbling, and out towards the living room, where the sun reflected off the snow is now blindingly bright against the grimy off-white walls. Amy turns the corner and sees only the silhouette of the balcony door opening. She scrambles after her.

"Hey, hey, what are you doing?"

Annie is leaning on the edge of the balcony in the blinding white winter morning, her hair moving in the breeze off the edge of the apartments, eleven floors up over the noise of downtown traffic. She's smiling blankly at Amy, almost posing, with a smirk and her neck bent right towards her. She turns around, settling down onto a bag of trash and lighting a cigarette in the shade under the edge of the balcony.

"I tried to kill myself too," Annie says. "Right before I saw your video, uh, and before the thing at the train station, I took a bottle of pills and I slit my wrists. It seems like things got really weird right around then, so that must have been when my body died, when I became just a spirit to guide you out of your childhood trauma or whatever."

"Hey, you're really starting to freak me out, Annie..."

Annie looks up at her evenly, talking like she hadn't heard anything. "It makes a lot of sense, if you think about it. It doesn't really matter if I die again. You're the only one who can see me, who was ever able to, and everybody else has just been watching the trash build up around me. Now that we've, you know, unified or whatever, my purpose is over. You have my full permission to move on." Annie laughs weakly, coughing.

Amy is shivering in the doorway to the balcony, the snow landing on her hair. She takes a deep breath. "Please, Annie, I really barely know you. I was being harsh, I'm sorry, but I need you to stick with me in this. I need to get you out of this apartment. You're capable of way more than this, outside of you being me or not being me or whatever else. I wouldn't have come down on you so hard if I hadn't spent my entire life fighting the urge to do what you're doing. But you've gotta come with me."

Annie tilts her head at Amy blankly. "What'd you think I was doing?"

"No need."

The wind blows quietly in the sun and snow as Annie takes a drag, flicking the cig away. Amy smiles at her and, gradually, Annie smiles back.

"I'm hungry," says Amy. "Let's get you together, and let's go get some food."

5.

Both nude, Amy sits behind Annie on a stool in the film of the soap-scum mirror. First she applies a little cream to her face, rubbing it gently into her half beard. She turns the tap on to maximum heat. It takes a while to heat up, but eventually the room starts to fill with steam. Amy has to run to the other room to get a razor blade in soft wax paper from her handbag, carefully slipping it out of its case and placing it between her fingers in order to run it over Annie without a sheath.

With slow, graceful sweeps, she pulls the blade across Annie's cheeks and jawline, taking the hair with it. She runs the blade under her mouth and over her lips, both of them hyper-conscious of every movement, both of them trying not to cut or to be cut. Amy runs her fingers across the now-smooth skin of Annie's face, and Annie shudders a little. Pulling her head back into place, Amy starts to rub in primer. Amy's fingers slowly press into her pores, first with greasy pancake-batter concealer over the scars and the stress acne, a little colour correction, a layer of powder dabbed over all this, foundation evening her out, sponging her, wiping off hard edges.

Annie cannot imagine that she is about to go out.

Amy streaks another line of a highlight across Annie's jaw, sweeping up into the hollow of her cheek, tucking a strand of her hair behind the ear, swapping out wet sponge for hard latex, patting hard. Their faces close together, Annie looks at the makeup on Amy's face, messed up and slept in, and sees the outline of the shape she's drawing now. Amy's hands carefully applying eyes, dipping the brush in the palette, pulling her eye open, running with the same precision as the blade across it, out and at an angle. She draws over Annie's high cheekbones and fills it in, then spreads the other eye, repeating the same in a long stroke, leaving nervous trailing sensations in its wake. She uses a finer brush. It all smells amazing. Amy curls Annie's lashes and she makes a little sound when her eyelids peel back. Amy brushes them out and applies mascara. Annie feels herself becoming powerful, heavy and sharp-edged.

They're both thinking about when they were teenagers and this was all new and fun and scary, though neither of them will say it out loud.

I am still me, Annie thinks, *wearing makeup*.

"You look great. Ready?"

Amy slides the bar out from the padlock and the door cracks open. In the hallway, Annie feels a need to hide her head, not knowing who in these halls might be able to identify her as the ghoul that lives in the unit 1104 trash mound. As they get to the elevator, Amy reaches her hand back, sensing resistance and giving Annie a little pull as the doors start to shut behind her, Annie seeing out of the corner of her eye a smirk on Amy's face, like she's won something.

Amy leads Annie, who is dragging her feet, arm in arm through the door, cutting the confident poise of a night out in cocktail dresses, although it's 1 p.m., the air cutting cold, the sun piercing the flat grey clouds between the still-drifting snow.

People are still staring at them, as Annie is in the process of confirming and reconfirming through a series of involuntary neck-and-eye tics every couple minutes whenever they walk past a stranger. She wonders if Amy notices them too. Amy does notice them, and mostly just feels bad for Annie. Amy's proud of her, though, making it this far out this early.

The stares get fewer, farther between and less ill-intentioned as they enter the gay strip, where Annie hasn't been since she was a kid. In her memories it was teeming with life, like every apartment behind every sublet curtain and above every shop was the most interesting situation you could imagine, and on every signpost and every storefront little flashes of pornography at all angles, announcing that any discomfort you, visitor, might experience will be tolerated but viewed with inherent suspicion. As a child she'd look with innocent curiosity at the leather harnesses in the windows of the specialty shops and process it on the level of *I wonder what that's for?* and nothing more.

It is all gone now. A few non-profit community hubs are left standing, the nightclubs are still scrabbling for survival, the handful of legacy sex shops, barred and windows blocked, searched regularly by vice squads, banks with rainbow signs in their windows announcing their pride, banks that used to. Amy bumps Annie towards the crosswalk.

"This is it. This used to be the after-hours spot when I was a teenager. It's a franchise now, but they kept all the same staff, so the vibes are kinda the same."

It's busy, which feels weird for 2 p.m. on a Tuesday; this must be lunch rush for the offices upstairs, Amy thinks. It feels completely different from how she remembers it. The decor is sterile and branded with the franchise's logo on every surface, and everything's been plastered over with a kitschy fifties aesthetic, cheap red leather on the bar stools and the booths. You can still feel the grime in the walls and in the floors, she thinks, and notices they were allowed to keep up some posters on the walls for punk shows they'd had there in years past.

Annie scans the room, preparing herself internally for some judgment or condescension that never seems to materialize. She makes offhand eye contact with a woman in a power suit whose makeup makes her look sharp and aerodynamic, cut from marble in shapes she sometimes tried, and reverts back to thinking this woman's eyes are coming to execute her for not passing. Nobody really gives a shit about them at all. Amy notices Annie's nervousness and pulls her along like a distracted dog, feeling herself pushing her anger with Annie down again.

They settle in on either side of a booth against a window facing the street. Amy settles in, her shoulders open, posture slack, bag on the booth seat beside her. Annie carefully positions herself against the corner at the window's edge, elbow bent against the sill, her mouth spasming at its edges periodically.

"Are you feeling all right?" Amy says quietly.

"Yeah. Don't worry about it."

"Okay. Because if I'm pushing too hard here, just say the word and we can go back home. I just thought maybe sudden exposure would be good for the first try, then we can start on a slow-build kind of from there."

Annie grumbles something approaching words as the waiter, a gaunt, pale man with long, deep-veiny arms, wearing a branded vest over an Alien Sex Fiend T, sidles up to the table.

"Oh hey, Amy! What's up with the cut on your face? And who's this?"

"Hi Adam, uh, yeah, this is Annie. She's my twin? Yeah. And, um, yeah, you know I get into some crazy shit."

"Jesus, Amy. What do you want?"

"Lumberjack's breakfast, a coffee with cream, and two orange juice. Annie?"

"A yogurt cup and a black coffee, please."

He scribbles down illegible chicken scratch in a hurry, and Amy interjects. "A second lumberjack's breakfast for me, then."

Annie makes a sound to try to interject, but Adam is already gone, back to the kitchen with the order.

"Please don't, I'm just not really hungry."

"Of course! Don't worry, the second one's for me too. Of course, if you ask, I can share, but I just thought the first one might not be enough."

Amy is beaming at Annie.She can tell from Annie's eyes now that they're not the same.

"I'm so proud of you. Look at you out here, doing fine, acting super normal. Isn't it nice? I haven't even really been out like this in a while, all that trying to chase you down between trying to stay active online kind of put me in the same position for a little while there, all cloistered away, but it's been so long since I've really just had a nice girls' day like this. It's been a while since I've even had, like, a close friend IRL, really."

"I would have thought you'd be a social butterfly."

"Not lately. There was this one girl, but it's been a long time and she doesn't really speak to me anymore."

"Did something happen?"

"Not really. It's just so easy to get caught in the swing of things with work and not get out and into the city sometimes. Fuck Vancouver, right? Like, Adam, I hadn't seen him in months!"

"The waiter?"

"Yeah! We hooked up once. Cute, weird little guy, we couldn't stay too close for too long. Seems to happen all the time. But because he works here, we still always see each other. It's never been a weird thing."

Amy turns her head to cast a melancholy look at him on the opposite side of the restaurant, and Annie can't help but feel a pang of jealousy, followed by a deep appreciation of the shape of Amy's sharp jaw and long neck, features she hates in herself but which seem to suit Amy perfectly.

Amy's shocked to hear herself speak this way, so bubbly and confident, and she realizes that she hasn't been able to put on this kind of charm in years. Annie seems so much easier to interact with than most of the other people she deals with, there's very little risk of pushback.

"Just old times," Amy says, pulling herself out of her train of thought. "I wanted to ask, by the way, what do you do for work? Are you in, like, coding or something? I just kind of guessed, like, agoraphobic trans girl with a fucked-up old computer in her room, seems like the programmer type."

"I wish. I don't really have any skills, so I just answer those online marketing surveys. You know the ones from the spam emails?"

"Oh good lord, girl, I'm so sorry. Aren't those things, like, way sub-minimum-wage when you take the time in account to set all your shit up?"

"I mean, it's fine. Plus, it's totally anonymous. I have an account with the company, but my actual submissions are unmarked, so I can really operate without any surveillance."

"Unless you count all the sketchy software you have to download."

Adam runs back with the drinks. "Ladies."

Annie feels great at Adam gendering her correctly but is starting to think he's playing it up. The door keeps swinging open, and a wave of chilly air hits her from up the wall every time it happens. She takes a sip of French roast, slightly colder than expected. It coats her tongue, then throat.

"Wait, why do you know that?"

"I used to work for a company called Chariot, in customer support. I felt so bad for those poor helpless drones getting chewed out on the other end of the chatbox, I can't imagine actually doing that."

Annie stares into her black coffee, affectless. "That's the same company I work for."

Amy nearly jumps out of her seat, gesticulating wildly. People at surrounding tables are staring at her. "Are you serious? We're working for the same people? Okay, that's too much to be a coincidence, right? Like, same block, same face, same job — there has to be some insane fucked-up thing going on there! Maybe they have, like, a headquarters or something. We could go see what information they have on us. Let me look this up..." Amy starts thumbing through her phone for the address.

Annie sighs. "Why? It's just gonna be all the same shit that's on our IDs. Bank info, that kind of thing."

"Did you ever get scanned? A lot of the surveyors do."

A look of horror crosses Annie's face. "Uh, yeah?"

"Okay, so they definitely know more than just the info on your driver's licence, Annie. But, like, somebody there has to be aware of this, right? This is the first thing that actually ties us together in terms of how we're actually spending our lives."

"I know what I trade for my info, and I'm at peace with it. I don't want to go knock down the door of some corporate office, Amy. They're just gonna toss us out. And anyways, they're going to be on holiday. Just please quiet down a bit?" Annie is staring at a group of people at an adjacent table who are all staring straight at Amy, who doesn't notice.

"Are you sure you don't want to go? I feel like they gotta have something to do with why we are the way we are. We might never know otherwise. You could spend the rest of your life in regret."

"I already do. Plus, we could get arrested for breaking and entering, spend the rest of our lives regretting *that*."

Amy deflates visibly, looks down at the table, seeming to remember herself. "Okay, fine, sure. Bad idea."

They sit in tense silence for a moment.

"So, what else are you gonna do?" Amy finally says. "Work your miserable job, you get enough for rent, enough for hormones maybe, cigs, booze, food, and then you just sit online the rest of the time? You need, I mean *need*, to get out of that situation. Why not move in with me? I stay busy, get you out of the house. We could just take off, start driving with no direction in mind. How pretty would that be?"

Amy wonders what's coming over her. A week ago, she felt like she was just as much a loser as Annie, and now she feels real in the way other people seem to her. A chance to start again innocently. It's intoxicating.

"It's a beautiful dream. I just don't have any money."

"I can cover you."

"You'd need to, and then you'd hate me."

"I wouldn't."

"I can't drive, so you'd need to."

"I don't mind. I could teach you eventually, either way."

"I mean, we'd sort of be homeless."

"For a little while maybe, but we'd figure it out. We always do. We'd live like — like cockroaches. Find a safe place, stay until the weather changes, move on. I have a little money left, we could go somewhere cheaper, live on our dumb internet jobs. Not much reason to be in a big city if you can't afford to go out and do anything."

Adam swings back through with the food, at first placing one full breakfast at Annie's side and one at Amy's, with the yogurt cup in the middle, before Amy pulls the second full breakfast to hers and pushes the yogurt cup towards Annie. Amy digs directly in, chopping sausage and egg into slices, mixing it into the hash browns, slathering the whole thing in ketchup and hot sauce, letting the yolk wet everything on the plate. Annie pecks at the yogurt with a teaspoon.

"So, is the expectation that I'd be camming with you then, so we could get by?"

Amy lifts a finger to indicate to give her a second, then speaks, mouth still full. "You could if you want to. Or not, whatever. Find another work-from-home job. Waitress again. Who cares? Anything's better than what you're doing now."

"Okay, because I really don't think I have the constitution for that kind of thing, and if that's the only option once we get out on the road — "

Amy's voice rings clear now. "We'll do whatever we can to survive, same as we're doing now. You're using the fact that you're desperate as an excuse not to leave your shitty situation, even though you know what you're already doing is hurting you, and now you say that if you leave that situation, you'll be desperate. You're still here because you're desperate. I need you to decide if you're comfortable where you are or not, because to me, it looks like you're really not. To me, you look like you still want to die but you're too scared to do it, and there's obviously more you can do than that. Anyways, I'm sure there's an audience out there for identical twins if we wind up back in my old gig."

Annie is barely touching the yogurt and sipping her coffee only periodically. The snow is picking up outside and it's already starting to get dark, the light from behind the grey sky fading fast. The lunch crowd has cleared out and the two of them are almost alone, the only other table a pair of seniors who'd just entered, in the opposite corner. Amy cleans the first plate in minutes, and starts cutting everything on the second plate together in the same way as she did the first. Annie is staring at the mess, the egg-and-sausage-and-hash-brown-and-hot-sauce assemblage of red-and-brown mash on the plate, wondering why someone would choose to do it that way. But she can't deny that she's hungry. Amy's starting to slow down on the second plate, it's clearly hurting her to keep going, but the smell of the sausage and the potatoes is still wafting out.

Annie wonders when the last time was that she ate meat, and thinks about Amy's blood trickling down into her mouth, how much her body seemed to call out for Amy's as a source of heat and nutrients as much as it did for anything else.

"Well, first we'll have to get the apartment cleaned," Amy says. "Maybe we'll go, maybe we don't, but there's really nothing keeping us here after that."

Adam hurries over as soon as Amy waves him over.

"Can we get a bottle of rosé? We're celebrating tonight."

"Sure, Amy. Just so you know, you're the last in my section, so, no rush, but when you guys could wrap up bills, that'd be awesome."

"No worries."

Amy's not touching the second breakfast at all anymore, and watches Annie watching it get cold. Annie, noticing Amy looking, keeps looking away as soon as she senses Amy's imperiousness around it, until Amy finally pushes it, cold, to Annie's side.

"I was waiting for you to ask. Come on."

Annie eats the remainder, cold and mixed together. She does not like ketchup, but it's more and better food than she's had at once in a long time. Adam, haughty, drops two wineglasses, specked with condensation, and a bottle of overpriced bottom-shelf rosé in a bucket.

"I'm so excited to get you out there," Amy says as she fills both glasses. "I'm sure we'll be the centre of the scene wherever we end up."

"Sure."

Annie has decided to take whatever crazy shit Amy says at face value from this point forward. She feels like she might have made a terrible mistake when she opened the door in the first place, but she's got someone making the decisions for her now. She's grateful.

6.

It's about 7 p.m. when they leave. The night air is cold and sharp, and the snow is still cascading down like a solid blanket, shards emerging from streetlights in fields of blue darkness.

The girls crash drunkenly back into the apartment, floating over trash to land in the stripped bed entangled, wanting to keep touching each other now that they can, exhausted and wet to their bones from the snow. The only thing they can use to warm up is the sheet in its mélange of piss, cum, blood, sweat, wine, and so many tiny holes from the bugs chewing away.

Amy, twirling a strand of Annie's stringy blond hair, breathes out slowly. Annie curls up into her again and they breathe together.

After a while, they get up. Amy suggests taking out the garbage first, and the two start taking two bags at a time, going from the balcony first, in that brutal air for a second, sliding sideways through the narrow hallway and back in the heat of the covered garbage room in the building garage. Amy keeps gagging from the initial lift of each bag, revealing the liquid and ripped bags dropping detritus out from underneath, but she doesn't comment beyond the involuntary response. By Amy's count, there are 231 bags of trash inside the apartment.

If the neighbours were ever watching for the ghoul to emerge from the infested unit, they could certainly find her now — two of them, hunched, bloody, pale, emerging back and forth with bags and bags, reflective black masses moving up and down the halls in constant transit, conversations loud and full of laughter, periodically hushed back to whispers when made aware of the time of night. After a few runs carrying two each, they decide there has to be some better way, and they decide they can at least take fewer trips down to the bottom. It's a cold night and nobody else really seems to be using the elevator, so Amy holds the door for ten-to-fifteen-minute intervals as Annie loads about a dozen bags into the elevator at once, two at a time. The first attempt fits about sixteen, but this doesn't really leave a comfortable amount of room for the two to go down, so they stick to about twelve at a time, and they stall the elevator for fifteen minutes or so on Annie's floor first, then again at the bottom level, propping open the back doors and letting the snow and wind back out into the lobby, over and over and over. After a few of these bigger trash runs, the floor starts to become visible in the apartment, with its coat of dead bugs, season after season of guests pasted along the floors and along the walls up to nearly ankle height where the black canyons had been. Towards the end of dealing with the garbage, Annie starts to crash and lies back on the bed, shaking and overwhelmed at how little night there is left to deal with the amount of work to do if they're going to leave the apartment by tomorrow morning, as they'd fantasized about all through the walk home, giggly and effervescent drunk, holding hands and leaning into each other; even though it's still only about 10 p.m., it already feels like they're running out of time with the amount left to be done. Amy asks if they need drugs to get it done, and Annie declines, a little afraid of anything but the familiar wine now. Amy is grateful for this answer, and a little embarrassed she decided to signpost this way. Last she heard, Clara left town.

Once the bags are all out, they agree the bed and its sheets are garbage in themselves. They walk it down the hall sideways, Annie thinking of anyone who might be looking out of peepholes to see two identical girls, bleeding down the hallway with heads covered by hoods, muttering insults at one another under their breath and smoking cigarettes, nearly on loop, in the apartment, outside at the dumpsters, in the hallways, in the elevators, the world becoming theirs to trash as much as the apartment ever was before. Annie is a little heartbroken to see her grand design, the world she created, so broken apart, its solidity and structure broken down into its core components and its underbelly exposed, but she's not allowing herself to feel any degree of missing or mourning, because she knows if she says the thought out loud, Amy will get mad at her, and if she thinks it without saying it out loud, she will hurt herself, pointlessly, it will come out, Amy will leave, and she will be left with nothing. This future will be gone, stillborn beside its disappearing predecessor, mocking her in her failure. She needs to grasp on and let it carry her where it will before it too fails.

Annie is not good at receiving feedback. Each time Amy prods her to change her grip, or tells her she's getting ahead of herself, Annie throws the accusation out that Amy's being unnecessarily cruel to her again, which in turn inspires Amy to be more insistent, thinking it's what she needs to stay motivated, or that if any advice is going to be taken as personal critique, she may as well go directly to whatever she's thinking rather than trying to soften things. But Annie needs things softened, and during particular peaks in their respective lingering mania she'll lash out or say she intends to cancel the plans, saying anything she can to have Amy reach back to her, comfort her. She also desperately wants to sit and rest, or for Amy to fuck her again, but Amy is hyper-focused on the task at hand, scrubbing baseboards and clearing shelves like a fiend. Annie's perceptions start to get a little foggy and she occasionally finds herself getting distracted on a particular small detail for a long time, like rubbing at one spot on the glass balcony door, spraying the cleaner onto it, wiping it away, and creating a seemingly identical spot, then starting the process over again. Amy has her back bent hard, using a steel-wool scraper against the floor to clear off all the dead bugs, mysterious sludge and egg pods. She's been at this for what feels to Annie like hours, her hands becoming wrinkled and burnt from the bleach. Amy can't help but think of Annie as a helpless little kid, taking the back seat all night and only seeming to take on any task when directed to, and hates herself a little for it.

They're getting to the end at four or five in the morning when Amy tells Annie to pack up the computer. At first she's completely frozen. The tower of the computer, its screen, the central mental interfacing point of the entire space — it's the last thing keeping this space Annie's, preventing it from being an empty room. This spot, the gaming chair with its foam spilling out from under cheap plastic, the headset microphone, crushed anime titty mousepad, the central organizing point of her life for two years. Now all she can think to do is reach her hand deep inside, between the nest of daisy-chained cables and peripherals, over years of careful construction, and start pulling cords. She pulls a fistful out, severing connections and hearing some faint electrical noise from somewhere in the rats' nest, then reaches her hand back in, makes a tighter fist, takes a harder pull, then reaches her left hand behind it as soon as her right is finished, until she's pulling back and forth, alternating hands. Fist in, fist out, guts after guts after guts, microprocessors, cords, hunks of plastic, tossing them over her shoulders, Annie feels feral, giving herself over in union with the machine. Dismembering some core part of herself, knowing that she's now entirely detached from her home, her income, her sense of self as it'd been built to this point. Whatever is left is what she's made with Amy in the past twenty-four hours.

She starts reaching into the back of the machine and bashing her fist against the plastic until it cracks and until it starts to hurt her hand to keep bashing, past the point where there's a gaping hole in the back of the machine, impaled over her arm from its bottom. Reaching into the gap, staring into the lights that had once produced the words of the boards, the individual pixels that produced Amy and brought her here, she grasps blindly and yanks her hand out, strewing circuits across the floor. Finally, she forces her hand backwards against the glass of the monitor, trying to rip a hole in the screen to be able to materialize herself as well. Amy, finally having made some progress on the bug-floor, comes around the corner to see Annie's arm penetrate the monitor, smashing the plastic siding, searing pain coursing up her arm and into her chest, her hands shaking.

Amy shakes out the last of the peroxide onto the wounds and bandages her with a roll of loose cotton from below the sink, the last thing left in the first aid kit after all the adhesive bandages had been used.

"You're so fucking dumb, you know that?"

Annie is shaking and squealing, her eyes bright and wide. "I just wanted it gone."

"Don't worry, you can use mine on my off-hours if there's time. Or we can find you one, or whatever."

"Do you even make that much money? Like, for the two of us?"

Annie folds over onto the edge of the tub and Amy holds her. "No."

After a night of scraping and mopping and scrubbing and breathing toxic fumes, patches of black mould and surviving silverfish, shitty Bluetooth speakers playing Björk's *Vespertine* on loop, they leave a note of Annie's intent to vacate at the front desk.

The property manager will not see it until long after the rent is due, and eviction notices will pile up at the door for months before anyone comes to check that it's empty.

7.

It's late in the morning but still mostly dark when Annie wakes up under the pink-and-red LED strip lights in Amy's bedroom. She looks around, realizing Amy is still asleep.

She could go right now. Back to the suburbs, back to her dad's place. He wouldn't be happy with her, but she wouldn't have to pay rent. She could live like a kid again, playing video games and making her little bit of money online to fund pleasure purchases. What could he do? He wouldn't turn her out. He couldn't have gotten that much worse. She probably still shouldn't come out to him, she thinks, better to take on the burden of recloseting than to take the risk of raising the conversation, thereby risking the last option she has if and when this whole road-trip fantasy falls through. Maybe he'd even take Amy in too. How would she even explain that? *Hey Dad, I have a long-lost twin! Hey Dad, meet my gay lover who looks exactly like me!* If they could make it past that point, they could at least take a breather for a little while, while they get ready for the trip across the country. She shakes herself and looks down at Amy's head on the pillow. She's breathing softly.

There are a lot of open questions, she thinks, but it's better this way. I have somebody.

She settles back into the bed. It feels like Christmas morning under the glow of the strip lights and with the big day ahead. She isn't far off — it's December 28 now. Looking up, she sees the mountains on the ceiling again — the same ceiling. She thinks about the apartment lying dormant across the street, knowing that if she wasn't haunting it when she lived there, she certainly does now, her imprint baked into the walls of that place for whoever comes next — a lingering musty smell, barely perceptible except on rainy mornings. Annie wants so badly to shake Amy up and drag her downstairs, to make her take her away from here as far as she possibly can as soon as possible. She watches Amy's chest fall and rise and thanks her silently for being there for the day it finally broke.

Amy does eventually turn over and Annie nearly jumps on her like a dog before they take turns showering and getting dressed. She briefly pitches a diner breakfast again. Neither of them are capable of summoning much energy, and the hours seem to stretch on as they shoot the shit in bed and talk in excited and nervous tones about what they're going to do once they go, the short winter day slipping past them.

"I'm really excited to get to do this with you."

Amy speaks softly, vulnerable. "Me too."

"Which way should we head first?" Annie says.

"East. I'm sure I've got a couch or two I can crash with some friends in Montreal."

"That sounds amazing. What do you think we'll do?"

"Keep working from home until we find something better. Live wherever we can for a little while, get really fucked-up and insular, gradually make our way to some kind of stability."

Annie doesn't say anything.

"We'll pack up anything we need from here, load the car, get going."

"You have a car?"

"Yeah. One last gift from my mom. Hand-me-down."

"That's sweet."

"It's just been rotting away in there for the most part, guess I'm finally getting some use out of it. I don't know if it even still runs."

Annie nuzzles into Amy, who glazes over a little.

Amy murmurs again, "Are you sure you don't want to go to Chariot? It'd mean a lot to me."

"No," Annie says softly. "I just want to get started with you. That's the only thing that matters to me."

"Okay."

Amy got the address when they were at the diner, still tabbed up on her phone, surrounded by uncanny stock photos and HTML text effects. It's right out on the edge of the city in an industrial lot. She decides she'll leave it be for now.

Amy walks through the flurry to grab them breakfast from a convenience store around the block while Annie packs their things. Left alone for the first time since they met, Annie thinks back to teenage fantasies of escape, to walking on a winter day like this, black metal in her earbuds, pretending on empty streets that it was the end of the world, that she was a wandering exile in a forsaken wasteland. She folds Amy's clothes and tucks them haphazardly in a suitcase and feels warm.

Amy is underdressed for the weather, getting her feet wet on the unshovelled sidewalk. It's hitting her that she has nothing to lose. How long has it been like this, how long would she have thrown it all away like this? She asks herself if she would have done this if Vivian had forgiven her. She hopes Annie won't leave too, once she gets to know her better. Amy still isn't totally sure what she did wrong, but she didn't think it was a big deal back then either, and everybody else certainly seemed to. She closely analyzes her movements now, unsure of what might upset Annie. I guess, she thinks, we have all the time in the world to learn about one another. She gets them each a blueberry Danish and a black coffee, and buys Annie a pack of cigarettes for the road.

Coming back in already exhausted, her coat soaked through, Amy hands Annie her Danish and the pack of smokes and they settle back into bed.

Annie speaks with her mouth full. "So, what are we gonna do first when we get to Montreal?"

"Probably meet up with some people, figure out where we're staying, maybe go out. Have a bit of a welcome party. The bars go all night there, I guess."

Amy's panicking a little, but she tries to push it back. Again she reminds herself, nothing to lose. How hard could it be to find a place to stay? Annie's unusually enthusiastic.

"Yeah, you mentioned having some friends out there, what are their names? What do they get up to?"

"Artists, mostly. And I've never really been out there, it's just people I've talked to online here and there. We'll have to figure it out when we land."

Annie pauses, looks directly at Amy now. "Can we really depend on these people if you don't even know them that well?"

"It'll be fine. You got everything in the bag?"

They lock the door to Amy's apartment for what they hope is the last time, leaving the bed full of crumbs. They squeeze through the green-chrome hallway to the elevator, into the underground parking garage. It's freezing cold, and Annie starts clinging to Amy's still-damp coat sleeve as they walk through the dim concrete space.

"Here it is."

Amy's car is a four-seat sedan, but it looks like a two-seat with the amount of trash in the back, which pains Annie to look at after last night. *How do I know I won't end up back in the same situation?*

They get on the highway. The aux cable is busted, so they listen to the couple tapes Amy has kicking around: *Janet Jackson's Rhythm Nation 1814* and Depeche Mode's *Black Celebration*. Annie focuses on the road, and the music makes her feel like that kid in the streets waiting for the end of the world. Traffic is bad. The tail lights of cars reflect from the body of one into the next, producing a sort of halo over the road. They drive past the mall where they both spent their teenage years unbeknownst to each other. Gridlocked between holiday shoppers, they trade stories of when the new wing opened, sitting in one spot for nearly an hour trying to keep themselves entertained as Dave Gahan drones on.

Sitting in the traffic jam, Annie smokes half the pack Amy bought her, elbow on the armrest and face pressed close to the window, open just a crack to let out the smoke. Amy's routed them towards Chariot, but she's not quite worked up the nerve yet to ask Annie if they want to take an impromptu detour. Once things start moving again, Annie jerks up her neck.

"Hey, we're not too far from the house where I grew up. Do you wanna see it?"

Great, Amy thinks to herself, *more distractions.*

Annie keeps talking. "And I mean, if my dad's down for it, we could crash for a little while. You know, save some money, get the plan settled?"

"I don't really want to get too settled with anything before we get out of here."

"But, I mean, if you don't really even know these people out in Montreal that well, how can we assume we're just gonna be fine when we get there?"

"It will be. Don't sweat it." Amy catches a touch of anger in her own voice saying this, and pares it back. "I'd love to come meet your dad. But we're there for, like, a day or two at most, okay?"

"That's fine. I'd at least like to say goodbye. I might never see him again."

"Sure."

Annie directs Amy towards the right exit. The lights in the low suburban houses are off, the houses are farther from the road, and there are fewer and fewer cars beside them until there's no halo at all. It's gone from grey to starless pitch, snow spraying through the darkness. Annie's a little tripped out being back where they grew up, on the surface of the moon, freeway signs with one light out, endless geometries of the same houses, black ice covering the sidewalks connecting them. Even a week out from the solstice, 3 p.m. seems a little early for it to be this dark and for the roads to be this empty. Eventually, the GPS dings and the freeway leads them into the greater light of the road, then the deeper darkness of the neighbourhood.

8.

The freeway absorbs its edges, the greenery sinking away as they reach the suburbs. The mountains disappear from the horizon like they've been absorbed into the earth, leaving only an expansive dead plain, snow-covered, utilitarian, dotted with houses spread farther and farther apart. The houses are just distinguishable enough from one another to clash; a misplaced arch or a gaudy turret are the only things changing on what are otherwise the same shapes, again and again for seemingly forever, faux wood and faux stone, glass, two-storey pseudo-lux. Despite the cold functionality of it, there's a strange beauty to this place, a stillness that allows the mind to wander. Annie stares into the windows of the houses they drive by, all as good as empty from the street. She cracks the window to smoke again, feeling the shock of cold against her face as the wind whips in. "Is there a way to be like this forever?" she says, half to herself.

Amy responds instantly, curt. "I don't know."

"Okay. I just really don't want to do anything that might fuck this up."

"Me too."

A pregnant pause between the two.

Amy murmurs, "So, are you and your dad close?"

"We were when I was a kid. Not so much now. I sort of cut them all off when I came out."

"So you're just popping back up out of the blue?"

"I don't know. I felt like I just had to close the loop if we're leaving."

"I get that."

There's another long, tense silence as Annie exhales. She's nearly killed the pack from this morning already.

Amy breaks the silence again. "I still really want to go to Chariot. Close the loop, like you said. I know you think it's stupid, or risky, but it's the only strand we have left to try to figure out why all this is happening."

Annie sinks into her seat. "Honestly, I don't care about knowing why. I just want to be here with you. I want to get out of here, and move on, and I'm really grateful to you for giving me that chance, so I really, really don't want to blow it."

"I know it's probably nothing, but it means a lot to me if you'd make the trip before we go. Don't you wanna at least try to figure this thing out?"

Annie reaches across the seat, gripping Amy's thigh. "It's so much nicer just having each other."

Amy sighs. "It is nice right now."

"Chariot's not gonna have anything," Annie says. "Door's gonna be locked over the holidays, it may not even be an office there. There's nothing we can't access online."

"Even if it's nothing, we may as well check. We leave, we turn around, we hit the road like we said we were gonna, or we come back to your dad's and plan for a while, or whatever you want. If you don't think there's anything there, there shouldn't be any issue in going, right?"

Annie looks out the window at the houses going by. "I'm scared, Amy. I'm scared of what might be there. And I'm scared of how you'll respond if there's nothing. Like, if you're even gonna want me around if it turns out this isn't going to fix all your problems."

"I would, I promise. But, would you really just be okay not knowing for the rest of your life, knowing why any of this happened to you?"

Annie's voice cracks a little. "I'd be happy."

Amy's quiet for a minute. They're getting deeper into the neighbourhood and Annie is getting more and more lost in thought.

"Hey, are we pretty close?"

"Uh, yeah, just this next exit."

"Okay."

They take a left past a dilapidated strip mall, old signs for liquor and smoke shops half-covered in worn For Lease signs. Past it is a row of houses on each side, older houses in worse condition, leading up to a cul-de-sac. Annie remembers the eyes in the windows of the houses on this street, watching her, ready to return her to her father's arms, to the warm car. The shape of the street brings her back to that vulnerable feeling, the protection and trust of the people around her, each house bringing back memories of empty days and long walks. Some of them she remembers waking in, and wonders if the families that looked after her on those nights still live there. She'd love to come back to them and thank them.

They take the corner into the cul-de-sac and find themselves facing a broad, empty field. The horizon seems to continue forever in the night, dotted with snow. A deer, standing in the place Annie's house should be, skitters off into the distance. Amy puts the parking brake on and lets the car idle, settling.

"Huh. Are you sure this was the right way?"

"This is definitely where it is."

"I mean, where it *was*, I guess."

"No, it's definitely here. Like, I was able to guide us here from memory, I know this house, I know this neighbourhood. I spent my whole life here. This is where my house is."

Amy pulls out her phone and desperately starts tapping away to reorient her map, muttering as she does. "Okay, let me just try to find it. Signal's a little weak out here, but we should be able to figure it out. Do you have an address for it?"

Annie's eyes widen and she starts to gesticulate with her left hand. "No! This is where I lived. This is where I spent my life. I *know this place*. I dream this place constantly, and there is a house here. My house. My dad's house."

Amy lowers her phone and looks at Annie with disbelief and dawning shock. "Do you know if he moved or, like, if they might have torn it down? I mean, you haven't been in contact for years, right? Can you text him, or . . . ?"

Annie pulls her knees up onto the car seat, the heat blowing against her. "I don't know... I don't know what's happening."

"Please, Annie, I want to help you. Are you totally sure this is the right place? We could go back to the apartment, figure out the specifics and come back, figure out where your dad is..."

"You're not listening to me," Annie says quietly. "It's not here. It was never here. I was never here."

Annie snaps the seat belt latch, swings the car door open and starts walking out into the empty lot, casting a long shadow in the headlights. Amy does not know what to do except to chase after her.

The headlights slice a cone of light into the field, overgrown with tall grass and with no clear boundary where a house might ever have been, the snow erasing everything.

"Listen, maybe this was a bad call!" Amy yells after her. "Maybe we just need to get going, we go get our new start, everything's going to be okay! Please, believe me. Everything is going to be okay!"

Annie calls back, livid: "You were right! I don't exist! I'm not here!"

"No, come on, we got past that, you're okay..."

"*Just let me go!*"

Annie sits down in the field, blank-faced. Amy catches up to her.

"Do what you should have done in the first place and spare yourself the embarrassment of keeping me around. Go be me for me, since you're clearly so much better at it."

Amy notices an old lady in a neighbouring house, pulling back her blinds to look out at the hubbub. She puts her arm around Annie's shoulder.

"Annie, get in the car. We're going to Chariot, and then we're moving on with our lives. Something's really wrong here, and we have to figure it out before we can move past it. I won't lie to you, this is fucked-up. This is a fucked-up situation we've found ourselves in, but I need you with me. So please, just get in the car."

Annie's muscles slacken as she places an arm over Amy, pulling herself up. "It was never there..."

"Please, Annie, people are looking at us. I don't want to get the cops called on us."

Annie sees the neighbour now too, hanging out of the front door to gawk. Someone unfamiliar, afraid of what these shouting weirdos idling their car in the night snow might do. Annie knew the woman who lived in that house, or she thought she did, and this isn't her.

"Okay."

Amy brushes some snow off Annie as they trudge back towards the car and settle in. The engine makes a wheezing noise as it starts up. The neighbour is still watching them as they drive past, leaving the field as empty as it'd been when they arrived.

Annie stares blankly as the highway blows by, from the suburbs onward into the industrial outskirts. She flicks the radio back on and Amy turns it down, burnt-out.

"You'd think you'd be happy not knowing, but you won't be," Amy says. Her voice with a slight edge to it that Annie hasn't noticed before.

Annie breathes like she's going to respond, but doesn't, staring out at the road blankly.

Amy, her voice soft, continues. "I have something I need to tell you. I convinced Sam I was you so I could get to you. And I don't really know anybody in Montreal. I've pretty much been doing the same thing you have, for a while now. I felt like you should know that. I'm sorry."

Annie turns away from her.

Amy continues. "This is my only option too. But I don't want that to come at your expense. If you want, I can take you back home."

"Please just drive."

9.

It's close to four but completely dark. Way out past the residential areas, everything turns into long, low boxes. Tan rectangles extend in every direction, presumably filled with shipping centres, all made beautiful under the blue night and the fresh snow. Periodically, the occasional truck still takes off from the back of one in a steady rhythm. Between each are empty fields, prairie biome left to run wild as the speculators argue over its cost. White jackrabbits dart between mounds of snow as owls circle far above.

The address on Amy's phone says the Chariot offices are on one side of one of the rectangles, but they keep driving and driving and it never becomes obvious which one it is. They overshoot it, turn back, and overshoot it a couple more times, before finally parking. They wordlessly get out and walk through the knee-deep snow halfway across a parking lot to an unmarked door, with no lights on inside. Amy pulls the handle and finds it locked.

"Let's just go back." Annie says. "Get moving."

"Wait, there are a couple more doors."

"Are you really gonna..."

Amy takes off. They trudge down the side of the same building and try pulling on a few more doors with darkened windows, but none of them seem to take, until Annie pulls on a door that unexpectedly jolts open. Heat radiates from inside and fluorescent lighting flashes on automatically.

Rows and rows of empty grey cubicles, out-of-date desktop computers with screensavers on. There's a whiteboard hung over a mini-fridge next to a coffee machine, which reads: "Milk and cream are for EVERYONE, anything else in the fridge is PERSONAL." Coats are still hung up. Amy starts to walk ahead and Annie ducks behind a cubicle.

"Someone must have just been here," Annie hisses at her.

"But it's been long enough that the lights were off. And we're just asking for some files, no reason we can't just walk right up to them and ask, right? They might just be closed for the holidays."

They walk carefully across the expanse of the cubicle room, moving to what must be the break room, which has several wide tables arranged facing each other. There are dozens of seats here. Annie wonders how many people would have to work here to need this much space. It smells like a high school gym. The break room leads to a smoke pit outside and to another work floor on the other end, the same as the first: rows of empty cubicles as far as the eye can see, the only visible clusters those lit up by the fluorescent overhead lights they walk under.

"I always imagined my parents working in places like this," Annie says quietly. "If they ever existed."

"Don't worry, they did. They must have. They loved you."

Annie mutters, feeling condescended to. "Thanks."

"Wait, look at that."

Somewhere far off in the darkness of the office, another light has flashed on. Annie dives behind a cubicle and this time Amy follows her.

"Shit shit shit shit shit, somebody's here."

"They're probably just cleaners. We're fine."

As the lights on the ceiling flick on, back and forth, in an S pattern, closer and closer up the hallways, they start to hear a deep whir. A man is pushing a carpet cleaner up and down the silent aisles of the office. Amy points and directs towards him:

"Okay, let's just follow the janitor."

Annie feels by turns embarrassed and terrified to be here, but too far gone not to follow Amy as she darts between cubicles. The cleaner's whir gets louder and louder as it makes its zigzag way across the office floor. The man pushing the cleaner is olive-skinned with slicked-back grey hair, wearing a jumpsuit with the brand of a contracting company across the chest, the name *Dave* embroidered just below the pocket. Amy recognizes the uniform from her training handbook, thinking he must have survived in the company a long time to get that embroidery, especially as a contractor. Probably did it himself. He's got wired earbuds running into his pocket and he's got a serene smile on his face, pushing the cumbersome handles around from his waist, making the patterned texture lining the carpet one smooth, consistent shape all the way along. When the staff get back in on Monday, everything will be in its proper place, and it will be like nothing has happened over the winter break.

After a few more S's, he drops the cleaner and walks back over to the hallway they'd entered from, carefully treading so as not to leave any trace of his backtrack, occasionally running back over it when he did. Annie follows, moving in the tail of the automatic lights. She pulls around a corner into a hallway and stares from the dark, careful to stay totally still. He stops in front of a door labelled Staff Only and fumbles with a massive key ring for a moment before picking one out, working the key in with a little jimmying and walking inside. Annie darts after him, taking off like she's running bases, seeing the door fall behind him. The possibility runs through her mind: This is probably a tiny janitor's closet, she will whip the door open behind him, they will stare each other in the face, he will tell her they are closed and ask her to leave, and she will apologize and go out in the snow to wait for Amy to follow after her. *Who knows how long she'll be, maybe she'll leave me out there.*

She manages to get her toe in the door just as it shuts, and slowly peels it open, waiting for the inevitable. Instead, she's faced with a narrow hallway with several doors on either side, leading towards a metal elevator at the end of the hall. The light above the elevator door is gold plated and lit in cherry red, an arrow pointing down. Annie slips off one winter boot and wedges it under the door, running back to the cubicle room, now blanketed in dark.

"He's gone!"

"What?"

"He went down a locked hallway to an elevator. I held the door, we should be able to keep following."

They hustle back down the centre of the rows of cubicles, the light following them. Annie finds herself staring at the cut on Amy's face, mostly scabbed over now. Amy has the discipline not to pick at it; Annie thinks about how she would have made it worse by now.

Annie pulls the shoe from the door and struggles to put it back on, trying to do it without untying it, giving up, untying it, asking for a moment, getting on one knee and tying it right there. Amy is trying to exude gentle calm but failing, and Annie is panicking sensing Amy's panic.

They get into the elevator and the floor jerks a little as the doors close, a mechanical screech coming from the hoistway.

On a gold control panel, several options are embossed in a deep-red sans serif:

WORKSPACE
SUPPLY
PARKING I
PARKING II
GYM
EXECUTIVE
CENTRAL OPERATIONS

"What do you think? Probably 'Executive,' right? Go right to the top?"

"No way they'll let us anywhere near there. Plus, it's still the holidays, they wouldn't be in."

"'Central Operations,' then?"

"Perfect."

Pressing on the gold button, Amy appreciates the really satisfying weight to it, with just the right amount of give. Nothing happens. Amy gives it a couple more frustrated jabs then tries "Executive," which lights up in cherry. The elevator jerks into motion, shaky at first and shaking a little when it crosses floors, which happens infrequently.

"What do you think is down there?" Amy says.

"Probably not anything that we can get into."

"Yeah."

The elevator keeps on rolling. It's a long pause.

"Amy, I really love you. I know it's only been a few days, but I do."

They're interrupted by another cacophony of whooshing and grinding as they move past another floor entry. Amy sighs.

"I love you too, though. And again, I'm really sorry for everything. We gotta stick by each other, right?"

"I don't think it was a great thing to do, but we're here now. It's okay."

"That doesn't make it go away."

"Thanks."

"How long have we been in this elevator, anyways? My legs are getting sore."

"My phone's dead, couldn't tell you."

They stand in the elevator making small talk for another twenty minutes and thirty-seven seconds as they make their descent.

~ ~ ~

The door opens behind them and they enter a narrow box of a room, wood panelled with orange-and-yellow shag carpeting. There's a pendulous glass lighting fixture, bulbous and white, hanging over the platform to a staircase heading down, concrete steps that exit the light after only a few steps, and over it a green neon sign that reads:

Below to EXECUTIVE and CENTRAL OPERATIONS

There are no other doors in the walls of the wood room, and no button to call the elevator back. They look at each other for a second, not saying anything, and then Amy grabs Annie's hand and they walk into the dark.

Space folds inwards behind them. The ceiling always seems to be closing in from overhead. The first hour is mostly trancelike silent determination, both girls' legs turning gradually closer and closer to jelly as they take each step, each step feeling the weight more and more as time passes. The concrete walls are covered with little perforations like follicles speckled across them all the way down. As in the cubicle room, overhead lights shudder on automatically when they walk underneath, then back off again, erasing their path. Annie feels herself relying more and more on the yellow handrail with its chipped paint, every texture in this space seeming to breathe through its pores, the rhythm of the girls' own breath beginning to match the pace of the walls' pulsations as their breaths get shorter and shallower. Annie's palms sweat and chafe against the chipped paint of the stairs' yellow handrail, irritating the skin on her hands and making her itch. She scratches them surreptitiously from time to time, and it gets a little worse each time she feels a burn in her back or in her legs and sets the sweaty hand back down on the metal handrail, the skin getting peeled away layer by layer by the rub, itch, rub, itch, scratch. But her legs and fingers can't stop moving, the legs in their perpetual march, the fingers syncopated, ticcing, gripping, tearing skin off their own cuticles and from between sweaty craters.

Amy tries to remind herself that she wants this, that she needs to keep a brave face, as she pushes forward through the pain. She suspects there's no coming back from here.

In the second hour of descent, letters start to appear on the walls of the staircase, spaced too far apart to read in individual bursts. They're painted on in what appears to be grease or wax, and are viscous to the touch, though no material comes off when Amy runs a finger through. The second hour reveals *H E A B*. They stop on a step at the foot of the greasy *B*. The stairs are angled slightly forward, and using them as a backrest hurts after just a few seconds, so each girl takes a step and they put their backs on either wall, legs extended towards each other.

"God, I'm hungry," Annie says.

"Yeah, but it's like, I can't even let myself rest or I'll fall asleep on these stairs and I'll never have the will to head back. We have to keep the momentum going."

"I hate this." Annie's voice moves up into her sinuses. She chokes a little on snot. "Why couldn't we have just stayed in bed? Was that really so wrong? What if there's no way back up from here and we're going to die?"

Amy's voice is hard through her exhaustion. "Doesn't matter anymore. All the choices that led us here were the ones that we made. Everything that came before is irrelevant at this point. I said I wanted to know the truth, and I'm going to get my answer."

There's a pause. Her voice softens.

"By the way, Annie, something's been bothering me."

"Yeah, go ahead."

"Why do you spend so much time on those chat rooms if you hated everybody on there so much?"

Annie breathes hard, swallowing some residual phlegm from her chain-smoking. She responds softly. "It was, like, the only thing I could do. Felt like the only real contact I could get anonymously."

"Yeah, but like, you know there's an internet outside of that. Even then, you could have a pen pal if you wanted to keep a low profile. But like, you don't sympathize with those guys' politics at all, right? Like, I never touched that shit because it was full of nazis. Sorry, I guess it just stuck in my craw a little."

"Oh no, I'm not really political at all."

"Oh. Okay." Amy, perturbed, raises herself back up onto her haunches and stands up. "Let's please keep moving."

By the end of the second hour and the beginning of the third, the air grows stagnant and begins to smell of blood. Their ears pop from the shift in air pressure as the descent grows steeper and steeper. Every step is agony, and at first the girls hide the sounds they make on each footfall, but eventually the pain is too great and the embarrassment subsides to the point where it's a full, low groan on each step. They begin to try to walk on their heels, as the particular point in the calf that stabilizes on a regular step stings each time. The rhythm and pace of their steps, which have been slowing since about mid-second hour, are now agonizingly slow, a complete process of mental buildup and comedown necessary for each one, which only makes each of them more aware of the total energy expended on each.

The letters continue. *A T T O*. They can't glean anything from this message. Nothing seems to make sense anymore, least of all the physical possibility of the depths they've now walked. Looking behind them and ahead of them, only ink-black murk, which seems to shift in peripheral vision for both of them.

"Are we going to die doing this?" Annie says, stopping again to catch her breath.

"What do you mean?"

"Like, is there an end? Or does it go on forever?"

"It can't go on forever."

"Do they want us to walk ourselves to death?"

"I will if I have to."

It is around 8 p.m., and Dave has long since finished his shift. The staff will be back on Monday; only upper management was in this morning. The girls have long since stopped communicating about bodily sensations. The wall reads *I.* They know they're never going to see sunlight again. There was a clarity that came with the walking at first, but now their bodies' needs have overcome any higher-level consideration and their minds are filled with pain. No sense engaged except vision and touch, everything hurting.

The nearest overhead light flicks on in the distance and sits over a flat platform, the first break in the stairway since the concrete broke off the orange shag carpeting hours ago.

Their muscles, finally coming loose, cramp on the flat ground, hurting worse than they did during the movement now that they start to recover. They grab each other's arms deep at the shoulder blade and sink together to the floor. They look up, and the imposing letter on the platform is *R*, looking down at them. The grease-paint runs along the wall, continuing from the *R* in a long stripe down. The stairs drop off in exactly the same way they have been doing for god knows how much farther. On the platform is a redwood door, with a gold nameplate in the same red text as the elevator: *EXECUTIVE.* Annie doubles over, hands on knees, and points at the sign between huffed breaths.

"Stop here?" she says. "I know we were aiming for Central Operations, but I can't do it anymore."

Amy struggles to stand, braces her hand on one of the walls just below the inky smear. She's breathing through her mouth, her eyes wide open.

"Come on," she says. "If there's anything at the bottom of this, they must *really* not want anyone to see it. This is here to distract us. We need Central Operations."

"Come on, I'm sure if there's some kind of record, or whatever you think you're going to actually get out of this, it's probably going to be in Executive, right?"

Amy runs her hand across Annie's cheek and pulls away, looking down the stairs. "I found it," she pants. "I can't wait, knowing it's in there. I don't care about the record, I just need to see it for myself. Please, come with me."

Annie takes a step back from Amy, looking horrified. "See what? You—you're not going anywhere, right?"

"Of course not."

Annie grips onto Amy, wrapping her up, holding her close and burying her face in her neck. She squeezes desperately. "Like, you're gonna go check this stuff out, but we'll meet back here and talk it through, right?"

"Of course we will."

"Okay. Please. I love you."

"I love you, too."

Annie looks over her knees as she watches Amy disappear into the dark.

She stands, taking a deep stretch in her calves, touching her toes and reaching up behind her. She loses her balance, sits down, stands up again more slowly. Annie cracks the door and peers inside.

There's a lobby with a table and two large velvet chairs. The smell of blood is gone, and the air is sterile, lightly perfumed. She sits at one and stares past towards the offices: a long, cavernous hallway with two glass walls on either side, containing two offices arranged in perfect symmetry with one another. Each contains a marble desk, a leather chair, a whiteboard on the wall (one empty, one covered in scribbles too far away to read), stone fireplaces facing one another with stone mantles, stuffed cougars prowling and perched over each. The panes of glass each seem to run hundreds of feet high and wide, the light ending before they do and their outlines penetrating a cloud of shadow overhead.

Annie sees a single figure in the distance down the hallway, not close enough to make out any details, moving gradually closer. The glass forms a kind of echo chamber around the hallway, and she can hear him clear as day. She stays in the lobby to listen.

10.

Amy leans hard into each step as she continues to descend, each impact now sending spasms across her entire body like leaning on broken bones. She can hear the voices calling louder and louder for her, the feeling of her mother's hand on her face. She is bracing her knees with her hands, trying to grasp at both guardrails and support muscles that have long since given out. The black grease line along the wall is continuous now, as if to say that she must proceed unbroken as it does. She feels the end of it all: every moment she's spent wondering what happened to her, what made her like this, why her life got so fucked-up, why some part of her was irrevocably broken in ways she will never recover, why she can never get it back. She lives in exile, the world is waiting for her to starve, she has been categorized as a toy for men to use until her purpose is expended and she's disposed of, this is all her fault, she could have sucked it in and dealt with pretending to be a man, that missing thing will always hang over her and will always torment her with its absence, what is asked of her is perfectly possible for anyone else, but this hidden eternal defect of hers will make it hurt too much, stress too hard, break bones and shatter her will where it would bounce off any functional person, they only see her as breeding stock and she can't even do it, listening to that kid in the dark having god knows what done to him every night forever, masking it all behind breaking her back even harder, pushing even more out, taking longer hours, making sure no one can see her cry, embracing her only when she's putting out whatever it needs you to put out that day, to promise final reconciliation not only in death but here on Earth, here in a sense of eternal happiness, no more struggle, no more turmoil, comfort like a child, someone always to take care of you and nobody angry with you when you fail to meet your responsibilities, all of which fall entirely within your grasp, total control, no pressure, no anxiety, healthy mind and body maintained through a sense of strong boundaries, child crying in the dark, no recompense for what black sunrise might lay on memory's horizon, yoga on Tuesdays, Thursdays, Saturday mornings, Saturday mornings feel the best, sometimes missing Tuesday night class drinking with friends, shrieking hangovers next day, food insecurity within days of resting, refusing comfort, punishing those who remind you of yourself the most, the thing tugging close, breathing in its perfume, hearing it on the opposite end of the wall, shaking through the grease, dripping at high temperature, sweat on palm on handrail burning burning slide, louder and louder and full of agony and so, so familiar.

Amy loses her balance and tumbles headfirst into the concrete. She lands initially on her shoulder, and bounces over her head, compound-fracturing her left wrist on impact. She's able to roll enough to avoid breaking her neck, but lands hard on her ribs on the next fall, skipping three steps. She bends a calf to try to stop the momentum, but she's moving too fast now and it snaps back behind her, foot flopping back in rapid, uncontrollable shakes behind her head, throwing off the trajectory and making the next rotation the one that finally bashes her skull into the concrete. The back of her head, foot now aside in the flailing limbs, meets the edge of a step and cracks, bleeding, and her vision gets fuzzy, she's still floating across storeys and storeys of concrete leading towards what she still knows are the only hard facts she'll ever know, head rush from blood loss and increasing forward momentum leading her towards truth. The blood on the steps matches the grease in its downwards movement, degrading under the increasing heat, hearing only the sounds of her own impact, thud and crunch across the concrete, until the caterwauling from below becomes audible.

The sounds of the neighbours in the walls. Air forced urgently from familiar lungs in panicked cacophony following all the way up the stairwell, the kid, thousands of her, she knows she is going to get there, she knows now that she is going to get there faster. After an eternity hung mid-air in silence, the next impact is spinal, making the flailing of her legs far less intentional, the last of the electricity she can will through her extremities proving its own existence by working itself through before all connection is severed entirely. The next impacts on her face and neck she barely feels at all, and she's halfway to sleep by the time she reaches the bottom of the stairwell.

Amy lies chest-down at the foot of the stairs. Her knee protrudes from its socket angled up towards the last step. Mustering the last of her strength, she turns her head upwards.

The grease paint on the wall forms a triangle, ending in a directional arrow that is running down below her. Digging her blue acrylic nails into the concrete, leaving white marks behind her, she scrapes the rest of herself across the ground, continuing forward on the basement landing.

Each pull takes with it some of her nails, which crackle and splinter with each pull, her foot bent farther and farther backwards, which only produces a soft pressing sensation, like pushing on a bruise. She presses herself up in a push-up formation, half military crawl, like an ascending yoga pose, and arm-walks as best she can towards the strip curtains hanging before her at the end of the platform.

She sees stars, fading in and out as she breathes. Glowing out from the open end of the dark hallway in front of her is the light that's been with her for her entire life, floating out distorted through a doorway covered by ribbons of transparent PVC.

11.

"Dr. Kaur, listen, I understand your concerns. But what we have to understand about the product is that it is *artificial*. Its anatomy may be extremely similar, yes, but the consciousness is built from the ground up, and I don't know if you've been to the core recently, but I can assure you, the way these things are made hardly resembles the miracle of birth. Okay, well, listen, I know a lot of folks in your circles like to fudge on what's real and what's fake *lived experience*, that sort of thing, but there's a real difference worth taking seriously there. Like, the whole *what if you could live a perfect life as a head in a jar* thing, people don't like it. People like to still see some things as real and some things as fake, as bad as you might like it to be otherwise, because no matter how hard you blur those lines, you can agree some things are more real than others. By anyone's standards, a *fake person* with *fake memories* can't be having *real experiences*. Even if the product can't tell that the experiences are fake, they're still fake, even once the product has been made aware of its situation. Even if you could, like, neurochemically describe exactly what's going on inside of one of these things in order to prove that it's the same as human thought, you wouldn't want to call that *consciousness* per se. It might be an extremely convincing simulation of consciousness — as displayed on the *surface* through its performance. But we need to make it clear to our stakeholders that it's impossible to tell whether or not the product has any real internal life, only baseline decision-making processes required to think through solutions to problems. It's impossible for us to know for sure one way or the other, same as any real person. Yeah, uh-huh. Some of the research makes it seem like they share memories, though the data on that's a little shaky. Uh-huh. I mean, right, but can you imagine if they *did* share consciousness? This shared database of memories, all over the world, all the times any individual unit would have seen itself die? How would you even, like, conceptualize yourself at that point? From your own standpoint, would you even exist, really? Do you just return to your body and say, nope, the thing that I am is still right here, that was just a thing that looked like me? Or do you say, I am nothing?

"We're assuming, when it comes to going wide with the product, that most people will take it as a relief. We've built our psychometrics around stuff people generally just aren't comfortable talking about, so I assume they'll barely want to get into this with us, if the thought even occurs. We need to focus on the framing. We're the ones coming at it from an optimistic perspective, you know, this could be the future! *Look at what we accomplished! Look at how cool it is!* And I mean, obviously, there's an intense empathy for the product too. They're martyrs! Whatever lives they could be said to lead, brutal as they may sometimes be, are the first step in the actualization of human potential, the movement from mere survival into a mass thriving, overcoming our physical limitations. Depending on what we find as we go further, they could even be a pathway out of aging and death, though that's way, way down the road as far as R & D goes. But still, anyway, I think post-drop we're going to see a lot of, like, reverent consumer treatment of these things, seeing them as, like, symbols of the post-work economy or something, maybe even people falling in love with them one day.

"Or wait, no, you're right, maybe if we're going to the unreal messaging regarding the whole consciousness problem, we might need to skip that one. I dunno, monitor the public response and we'll see, we can encourage teaching the controversy.

"But really, you can't tell me you don't feel a little bit nearer to God when you're in the room with one of those things, and not just because of where they came from. I mean, we've seen huge success when the product, independently and of its own volition, seeks sex work as a form of supplementary income, that's a huge proof of concept on that side of things. Anyways, the ones *you* saw on the cameras were dressed as women, right? That's something we've been watching as well, not incidentally related to that above thing, supplementary streams of income. We still don't really know why, but it's a demographically noticeable chunk at this point, and I can't stop myself from thinking about it sometimes. Why do they do that? Is it a sex thing? Trying to find some kind of agency? There's been some internal rumblings about whether this is a problem in the memories we choose for them, but it infects their memories too. They just seem to land like that, nothing else quite like it we've found. You wonder if it might have been some defect in the original, whoever he was. But anyways, I could talk about this stuff all day, so I won't bore you, but I think it's beautiful when people can express themselves. Mm-hmm, yeah. We have to treat them like human beings as much as we possibly can. Right, okay. Yeah. Talk soon, bye."

The figure bounces down the hallway, whose royal-blue walls seem to stretch as far vertically as the distance Annie and Amy had walked. His footsteps echo up.

"Hey, Annie!"

She double-takes. He has grey hair, a salt-and-pepper beard, and bright-blue eyes like a husky. He's wearing a midnight-blue three-piece suit. The vest is a little too tight.

"Good work getting down here. Listen, nobody's gonna hurt you while you're in the building. You've been in a lot of places you're not supposed to be, so there might be some consequences later. But you're safe right now, so try not to worry. It's out of your hands now."

Annie tries to respond but can't think of anything to say.

"You made the right choice stopping here. I'm sorry to be the one to tell you, but your friend isn't coming back from down there, and if you follow her, you won't either. You should head back up those stairs."

He's stopped about twenty feet away from her. Annie can tell from his face that he's remorseful.

"Thank you for your time."

She opens the door, still out of breath, and starts back up the stairs.

12.

Dragging her body through the threshold of the plastic-shutter door, Amy is met with *The Abattoir.*

A tower of black grease and liquid chrome, demarcated with ridges and protrusions that seem to have been carved over eons like a karst spring. It extends an endless height, its base deep out of view feeding a system of interconnected roots that run much farther than the facility itself. The tower is constantly moving while maintaining its shape, undulating under unbearable pressure. On the roiling surface of the material, the beginnings of faces. Each face is at a different stage of its development, and with different sets of markings, scars, expressions, skin weathering or lack thereof, but all exactly the same in their features, an eternal mosaic of the possibilities contained within the single life it has enfolded into its multitude. For Amy, it's like looking over an infinite number of funhouse mirrors. Surrounding the tower's roots is the soil in which it grows, bodies writhing in filth, shitting into each other's open wounds, each a mass of red pores absorbing and recycling the waste of the others and feeding off the pure energy emanating from the mass. The bodies are wrapping limbs around each other in a constant half embrace, half wrestle for control, pushing towards the top of the base of the tower, trying to move upwards into the light. The bodies, too, are at every stage of life and sit as infinite iterations of the same singular possibility. All have penises, though some also have breasts, and sometimes the bodies rub together blind, getting themselves off, mixing cum into the stew of shit and meat they swim in. The biomass trench seems to go on for miles in each direction of the tower, past the visible horizon, full of constant movement.

Rising from the mass are a pair of grasping arms, thin strands of silver liquid metal, themselves teeming with life, extending into long fingers that pick up individual bodies from the biomass below in a pinching motion, grasping around their ribs and raising them farther and farther into the heavens until they are blind to the others, but level with the upper observation decks where Amy watches them work. Once at this elevation, the body has its face grafted on under extreme heat, steam encompassing it, and the limp body is lifted skyward towards its grander purpose. Its eyes light up mid-ascent as it hurtles towards the world.

However, if the body is rejected for release, the fingers begin the process of recycling the genetic material. Then, the needle-like fingers of the tower's arms pick across the recycled body, first removing unnecessary extremities, each in the same pinch-like crush-and-squeeze motion: fingers, toes, eyes, then hands, feet, tongue, lips, nose, genitals, before sliding beneath the skin and slowly working their way up across the body, degloving skin from muscle. The skin is only pierced once the twin fingers meet at the top of the neck, pinching through and plucking its doll-like head and dropping it into the pool below. The skin is slowly worn down from the headless body, shaken off, leaving a pile of twitching muscle still held carefully in the palm of the hand, which then, with lightning-fast, precise movements, picks through any bones and pieces of the central nervous system that might contain any potentially useful data or that can be incorporated into the tower itself. The fingers of the hand then gradually ball into a fist, reducing the remaining semi-solid mass into pure nutrients, which are spread and showered over the biomass below, feeding back into the tower and redistributed by the writhing of the individual biomass components against each other. The bodies, which cannot speak and do not eat so much as absorb the nutrients, shake with pleasure upon the delivery of fresh nutrients, as the pool around them can grow toxic and stagnant over time without this periodic reintroduction. Each arm is in a near-constant state of searching, with very few bodies selected for life on average, the process taking approximately twenty minutes per body.

The tower produces an immense amount of heat, which keeps the lake of human refuse surrounding it at a boil and which requires Chariot staff technicians to wear special equipment when they come to observe it, which isn't often, as the tower operates entirely on its own, regardless of its purported owners' whims. The tower was not built by Chariot so much as it was discovered and claimed by them, and the heat it produces is channelled into the electricity that powers the rest of the facility. The cylindrical walls surrounding the tower go on for miles across, and the feeding pool has been dug into a hundred-foot trench along the bottom of the room so that observation decks can be maintained above.

Amy sits under the plastic shutters and stares in awe. The ghost is totally silent for the first time in years. She watches the arms upraised at the clawed fingers carrying a body skyward, giving them their moment in the light, and for a moment, as the limbs bend back in ways that seem like they'd hurt, the fingers form a circle. Those fingers and hands form their circle in shadow and snap shut, as Amy experiences a sense of peace and tranquility for the first time since she first saw them.

She pulls herself towards the edge, feeling the metal grate of the observation deck clearly with her fingers, everything clear now, and she shrugs herself over the side, one hundred feet into the mass below.

IV. OUT

Simply the thing I am shall make me live.

—*Shakespeare,* A Winter's Tale

1.

The rain patters softly overhead and the concrete glows lilac then green in the lights of the underpass below the train station. After-work crowds are piling out of the shopping mall across the street as the lights come on and they march towards me with their umbrellas overhead. I'm singing softly, my voice covered in reverb from the little karaoke machine I've set up and from the edifice above me. Some of these people must know this song, right? I try to see myself from outside, and I can't believe I've resorted to this, someone dropping coins in my case as they go by. *So brave.* Not that I really need the money right now, but I want to try for Dwayne.

After I left that place, I found myself waking up in strangers' houses. Like when I was a kid, but all over the city. I couldn't tell when I was doing it on purpose or if I was sleepwalking; I was blackout drunk a lot of the time and the lines between wakefulness and sleep were blurry. I didn't care if anything bad happened, I just refused to sleep on the street, no matter what. Sometimes it was someone I had some faint memory of, some half-remembered acquaintance from school or from my old job, or someone I'd clearly picked up at a bar somewhere, other times it was a random stranger, and often they'd wake me up with panicked shouts, demands to get the fuck out. Once in a while I'd wake up before anyone else did, and be able to sneak out without any interaction at all — that was best. No risk, just a game of trying to piece together who the prior night's patron was from whatever family photos and knick-knacks they have lying around as I make my way back quietly out into the snow. Regardless of what had happened between us, it was usually someone who was at least friendly, and I'd take their number down and stay in touch, so that I wouldn't need to risk it with new people as often. It was a lot easier to make and keep friends now that I had no structure holding me back and nothing to lose.

Every morning for the first couple weeks, I would text Amy, just a quick *love you* or *miss you*, though after some weeks it sank in that the man in the basement had been right that she was gone. I filed a police report, but nothing has happened yet.

One night, I set up at a bar in my old neighbourhood where the owner would let me come and sit sometimes when it got cold, an old, sticky, maple-lined sitting room with a dozen dartboards in the basement. I'd usually come and watch the old folks come and go from this place every day, and sometimes someone would strike up a conversation with me, even buy me a meal on occasion. One night I met a man, he looked like he was in his fifties, and said his name was Dwayne. He asked me about who I was, and where I'd come from, and I told him, *oh, you know, I'm twenty-one, and I'm between jobs and places right now, but I'm working on it,* and he told me how normal that is at my age and how I shouldn't get too down on myself about it. When I asked him about himself, he told me how much he hated his boyfriend, a heroin addict named Charlie he'd met at the facility where he was a social worker. As soon as they'd started dating, he dropped out of rehab, which Dwayne thought was very, very selfish, especially since he was giving him a leg up by letting him stay at his place rent-free. I nodded along, and told him about how sometimes it's your own fault for letting people take advantage of you, and it sounds like a bad relationship that it might be time to let go of. Dwayne agreed, but said it wasn't that easy, you know, he was the one who put him in that situation after all, and maybe he would still be in rehab if it weren't for his care worker exploiting the power he had over him. I told him I could see his point, but that he ought to forgive himself, and that seemed to stick with him.

After that, I'd go back to that bar every night, and when Dwayne was there, we would go for walks together along the riverside, and he would tell me all about his past life as a long-haul truck driver, seeing the country from the perspective of its warehouses and truck stops at late hours, all the predation, weird creatures that skulk around the dark corners of the supply chain where nobody looks. I told him one night that I was only now really getting to have adventures of my own, and he told me I needed to savour them.

Towards the end of that walk, Dwayne told me his boyfriend hadn't been home in several days. He told me he was scared and worried, that he had put word out to all his co-workers and to all the in-patients at the centre for anyone to report where he was, and told me to do the same. I told Dwayne of course I can do that, though I didn't really have connections the way he thought I did. I told him if he ever needed anything, he could call on me any time, and offered to help get him home, which at first he brushed off, but I knew where his place was since I'd sometimes double back if I had nothing to do and nobody else to call, though I'd always been cautious to go early knowing the boyfriend was on the couch, so eventually he yielded, and when we arrived back there, after making a pot of tea, Dwayne asked if he could suck my cock. I agreed, and dissociated hard to make it through for about twenty minutes before realizing I wasn't going to be able to come for him. He was okay with that, and he asked me kindly if it had been okay for me, and I told him, yes, I loved it very much. He said it had been a little weird for him because he hadn't been with a woman since he was in the closet, around my age, which only troubled him more. I told him we didn't have to do anything like that again if he didn't want to. I slept in his arms.

I stayed there with him every night for about two weeks before Charlie came back. It was the middle of the night, and I heard pounding from downstairs. It was a legacy building, palatial brick with a white plaster dome roof that'd been built in the 1800s, and it had one of those terrible old radiators with the rattling bars. I assumed at first that that was the source of the noise, it was cold and we'd tried to turn the heat on, but it only came on about ten percent of the time, the other ninety it produced that awful sound, followed by no heat at all. But Dwayne was familiar with this, and had this strange sort of relief in his expression as he ran out of the apartment and down the hallway. Dwayne came back into the room with a guy who was presumably Charlie, and as soon as they were across the threshold, they were screaming at each other, bringing up every past slight to try to guilt the other into backing off, but it just never seemed to break. Charlie started crying at some point, pointing at me and calling me *that thing* and saying I was his *replacement*. I tried to get a word in, but the two of them wouldn't let me, just barking at each other yet louder each time, until eventually they'd shoved each other into the bedroom and for a while I could hear a slow, continuous *thud* against the wall at a stable rhythm as I fell back asleep, this time on the couch.

I'm still staying there, on the couch, and Charlie comes and goes as he pleases. Sometimes he's mad at me just for being there, and we end up in a shouting match when I try to defend myself, eventually needing Dwayne to step in to calm him down. Other times he doesn't care at all, we watch TV and get along fine. I learned he used to drive trucks as well, and that was how he and Dwayne initially bonded. He also told me that Dwayne only pretends to get drunk when he goes out, that Dwayne's actually flat sober and loves to tell people otherwise to get their guard down. Both of them love to tell me all the worst things about the other, and I always nod along and agree with whoever I'm speaking to at the time, just hoping to keep the peace, liking them both well enough.

One morning, after a particularly bad fight the night before, the two of them sat me down at the kitchen table and told me I was going to need to start paying rent to stay there. I begged and pleaded and told them no one wanted to hire me now, you know how hard it is for someone like me, that sort of thing, and they agreed that I could only stay on the condition I was at least looking for work. I was a little pissed, I knew Charlie was still just sitting at home watching TV all day, but I guess it was his place first, and Dwayne actually wanted to fuck him, so I couldn't really argue. During the day I would go out with a stack of resumés and apply for jobs, riding Charlie's bike around in the rain downtown, plastering coffee shops and fast-food restaurants, and I got a lot more replies than I'd ever expected to my resumé, but they would always ghost me as soon as they received my references. I tried it back and forth, including or removing Chariot from the references form, but it never seemed to matter; they'd always ask for it, and never talked to me again once they got it. Eventually, I just lied to my hosts that I was out applying for jobs and would come out here instead with this karaoke machine I found in Dwayne's basement and a little cash box to collect change from the people going by. They're happy to have the extra money, though I'm sure they probably know I'm begging by now.

The rain's been good because people are crowding around me to stay dry, and it doesn't seem like the cops are gonna shut me down today. An old man said I was beautiful earlier, I didn't know how to take it, but it didn't seem like he was lying either. Every day around 4 p.m., I think I see a commuter who looks a lot like me, and for a second I think it might be her, but it isn't. I can tell from the eyes now. I keep my head down and focus on staying on pitch. The lights overhead are blue, then green, and back to lilac.

2.

You witness a mine collapse on the news, ninety-nine of those new same-face boys trapped on a mountainside in Peru. No one lives. The minerals they had been sent to source are recovered, but no bodies. You watch helplessly, thinking of the interconnectedness of things, how you would not know how to live without eternal access to infinite natural resources, infinite knowledge, infinite labour devoted to the extraction of both. You try to think through some way things could be different, but you are not able to. You push yourself to your far limits just to take some care of yourself, and it seems impossible to even keep yourself afloat, let alone someone else, let alone so far away. But that same face starts to appear on TV more and more, and the desperation in his eyes summons something in you that you don't know what to do with. It's impossible to tell what the consequences would be if you acted on these feelings, and frankly, it's unreasonable to expect that much of you. You begin to feel increasingly defensive of your tenuous position, and begin to support increasingly punitive measures against those who would challenge it, though you would never personally hurt anyone, of course. Eventually, things change whether you want them to or not, and you withdraw further and further inwards, bringing your family with you, building a great fortress and placing yourself as far as you can from the terrible things you saw. Your children, who grow up inside fortress walls, are able to conceptualize even less about the outside world than you can, but are now tasked with inventing entirely new ways of being in order to fill the vacuums of power and meaning left by the failed world you created. You are disgusted with them for their arrogance, and withhold all but the most basic necessities. They are disgusted with themselves, no matter what they do, and are never sure why.

Thanks

to emily, cat and athena, for taking a chance on the dead thing i left on your doorstep.

to louise, without whom this certainly would not have been finished, let alone seen by anyone.

to emma, for years of friendship and help with research on this book.

to kaytie, for everything.

to mom and dad, promise i'm fine now.

About the Author

aoife josie clements was born in calgary, alberta. she makes music under the name ravine angel.

About LittlePuss Press

LittlePuss Press is an independent feminist press run by trans women. We believe in printing on paper, intensive editing and throwing lots of parties.

A Note on the Type

This book is set in an uncannily twinned pair of fonts by Zuzana Licko: the serif Mrs Eaves and the sans-serif Mr Eaves.

Regarding Mrs Eaves, in which the body text of this book is mostly set, its designer notes: "There is something unique about Mrs Eaves and it's difficult to define. Its individual characters are at times awkward looking, the W being narrow, the L uncommonly wide, the flare of the strokes leading into the serifs unusually pronounced. Taken individually, at first sight some of the characters don't seem to fit together. The spacing is generally too loose for large bodies of text..."

We hope it left you slightly uneasy.